ON THE EVE
OF UNCERTAIN
TOMORROWS

Neil Bissoondath was born in Trinidad in
1955. He emigrated to Canada in 1973 and
studied French at York University,
Toronto. He later taught French and
English as a second language while beginning his writing career. *On the Eve of
Uncertain Tomorrows* is his second book of
short stories, and follows his novel,
A Casual Brutality. Neil Bissoondath lives
in Montreal.

By the same author

Digging Up the Mountains
A Casual Brutality*

* available in Minerva

ON THE EVE
OF UNCERTAIN
TOMORROWS

NEIL
BISSOONDATH

Minerva

A Minerva Paperback
ON THE EVE OF UNCERTAIN TOMORROWS

First published in Great Britain 1990
by Bloomsbury Publishing Limited
This Minerva edition published 1991
by Mandarin Paperbacks
Michelin House, 81 Fulham Road, London SW3 6RB

Minerva is an imprint of the Octopus Publishing Group,
a division of Reed International Books Limited

Copyright © 1990 by Neil Bissoondath
The author has asserted his moral rights.
A CIP catalogue record for this title
is available from the British Library
ISBN 0 7493 9137 5

'*Kira and Anya*' first appeared
in *Saturday Night*, May 1990.
'*The Power of Reason*' first appeared
in *New Virginia Review*, Vol. 7, 1989.
'*Things Best Forgotten*'
first appeared in *The Literary Review*
(Fairleigh Dickinson University, Madison, NJ)
Vol. 29, No. 4, Summer 1986.

Printed and bound in Great Britain
by Cox and Wyman Limited, Reading, Berks.

For
Shelley and Ved
with love

Contents

On the Eve of
Uncertain Tomorrows

IT IS THE violence of beating wings that attracts Joaquin's attention.

Two pigeons, colour only hinted at in the half-light, press in fluttering desperation against the chickenwire enclosing the little wooden balcony. They are too engrossed in battle to notice him at the open door. The air — though soft with the underlying warmth of the spring Jeremy Windhook, the lawyer, says is coming — feels cold, and he folds his arms against its subtle bite.

The wings of the birds flare like pouncing condors, the male — Joaquin now understands — pinning the female beneath him. He sinks his beak into her neck feathers, inflicting submission; steadies himself and, avoiding the ineffectual battering of her wings, awkwardly mounts her.

In the distance, past the complex geometry of withered buildings — garages, storerooms, walls of tin and brick —

pressing in on the rear of the rooming-house, the colourless towers of a few tall buildings of the city sit one-dimensional against the sky. They suggest an unknown life, a world of blood and flesh and everyday ambition, a life within his sight but not, still, yet, within his grasp.

The wings scratch and scrape at the wire, batter at it. Create, in their terrified clamour, a raucous plea for escape.

His heart races, temples engorge with blood. Lucidity slips, his mind an ungraspable swirl, as he steps out onto the balcony, knowing for the moment nothing but the noise of the birds.

Slaps at the wire with the back of his open hand.

To no sound, no effect.

They cannot — will not — take note of his protest.

He stands back. Horrified. Witness, in the quiet of the morning, to unwilling coupling, an avian rape. It is the way of nature, he tries telling himself. But they are unattractive birds, with panicky, red-rimmed eyes, and this lack of beauty denies them his sympathy: they call to mind infection, physical corruption.

It is all over in seconds. The male has answered the call of nature, the female has been violated. Then, unconcerned, their congress concluded, they wing away in separate directions, are quickly swallowed by the dark grey sky.

Only then does it occur to Joaquin that the wire netting wrapped around the balcony is there not to keep the pigeons in but to keep them out, its function reversed. And he is the one confined, by the chicken wire and by so much more.

"They say that the waiting is the worst thing." Amin, who

says he will one day take the name Thomson, carefully pours the boiled coffee into their cups. "But it is not so, I believe." Joaquin silently admires Amin's delicacy, the economy with which he speaks, moves, handles objects, as if he has an abhorrence of excess.

Amin, usually not an early riser, has been up for a while, fussing and puttering in the bathroom. His curly black hair glistens with a shampooed freshness. His every movement tosses off a perfume that conjures for Joaquin a sweet but sweaty armpit. Amin is wearing the outfit that Jeremy Windhook brought him last week: a simple white shirt, pleated trousers, dark socks. It is a specific look that Jeremy Windhook seeks, that of a genteel poverty, an effect he must labour over for people like Amin, who, in their hunger, can so easily look brigand-like. Amin has taken special care this morning. He has showered, he has shaved, he has even clipped his nose hairs — for today, Joaquin knows, is his tomorrow; today is the day that will determine whether tonight he celebrates, or whether tonight he cries.

"The waiting is simple, after what we have been through." The words swish easily from between his barely parted lips, as if he speaks only with his tongue. "The hard part is not knowing what tomorrow will bring for me. Where will I be? What will I do? Will I be happy, or will I be sad?" He lets the condensed milk flow long and thick into his coffee, stirs it without letting the spoon clink against the side of the cup. "These are sad questions, my friend, to ask about tomorrow. No man should have to ask them, I believe."

Joaquin takes his coffee cup in both hands, blinks rapidly at the steam as he raises it to his lips.

"You did not sleep last night," Amin says.

Joaquin smiles minutely at him. The coffee is bitter, the boiled grounds gritty between his teeth.

"I see it in your eyes, my friend. It is not good, I believe." He sips from his cup, adds, "Eh?" Amin has an ear for language. The exclamation is one of his new acquisitions. Joaquin thinks he is having an affair with one of the secretaries in Jeremy Windhook's office, although Amin says she is only helping him with his English.

Joaquin gives him a thin smile, an acknowledgement of his concern. But he is not sure how he really feels about Amin; he's too self-confident, in the sly way of the street-survivor. Joaquin worries when Amin claims a communality of experience with him. He has never spoken to Amin of his life, has listened with silent skepticism to Amin's eagerly offered autobiography of civil war, starvation, forced conscription. Joaquin wonders whether Jeremy Windhook has told Amin his story; but Jeremy Windhook has never mentioned any of his other clients to Joaquin, so he has no reason to believe this. He thinks instead that Amin is simply assuming the comradeship of those involved in the same enterprise. It is, he thinks, a sign of Amin's struggle with his isolation, the isolation they all share.

Amin reaches into the cupboard for a box of crackers, stuffs two into his mouth with one hand as the other digs into the box for more. He no longer bothers to offer them to Joaquin, knows he does not like their salty dryness.

In the silence disturbed only by Amin's crunching, Joaquin wonders whether he should tell him about the pigeons — it seems somehow important — but Amin's camouflaged nervousness reveals itself in the desperation of his jaw.

4

Joaquin knows that his tale of the pigeons will force Amin's natural melancholia to the surface, will smother his summoned ebullience. So he says nothing.

This day has no dawn.

It is the sun, in any case, and not mechanical precision that marks Joaquin's sense of time. Midday or midnight on his illuminated alarm clock is meaningless. So it is only with the lightening of the sky, its dimming of the lights in the distant buildings, that the day after tomorrow truly becomes tomorrow.

Tomorrow: it is like a forbidden woman, enticing, creeping into his daydreams, invading his fantasies. It robs him of sleep, grates his nerves into a fearful impotence.

It was earlier, when he couldn't stir except with the greatest of effort, when the stillness that gripped his body threatened to harden into a conscious permanence, that he struggled from the clasp of the blankets and trudged the cool confines of his room. He was thankful, in those moments of struggle, for the nightlight — the glowing Mickey Mouse face Jeremy Windhook's little daughter no longer needs — that held the darkness at bay. Joaquin cannot abide darkness. He has had too much of it, has experienced too intimately the concrete and imagined terrors of it. So he stalked his room in the thin glow, three paces one way, three paces the other, the scuffed boards squeaking like mice underfoot.

Stalked through the figures and effigies of nighttime evocations: the slow tearing of nails from fingers, the cracking of bone, the bite of saw-toothed metal into nipple. Liquid coursed thick and warm across his stomach. The gurgle of strangulated breath caught his throat, a blindfolded darkness

pressed in on his eyes. Pain came in vivid memory, flushing
hot and cold through his belly and into his chest. His hands
throbbed, nipples burned —

Space: he let himself quietly out of the room, padded
through the darkened corridor to the kitchen. To the tyranny
of shadowed things: the fridge, the stove, the sharp angles of
cupboards. The tap dripped rhythmically, maddeningly, into
the aluminum sink. He tried the light, but it wouldn't work —
the bulb had blown the day before and no one had bothered
to change it — and so he opened the door to the little balcony,
for space, for air, for escape from the demons of his mind.

Amin, satisfied, belches contentedly into his cupped palm.
In the webby light, the hairs on the back of his hands and
fingers stand out like stiff, black bristles. He offers more
coffee and Joaquin accepts with a nod of his head. Amin
refills the cup, careful not to pour in too much of the sediment.
He empties the grounds into the sink, rinses the pot, places
it on the counter; turns on the stove and, hands clenching
and unclenching in his pant-pockets, waits for the burner to
redden.

From within the house float the distant stirrings of the
awakening others: doors and floorboards creaking, the splash
of water and the tremble of old pipes, throats discreetly
cleared. They are seven in all, the Magnificent Seven, as
Jeremy Windhook mumbles in moments of exasperation:
Joaquin, Amin, a Vietnamese couple, a Haitian, a Sikh, a
Sri Lankan. Except for the Vietnamese couple — the man
restless, the woman watchful, the two hard-eyed in the way
of the ravenous — who spend much time walking the streets
of the city, the others keep to themselves, frittering time

away in newspapers, television, comic books, or the solitary flipping of cards. Joaquin prefers it this way — life has taught him that the friendliest smile may conceal the sharpest teeth — but he is secretly grateful, too, for Amin's extroversion, the ease of his conversation, the way he will begin talking as if he has been asked a question when he has not been — or as if he is anticipating the questions he may be asked and is eager to provide the answers. Amin fills empty time, provides distraction, but not in the impersonal way of the television; this is what Joaquin appreciates about him, why Joaquin will sit and listen to him, watch the graceful and communicative gestures of his hands, watch his smoke turn the air a soft blue-grey.

Amin takes a cigarette from his shirt pocket, holds the unfiltered end to the glowing element until a thin curl of smoke rises from it. Flicking off the stove, he pulls carefully at the cigarette, encouraging the fire, sucking until the end glows healthily and smoke billows from his nostrils. Sitting on the chair with an uncommon energy, he crosses his legs, looks intently at Joaquin through narrowed eyes, says, "I will tell you why Thomson."

Joaquin already knows why Amin says he will one day change his name to Thomson, but he does not interrupt, for to do so would be to disrupt Amin's optimism, his insistent planning for tomorrow; and thus to disrupt his own. And what else do they have, people like him and Amin and the Vietnamese and the Haitian, but fantasies of tomorrow, how it will be, how they will be? Besides, he likes the deliberation Amin has brought to the enterprise. It shows an initiative he wishes he himself had.

"Because no other name will do, I believe." He sucks at

the cigarette held between thumb and index finger. "Canadian people respect certain names, but sometimes they fear them, too. Names of men who are rich and who are bright — maybe too bright, eh? Rich, bright men must not expect popularity in this world."

Joaquin nods in agreement. Amin speaks like a man of the world, a man who understands much beyond his circumscribed experience — and who is he, this Joaquin, electrician by profession, union organizer by necessity, to contradict him? So he listens to Amin, believes he is learning something useful.

"So Thomson it will be. Rich, and bright, no doubt. But not a name that makes simple people — what is the word? — thrimble?"

Joaquin nods again. He thinks of the word *temblar*, raises a quivering hand before him.

"Yes, it is thrimble, I believe. This, the name Thomson does not do to simple people. Respect, yes, and admiration. But thrimble, no. So this is who I will be, eh? Amin Thomson, Canadian."

Joaquin smiles thinly at Amin, envies him his certainties.

Amin goes to his room to finish getting dressed. The Vietnamese couple — eyes of a hounded intelligence — come quietly in. With a challenging glare at Joaquin, they slam the balcony door shut and — an eye always on Joaquin — wolf down a couple of peanut-butter sandwiches. They are gone after only a few minutes.

The Sikh, his hair twisted into a knot on top of his head, comes in, makes coffee, and drinks it sitting across the table from Joaquin. They nod at each other, but neither speaks.

Outside, the day proceeds through heavy cloud. Pigeons, soaring in the distance, present swift silhouettes.

To Joaquin, the day already feels old.

He looks at his hands, as he does at least once every day. They continue to heal. Slowly. Very slowly. They will never be as they were before, although the doctors tell him greater flexibility will return in time. He will never again hold a screwdriver or a pen — it is how they put it, confirming the expertise of those responsible — but he may, with patience, be able to type.

Jeremy Windhook, a solemn young man intent on evidence, proof, *the full story*, tells him with no hint of irony to look on the bright side. Show them your hands at the hearing, he says, keep them in plain sight, *front and centre*. They have never seen hands like yours. Let them see the fleshy cavities where once there were fingernails, let them see the knotty lumps of crushed knuckles left untended, show them the scars on the back where once flesh was sliced through to the whiteness of bone. Throw the scars at them, he says, bring home to them the enthusiasm with which your hands have been redesigned. Evidence, yes. Dramatic and irrefutable. Jeremy Windhook cannot see his hands without blanching, but it is as if he is in love with them, he speaks of them like a teenager ruminating on imminent coitus: with fascination, with fear.

And what more do you want, Mr. Lawyer? Joaquin thinks. Maybe that I sit there naked so they see the greater mutilation? The hardened welts on back, chest, buttocks?

Tell them about the whip of steel cable, he urges.

The tattoo of cigarette burns on my stomach?

9

Marlboros, weren't they?

The circle of ragged flesh that has replaced my left nipple?

Make them feel the bite of the sharpened pliers.

All the practised disfigurement to which I have been subjected, Jeremy Windhook?

But no, Jeremy Windhook has had pictures taken, from every angle. His briefcase is stuffed with medical reports — the language cool and factual, menus of distress that Joaquin has seen — detailing anal violation, organ disruption, bodily dysfunction. It is amazing, Jeremy Windhook says — with fear, with fascination — that he survived.

Joaquin is relieved when, as the Sikh leaves, Amin returns. He is wearing the sombre grey jacket that is the final touch to the outfit Jeremy Windhook has provided. He sits and laces up his shoes. They are of brown leather, do not match the rest of his clothes, but they are freshly shined. He has decided not to wear the tie. Ties, like nooses, make him nervous. "Do you know, Hakim —" It is Amin's name for Joaquin, his closest approximation. "— that it takes thirty-five gallons of sap to make one gallon of maple syrup?"

"Sap" is not a word Joaquin knows.

"It is juice from a tree," Amin explains. "They take it the way doctors take blood. Then they boil it to make a sweet syrup. It is a Canadian delicacy, I believe."

Joaquin knows where Amin gets all this information, from his friend the secretary and from the newspapers he is always reading. He hopes that one day he, too, will acquire such knowledge.

Amin suddenly stares at him. His eyes, of a glittery and

undiluted black, are steady and imploring. "You know, Hakim," he says, his voice breaking, "you know."

Joaquin nods: he knows.

"It is not too much to ask, I believe. A simple life. Khappiness. We forget to enjoy it when we have it, we let it wash over us like water — and then it is gone. If only we knew how to record it, like a film, so that we can recall it and comfort ourselves with the memory. But our brain — it is not strong enough. Khorror will come back with all its power. Khorror will frighten us many months later. But khappiness? Khappiness many months later will make us sad. This is the thing, Hakim. We, you and me, have too many prisons —" He taps at his temple with a finger. " — here." His breathing goes raucous. "We must learn how to make the keys, Hakim, for when our tomorrow comes."

If our tomorrow comes, Joaquin thinks but does not say, for he wants to believe Amin is right yet fears, too, to believe it.

The front door bell buzzes twice. Amin glances at his watch. "Jeremy Windhook," he says.

They hear the door being opened, the Haitian's gravelly voice greeting the lawyer.

Amin stands up tucking his shirt more neatly into his pants. He buttons the jacket, runs his hands through his hair. "Well?" he says.

Joaquin examines him, finds him stiff-looking. He reaches out and undoes the jacket button.

Just before Amin leaves, he glances through the window at the sky. The clouds are thinning, beginning to break up. "Look, Hakim," he says, "the sun! It is a good sign, I believe, eh?"

Joaquin stands up. He cannot speak. Instead, he offers his damaged hand and, for long seconds, they share a firm handshake.

The day advances steadily into the forecaster's prediction of bulky cloud rifting into periods of delicate sunlight. The streets are dry. Cars rumble by spouting music, tires gritty on the asphalt. A sheet of errant paper, whipped along in the wake of the traffic, rasps on the sidewalk. The air teems with sharp, clean sounds unfamiliar from his months of winter waiting.

Joaquin removes his mittens, unzips his parka, the perspiration that is like that of fever drying instantaneously under his clothes. His senses awaken then, nudged through the heaviness of his fatigue into a heightened mindfulness.

There are people all around, people hungry for the sun like prisoners emerging into a prison yard after a too-long, too-dark night. They lounge smoking on benches in snow-bound parks, they haul chairs onto their tiny balconies to read or to daydream. Coats are bundled, convertibles converted, sunglasses unfolded. A man and a woman walk by, arms around each other. The woman says, "Spring's around the corner." The man, with a laugh, replies, "Yeah, but it's a big corner."

Joaquin smiles at the little joke. He is enjoying the growing lightness in his legs. He has always been sensitive to weather and is pleased — it is like a sign of a returning normalcy — to find his body reacting with such vigour. For the first time, he feels the city to be a friendly place, an entity apart — so different from the sterile and hermetic offices of officialdom that he cannot imagine the immigration officers he has

On the Eve of Uncertain Tomorrows

encountered leading normal lives, relaxing in sidewalk cafés or hugging loved ones. He knows that they must: knows that they watch television, read newspapers, make love. But the implications of their professional functions are, to him, too enormous. Surely they must be immigration officers all the time, as doctors must be doctors all the time, or policemen policemen all the time. So it is, he thinks, so it must be with all people who wield the powers of life and death.

Soon he has left behind the snappier streets, the expensive boutiques and neon-signed cafés and renovated condominiums giving way, as he approaches St-Laurent, to stretches of run-down housing, Korean supermarkets, Portuguese restaurants. The laneways, bordered by crumbling garages, are still dense with snow and dirty ice. Two men in bloodstained lab coats — like morgue attendants, he thinks, clearing the site of a vigorous massacre — unload slabs of fresh-cut meat from a delivery van, while a young boy, attention wandering, sprays a jet of water at the sidewalk.

He turns right at St-Laurent — which Jeremy Windhook calls Saint Lawrence — and walks hurriedly up its length, the crowds here denser, more intent on their business; past the cut-rate stores and dark restaurants, the specialty-food shops and the sex cinema, turning off at last into a quieter street of curtained windows and peeling doors and, quickly, in a movement that feels furtive, into the shadowed cocoon of *La Barricada*.

Miguel, ever watchful, spots him the moment he enters, nods to him, his eyes only slowly losing their suspicion. Satisfied, he puts the beer flute down on the counter and turns away, to prepare, Joaquin knows, two glasses of his spiced coffee.

Miguel keeps his eyes open; is owner, bartender, cook, and watchman all rolled into one. He has installed a bell that warns him when the door is opening; looks for grim men in jackets and ties with badges to flash. They have never come, but all the regulars know that, should Miguel break the beer flute, those who must are to use the door to the second floor in the common washroom while the others, feigning fear, create diversion by heading for the rear exit. It is not a perfect system, but it is a system; it offers a fighting chance — and that, Joaquin appreciates, is all that anyone truly wants.

It is a curious place, small, with whitewashed walls and fake beams overhead, bits and pieces of his country, his continent, scattered around. Baskets hang from the ceiling, shawls cling to the walls, drums and Pan flutes dangle from crooked nails. Travel posters show Andean heights, Machu Picchu, the modernistic sterility of Brasilia. Quietly, as if wafting in from a great distance, the sad music of the mountains lingers just out of reach, a fading memory even before you can seize it.

On one wall, someone has painted lace curtains framing an open window. Through it stretches a field of trimmed grass, trees, flowers, and, in the distance, stark against a perfect and unreal sky, a line of women colourfully dressed but strangely lifeless. Joaquin finds it a profoundly unsettling work, a vision of a rural paradise in which humans are trespassers. A beautiful and angry work, a work of despair. He sits always with his back to it.

Miguel brings the coffees over, the empty beer flute balanced between them; sits in front of Joaquin with elbows on the table, chin resting on his interlaced fingers. He is a handsome man, his curly black hair, infrequently cut, generously sprinkled with silver. He sleeps little, always looks tired; tends *La Barricada* until late at night, then works into the early hours of morning at the jewellery he fashions as a lucrative hobby. It is these bracelets and earrings and intricate necklaces of silver that keep *La Barricada* afloat; he wholesales them to jewellery shops on St-Denis, enters the profits into the café's books as dinners served and coffees consumed. He sips at the coffee, licks his lips. "You heard about Flavio?" he says in a flat voice.

Joaquin thinks of the sad-eyed young man he's often seen sitting by himself in a corner of the café. Remembers his discomfort at Flavio's hermetic absorption.

The truth is that Joaquin would not come here if he felt he had a choice. The furniture, of worn wood, is too decrepit, lends the place a dismal air, emphasizes somehow its sense of spirit broken into timidity. It is like a closet for the soul, built for containing dusty memories of lives long lost, for perpetuating the resentments of politics long past. Here, he thinks, there is no tomorrow; here, yesterday becomes forever.

"They're sending him back."

Back — a fearful word.

Yet where else is he to go? A chic café on St-Denis? A glitzy bar on Ste-Catherine? He's tried doing both, but in each everyone — or, at least, so it seemed — noticed his hands. Here, too, they are taken note of, but the response is not of questions or queasiness. No, here his hands are accepted as simply part of the universal damage; they evoke no shy curiosity, no willed sympathy, no embarrassed revulsion. Everyone either has endured more or knows of someone who has. And everyone has loved ones who have been, as

15

Miguel says, "thrown through the Devil's Doorway". It is why he is drawn to *La Barricada*, why he feels safer here than anywhere else.

"They say he wasn't involved in enough union activity."

Enough — what is enough?

"Not enough to endanger his life."

Joaquin shivers, twice.

More reason for discomfort: in the corner where Flavio sat, a young woman, Teresa, whom everyone calls Tere, sits biting her nails, or rather not her nails — they are too eaten down for that — but the flesh around them. Joaquin has seen the blood on her fingertips. Miguel has told him Tere's story. They had their Canadian papers, Tere, her husband, and their two children; but on the night before their departure, with their farewell party in full swing, the door burst open. There were scuffles and screams, a brief burst of machinegun fire; and her husband was gone. Embassy officials reacted quickly; saw Tere and the children safely on the plane north, lodged a protest with the government, and demanded that a search be launched for her husband. But they knew — Tere knew — that all the official steps were just a cruel bureaucratic joke.

So Tere arrived, distraught, with the bewildered children; was met by a social worker who took her to a furnished apartment, left her there with mimed instructions — Tere spoke no English, the social worker no Spanish — that she was to prepare dinner for the children. The social worker returned an hour later, to find the apartment thick with smoke and the legs from two of the dining-room chairs smouldering in a cooking fire in the middle of the living room. Someone thought of calling Miguel, and it was up to him to tell Tere,

16

two days later, that her husband had been found shown through the Devil's Doorway. They had identified him by his ring and clothes; it was all they had to go on, considering the condition of his head and fingers.

Miguel made arrangements. A woman he knew in the community looks after the children while Tere attends English classes or, as she has taken more and more to doing, while she comes here to *La Barricada*. It has been six months, and Miguel doesn't have the heart to force her to do what he knows she should be doing. She is torn, Miguel has told him, between returning to her country, where she still has family, and staying here, where her children have a future. She is, Miguel feels, herself seeing the outlines of the Devil's Doorway through the writhing of her demons.

Miguel says, "If Canada will not give Flavio a visa, then God will." Miguel is, in a curious and personal way, a religious man. He can, for hours and with feeling, quote the poetry of the Nicaraguan Cardenal.

Three men huddle in another corner. Two of them are crouched over the hand of the third who sits bolt upright in the chair, eyes shut, lips grimly set. On the table beside them are a box of bandages, a roll of cotton wadding, a bottle of rubbing alcohol, a pair of scissors, and an open package of razor blades.

With a twist of his eyebrows, Joaquin asks Miguel what they are up to.

"Medical care." Francisco, he explains, cut his hand badly at work a couple of weeks before. He was washing dishes, a glass broke. He had no choice but to go to the Emergency. When they asked him for his medical insurance card, he said he'd forgotten it at home. They sewed up the cut, and warned him to bring the card the next time, when he went to have the stitches removed. Francisco was already paying fifty dollars a week to use someone else's social insurance number, and the man wanted two hundred for use of the medical card. Francisco couldn't afford it, so his friends — one a hospital orderly — were removing the stitches for him. The nightmare, Miguel adds, is if an appendix bursts. . . .

In the corner, Francisco draws a sharp and lengthy breath.

Joaquin thinks: just another day at *La Barricada*. He knows, and appreciates, that he is among the least damaged, least desperate of Miguel's clients. It is maybe, in the end, why he continues to come here, not just for himself but for Miguel, too.

Miguel prepares lunch for everyone, cheese sandwiches with sticks of carrot. Tere remains at her table, nibbles at the food. Francisco's friends have to leave and Francisco, his right hand roughly bandaged, joins Joaquin and Miguel.

As they eat, Francisco complains about the man whose social insurance number he is using. He is a blackmailer, he says, this man who seemed so sympathetic at the beginning. Even though Francisco has not been able to work for two weeks, the man continues to demand his weekly money, is threatening to tip off Immigration if he is not paid in full.

"Who is this man?" Miguel asks.

"Just a man," Francisco replies.

Joaquin, eating, listening, appreciates Francisco's reticence, understands it. He knows — from the moment his mother's phone call reached him too late at work; through the hours? days? of darkness to the unexplained release, followed by the harrowing weeks of movement and concealment during the transit north — what it is to be an illegal, understands the fears that lead to continuous vagueness and, eventually, to an invented self. He wonders what Francisco's real name is and for several minutes, as Francisco and Miguel dissect the situation, he tries different names, looking for the one that best matches Francisco's face. It is a haggard face, older than its years, severely scarred by acne; a face that Joaquin could only learn to trust in time. He is neither a Juan nor an Antonio, Joaquin decides, nor a Raul nor an Andres. Luis is too soft, Carlos too round. Alberto, Federico, Mario, Manuel — none quite fits. And then, as he finishes the first half of his sandwich, it comes to him: Francisco has the face of a Jorge.

Jorge. The name echoes in his head, the consonants a harsh whisper. His hands begin to throb and he is forced to drop the carrot stick he has picked up. Francisco and Miguel glance quizzically at him, but return to their conversation after he forces a smile. He tries clenching his hands in his lap — their stiffness prevents the forming of a fist, he can squeeze only so far — but the pain he feels is not a physical one, will not go away so easily.

The pliers, Jorge. No, not those. The smaller ones.

It was his mother who came to him in those moments of searing pain, her teary face alternating with a darkness deeper than that of the blindfold.

You see how he clenches his fist, Jorge. He knows what we want to do, don't you, friend?

A face ageing instantaneously at the news of a daughter's dismemberment. A darkness sparkling with comets and exploding stars.

Any sharp knife will do. You just pull it down, from the

19

wrist towards the fingers. See? Everything opens up. Including the fist.

Dark hairs greying before his eyes. The darkness growing brittle.

You put the pliers just so, getting a tight grip. If he's a nail-biter you have to push it into the flesh, but we're lucky with this one, he's not the nervous type, are you my friend? So you work it as you wish, a quick tug —

Face dissolving. Darkness shattering.

— or a slow twist, ripping it away —

Colours, and a roaring in the head.

— either way is effective.

Then only the face, smiling a soothing smile.

Jorge.

A long silence. Then —

Miguel: "Ten minutes?"

Francisco: "At least."

"Maybe a problem with the stomach —"

"Fifteen, even."

"That long?"

"Maybe longer —"

"Joaquin?"

"Yes —"

"Well? Ten, fifteen, longer?"

"Yes, possibly."

Miguel's eyes flicker at him — an annoyed, inquisitive look, a look that in an instant realizes, absorbs, questions Joaquin's distance — then focus on a point past him.

Joaquin turns: a plate with an untouched sandwich, an

empty chair pushed back from its table. He realizes how distant he has been, he never noticed Tere leaving.

Miguel considers the chair, the nail of his little finger working at a piece of food stuck between his front teeth.

Francisco drains his beer, draws the back of his hand across his lips. He, too, but with less intensity, considers the empty chair. "So," he says.

"So," Miguel echoes.

Joaquin looks from one to the other. His hands, forgotten, relax in his lap, the pain ebbing.

Miguel dislodges the piece of food, flicks it to the floor. Abruptly pushes himself from the table. The beer flute tips, teeters, crashes onto the table top. He frowns at the pieces of broken glass. And then he is running, knocking chairs out of his way.

Blows of his fist on echoing wood.

Joaquin turns, to look.

Miguel is kicking in the bathroom door.

The stickiness that will not wash away from his hands dries quickly in the cold air.

The sidewalks are less crowded now, the streets busy with home-bound traffic. The sky, in the glow of the setting sun, is a brittle, icy blue.

Joaquin walks slowly along with his hands secure in his coat pockets, the air washing cool and fresh through his lungs. He feels good, strong; enjoys a physical self-possession too long absent.

On impulse, he stops in at a fruit and vegetable store, buys a couple of oranges. The woman smiles as she hands him his change, and he realizes with a gentle jolt that he feels less distant from these people now, strangers become a little less strange not through any act of their own but — in a twist he cannot understand — through an act of *his* own: in this city, he has helped save a life.

It was his fingers, useless for so much, that Miguel pressed to the cuts on Tere's wrists, his parka snatched from the back of his chair that Francisco threw around her shoulders. Miguel and Francisco, faces glistening with sweat, fingers nimble and efficient, worked quickly with the cotton wadding and bandages.

Tere didn't fight, sat flaccid on the toilet cover, glazed eyes passively watching them. She had rested her hands on the edge of the sink but, growing weaker, hadn't been able to hold them there. The tiled floor was slick with blood.

Francisco's bandage came loose. Joaquin saw the fragile blending of the wound, pinpricks of blood forming on the pulpy skin. Francisco ignored it in the greater urgency, and Joaquin thought with a prickling shame of his judgement of him. This intensity, this urge to heal: he was wrong: Francisco was not a Jorge, he just had a misleading face.

Afterwards, Tere begged them in a voice weakened and fearful not to abandon her to the hospital. Her verb struck them all, prompted among them glances of uncertainty. They had stanched the blood flow and Miguel, soothing, reassuring, murmured his assent. While Francisco disinfected and rebandaged his own wound, Joaquin and Miguel helped her upstairs, to the bare room in which those who had to could take refuge. She curled up on a mattress on the floor, one hand resting lightly in the other. Miguel gently checked her bandages and, glancing backwards at her, led Joaquin from the room back down the narrow stairs. He would keep her there, he said, would make the necessary arrangements for the children.

Miguel cleared away the broken glass, poured them each a beer. They drank in silence, absorbed. *La Barricada* seemed to have gone inert. The music was off, there was nothing to say.

Eventually, with nothing more than a nod, Francisco left. Joaquin put aside his unfinished glass of beer, offered to help Miguel clean up the bathroom. Miguel refused with a shake of his head; he seemed, in the aftermath, to have no defence against his fatigue; said he would close the place for a few hours, work at his jewellery.

Joaquin walks along, the oranges tucked into the belly of his half-zipped parka. He is not unhappy that Miguel refused his offer. He did not, in truth, relish the thought of returning to the washroom. Much prefers being out here on the sidewalk, in the grip of his sense of having taken a vital step, looking in on the bars and cafés and little restaurants moodily lit behind glass, at the warmth and suggested security of their growing animation.

He lengthens the way back to the house, following streets never before followed, turning left or right or retracing his steps on pure impulse. As the sky darkens into night, windows frame lamplit scenes of comfort and domesticity: a couple preparing salad; two children tugging at a toy; a man absent-mindedly twirling a glass of red wine by candlelight; a woman shuffling through papers in her briefcase. Joaquin drinks them in, these little domestic spectacles; they are so trivial, so inconsequential, so attractive in their banality. And as he watches a cat prancing in pleasure at the opening of a food can, Amin's words come forcefully back to him: *A simple life. Khappiness.*

A faint throb in his hands: Is it too much to ask?

In the sitting room, the radio is on low in the background. The Haitian and the Sri Lankan, both slight, shy men, are hunched over the coffee table playing cards. They glance up without interest as Joaquin comes in, watch without acknowledgement as he removes his parka.

He wonders whether Amin has returned yet, but thinks it best not to ask. It would be like prying, would be frowned upon.

In the kitchen, the Vietnamese couple stands guard over a vigorously bubbling pot. They do not take kindly to his looking in so he goes to his room, puts on the overhead light, and sits on the edge of the bed. His mood, seized in the peculiar tensions of the house, robbed of air by the confines of the room, begins to evaporate. A familiar unease reasserts itself, a vice tightening in his intestines. He takes an orange, nips off chunks of the rind, chews them, the tanginess puckering the fleshy insides of his mouth, invading his nasal passages. It is not a pleasant taste, but is one he has grown to appreciate: for a week during his journey north, fresh oranges were his only sustenance; there was no part he could afford not to consume. The flavour calms him and he closes his eyes, returning in imagination to the scenes witnessed long minutes before. The salad, the toy, the wine glass. The cat circling in hungry anticipation —

24

The buzz of the doorbell jars him back to his room. He listens: the front door is opened, voices murmur.

Careful footsteps approach his door. He thinks: Amin. Drops the orange onto the bed, stands up, opens the door at the first knock.

No, not Amin. Jeremy Windhook. A jacket is draped over his arm. "For tomorrow," Jeremy Windhook says, holding the jacket out to him. "Eight a.m. sharp. Be ready."

Joaquin takes the jacket, recognizes it. "And Amin?" he says.

Jeremy Windhook hesitates. Then: "Amin was refused."

"Refused?"

"They've classified him an economic refugee."

"*No entiendo.*" Joaquin thinks: Are you less a refugee, Jeremy Windhook, if you are in danger of dying from hunger rather than a bullet?

"He doesn't qualify under the UN definition. He'll be deported tomorrow."

"To his country?"

"To Germany."

"Germany? Why Germany?"

"Because he made his way here from there."

"But if they say he is in no danger in his own country, why do they not send him back there?"

"Because —" He shakes his head. "Because it's the rule."

"Why, Jeremy Windhook? Tell me why."

"I don't know why."

"Is it so that another country will do the dirty work for them? The Germans will send him back to his own country,

25

I believe." As he says the last words, Joaquin hears Amin's voice. "And he will die."

Jeremy Windhook says nothing in reply, silently eyes Joaquin.

"You can do nothing?"

"Nothing."

The word hangs hollow in the room.

Jeremy Windhook turns, leaves.

Joaquin tosses the jacket onto the bed. He sees Amin in a room he cannot imagine. He is sitting, his face in his hands, in despair: "Amin Thomson," he whispers. "My name is Amin Thomson." Joaquin swallows hard, wipes his eyes on his sleeve. Picks up the orange and makes his way to the kitchen.

The light is off. All that remains of the Vietnamese is the lingering odour of their dinner. He goes to the door, stands, looks out. His hands throb, and he watches for the pigeons, waits for the dawn, here on the eve of his uncertain tomorrows.

Kira and Anya

THE HOUSE IS larger than she expects — or at least, set back from the road as it is on a rise in the land, it gives the impression of a decades-old massiveness. What, after all, would one man do with three floors and a basement except rattle around in their emptiness? Staring up uneasily at its shuttered self-possession, at the chilly inanimation that gives it the look of a domestic fortress, she marvels that Seepersad has managed in a city of almost unrelieved flatness to obtain so dominant a perspective. It is like a statement of self-caricature; is so like the man, so like everything she has ever heard or read about him.

The strip of lawn fronting the house — the grass healthy though roughly tended, patchy in the centre and scraggly at the edges — is cut off at the sidewalk by a steep slope of stacked rock, access to the front door afforded by narrow concrete steps. To the right, a small garage has been tunnelled into the hill, its electronic door, showing only as a stiff, tilted skirt at the top, broken and rusted into place. Wild ivy, sprouting from among the rocks above the lip of the cavity, sends tendrils trailing down across the gloomy mouth in a fringe of straggling coils. Their tips glance off the blue hood of Seepersad's car — an overblown American boat of the fifties — the front of which protrudes from the garage. The vehicle is in a state of advanced disintegration, the paint faded, headlights smashed, chrome ripped and rusted, tires flattened.

She gathers up her handbag and tape recorder, hugs them close to her body, brushes past the vines, and sidles into the garage. The air is dank and musty, thick with the odours of decay and stagnant water. The car fills the garage, less than a foot separating it from the concrete wall. As her eyes accustom themselves to the darkness, she sees that the overhead lightbulb too is smashed.

In the dim light, the car looks as if it's been in an accident, a rolling, tumbling accident rather than one of sudden impact. The windows are shattered into an opaque milkiness, the roof and trunk severely dented, the edges of the warpings rusted a deep brown. But it is the interior that points to a fuller story, a story of greater deliberation and mindfulness. The light blue leatherette seats have been scoured and ripped into bales of flayed skin, the exposed stuffing bubbling past rusted springs like suppurating guts. The dashboard, the radio slot a toothless mouth, has been reduced to a string of smashed dials on a battered field, ends of wires hanging forlornly from empty sockets.

In the silence of the garage, the devastation before her is unsettling. Senses sharpen further: bellying nets of cobweb descend from the ceiling, the air thickens with the desiccated grittiness of ancient animal excrement. She wants to walk back the way she has come, back to the subway along the residential street somnolent in the summer heat. Her breathing strangles, goes raucous with tension. But she is expected at the house above. She glances at her watch. It is time to mount the concrete steps, knock at the front door, face now with fear what she has long anticipated.

"What's *she* doing here?" Kira and Anya say in unison, Kira from the living room where she has barely unslung the handbag and tape recorder from her shoulder, Anya from the threshold of the front door that Seepersad has just opened to her hesitant knock.

"Same thing as you," Seepersad says to neither and, so, to both. "You two know each other?"

"Know each other?" Kira says, hoisting handbag and tape recorder straps back onto her shoulder. "I don't know what game you're playing here, Seepersad —"

Anya's shadowed eyes punch into him like staples. " — but I don't want to have anything to do with it."

Seepersad is immediately taken with Anya, thinks her attractive even though her teeth are so pointed they almost look sharpened. He says to her, "Is this the first time we've met? You're familiar, somehow."

"We've never met. We move in different circles." Her eyes remain fastened on him, curious, unsettling, as if she is examining a rare relic.

"I have no circles left," he says with a shrug.

Kira takes one step towards the door. "I'm leaving."

"No," says Anya. "*I'm* leaving."

Seepersad tugs Anya into the vestibule — her resistance is less than he expects, he is surprised at the ease with which she submits — and closes the door. "Nobody is leaving," he says.

Kira, clenching her fists at her sides, steps towards the door, but the vestibule is tiny and with two people already there — Anya, also with her purse and tape recorder, both bulkier than Kira's, and Seepersad, a man older and shorter and wider, a man more powerful-looking than in his photographs — there is no room, she cannot get by; does not, in the end, even try. "Just try and stop me," she says, but feebly, the threat an absurdity even when only a thought, shrill — and she hates that — when actually uttered.

"Sit down, sit down," says Seepersad, enjoying his fussiness, making a show of it. "Make yourselves comfortable, ladies. Anywhere you like." On his hands still, on the skin of his fingers, like smudges of silk, like smears of a fine and tingling powder, is the feel of Anya's blouse.

"Hey, old man," Kira says. "I'm no fuckin' lady, got that?"

In his nostrils, the thrill of her perfume: the thrill of a subtlety long forgotten and suddenly, maddeningly rediscovered. "Got it," he says. "You're no fuckin' lady." He looks at Anya. "And you? Are you a fuckin' lady?"

But Anya ignores him, may have not even heard him. She is in the living room now, both hands — fine hands, he notices with a tremor, slim, with long fingers ending in nails carefully shaped and modestly, almost imperceptibly, lacquered — clinging at the purse and tape recorder straps as if she is fearful of attempted theft. She stands across the

Persian carpet from Kira. As if making up her mind, she looks back at Seepersad, then at this other, coarser girl who wears her lack of attention to herself — her skin neglected; her face unmade; her hair unwashed and untended and tugged back into a ponytail — in the most immodest of ways, as a reverse vanity, self-regard refracted to the world through a splintered mirror.

Seepersad tries to read the look on Anya's face, but the only hieroglyph he can decipher makes no sense: what, he wonders, could Anya possibly have to fear?

Kira thinks: So what did you expect? Fangs and horns? Claws and pointed ears? Yes, of course. All that, and the smell of old blood.

The realization startles her, strikes her as — she struggles with the word, rejects it, but it comes insistently back at her — so *childish*.

You've seen the photos, she thinks, all the old newspaper photos of him: Maxim Seepersad shaking hands with Richard Nixon, Maxim Seepersad embracing Leonid Brezhnev, Maxim Seepersad puffing cigars with Fidel Castro, Maxim Seepersad glaring at Harold Wilson, Maxim Seepersad toasting Pierre Trudeau. Seepersad at play, Seepersad at work. Seepersad eating, drinking, sleeping. Even — from a failed attempt at political blackmail — Seepersad making love. Seepersad young and slim and dark-haired. Seepersad old and fat and grey. You've seen them all, she thinks, so why should he surprise you now?

But she dismisses the question, retreats from the discomfort it brings. Forces herself to think of the other photographs she's seen: of weeping relatives choking on tear gas, of political protest shattered by gunfire, of blood and broken bodies.

Thinks: The only photograph you haven't seen is of Maxim Seepersad dead.

Kira says, "So what gives, Seepersad? What's the idea?"

"Idea? I don't follow you."

"So what's the deal? What are we both doing here?"

"I'm sure I haven't the faintest idea what you're talking about, my dear —"

"You agreed to an exclusive interview with me, Seepersad."

"And with me, too," says Anya.

Seepersad smiles wearily at their accusing faces. "Kira," he says. "Anya. Forgive me. Forgive an old man. A forgetful old man. Your requests reached me at about the same time, I mixed things up."

Kira and Anya sigh in unison. They are unconvinced.

"I am not a well man. I have been ill. My energy is not what it was. Two reporters. Two interviews. I thought they — you — were one and the same."

"You haven't changed one little bit, have you, Seepersad?" Kira sneers her words at him. "Ten years after they sent you packing. Still the old cat-and-mouse game. The same dancing around —"

Seepersad laughs heartily, his tone one of unembarrassed admission.

"Mr. Seepersad —" Anya spits his name. She is exasperated at his arrogance.

"Why don't you call me Max," Seepersad says.

"Yes," Kira says sweetly to Anya. "Why don't you?"

Anya thinks: How disappointing. He hasn't even farted once. Oh well, there goes that first line: *Maxim Seepersad lifted his leg like a dog about to pee and broke wind.* Would've been nice. Great way to confirm his character from the beginning, not to mention all those stories about his personal habits. A man without compunction. The great public nose-digger. The great public ear-cleaner. The man who will scratch any itch anywhere any time. What was that other story? He'd clipped his nails at dinner with the Queen Mother, then proceeded to suck loudly at his teeth and clean them with a finger? And hadn't he sat before the cameras in the Oval Office and plucked nose hairs from his nostrils? Both apocryphal, probably. Unfortunately. Strange, too: it'll be no problem to ask him about the stealing he's condoned, the murders he's turned a blind eye to, but to try to confirm these personal stories, that's another matter. They form a line. Step beyond that line and you're no longer confronting him. It's weird, but somehow, in a way that's hard to understand, you'd be joining him. But, God, it's not easy to get that public farting out of your mind.

"Seepersad interview," Kira says into her microphone.

"Maxim Seepersad interview," Anya says into hers.

"I'll tell you," Seepersad says suddenly from his armchair. He crosses his ankles, clasps his hands on his ample belly. "The big boys — the *Globe*, the *Star* — they ignore me. Then, out of the blue, two calls. One from a left-wing rag —" He nods at Kira. "And one from a right-wing rag." He nods at Anya. "No one expects — what's the word? impartiality? fairness? — from you or the papers you write for. You're not journalists, you're crusaders. So I thought we could have some fun, the three of us. The same interview, at the same time, in the same place. The same words, the same ideas. So let's see what they do with them. The monster in one, the hero in the other? Or two monsters or two heroes? Maybe no monster, no hero. Maybe just a man doing his best in trying times —"

Anya says with restrained skepticism, "What is this, Mr. Seepersad? Loneliness? A plea for understanding?"

"Understanding!" Kira exclaims, turning to Anya in mock horror. "What's wrong with you, girl? Can't you see when you're being set up?"

Anya turns angrily to Kira. "Listen, you! You ask your questions, I'll ask mine, all right?"

"Touchy little bitch, aren't you," Kira sniffs, faking defensiveness. "No wonder he's one of yours."

"Ours? You mean yours."

Seepersad smiles benevolently. "Now, now, ladies, you can both have me, I'm more than enough for the two of you." He gives another hearty laugh.

To Kira it is as if he is drooling with desire: the lips that she sees slicked and twisted with humour, the teeth revealed behind their tautness discoloured and widely spaced. She wonders why she never noticed this before in the photographs, this imperfection of the teeth, and she realizes — even as the saliva in her mouth thickens, sours — that in none of the hundreds of shots taken of him is he smiling. "Okay," she says with a heavy tongue to Anya. "Go on, ask your goddamn questions."

Anya leans forward, face attractive in its seriousness. "Mr. Seepersad —" she says.

"Yes, Anya."

"The tenth anniversary of your ouster is approaching —"

And Seepersad averts his eyes, turns to the open windows. Outside, houses and trees across the street shimmer in the summer sunlight. But it is not this that he seeks, not this brightness, not this exposure. His gaze wanders across the room, past the two girls — girls, yes, young enough to be his granddaughters, sitting here with their questions and their restrained malevolence — to the painting, large, in heavy oils, hanging on the far wall.

A river, quiescent, of water the colour of damp concrete, hedged on either side — no banks here, no hint of the natural — by paved walks. A canal, then, a construction not of romance but of commerce. Beyond the far edge — the narrow walk hazy, gilded by an achieved lightness of hand — lies a road the colour and texture of rubber. The road is deserted, and not just temporarily: it holds the deeper quality of a passageway never used; seems suffused with the peculiar emptiness of the abandoned. On the other side of the road stretches an unpeopled square. The word *piazza* comes to Seepersad, conjures up his brief and inconsequential audience with Paul VI, a man brittle with the sexless desiccation particular to priests. Its cobblestones of dull gold extend across an expanse that dwarfs the buildings lining its distant periphery, attached, many-storeyed buildings — faded blue, faded yellow, faded green, heavy doors sealed, tiny windows darkened — of imposing and impenetrable façade. And above the hush and inanimation a sky of fragile presence wavering between a powdery blue and a smoky grey.

Seepersad thinks: Yes, that is where I belong. Right there. Right now. In that wet air thick with the smell of the canal.

That sickly-sweet Venetian stench of modern detritus steeped in ancient waters. Coddled by the reassuring architectural extravagance of that other, far grander age. When the society of man was more certain and one's position in it — fought for, carved out, claimed — was more clearly defined. Under that sky, so —

Anya says, with just a hint of impatience, "Did you hear my question, Mr. Seepersad?"

Seepersad blinks away his reverie, smiles thinly at her, as if emerging from a pleasant dream. "Yes, Anya. I heard your question." Something to do with stolen money, secret bank accounts, swindles and smuggling: the usual thing. "Well, what can I say?"

Kira alone returns Seepersad's smile, but with a knowing edge. She glances at Anya. "You've done your homework, I'll say that for you."

Anya ignores her, purses her lips — fine, shapely, lightly glossed — and awaits Seepersad's answer.

"Kira —" he says.

"Anya," says Anya. "The question was mine."

"Yes, forgive me." Seepersad, to his surprise, finds it more difficult now to perceive differences between the two, now that the questioning has begun. A query of this kind — informed, cutting — he would have expected from Kira. It is, suddenly, as though they have appropriated the room, they the hosts, he the visitor, they the possessors, he the possessed. Light perspiration slicks his forehead. He wipes at it with the flat of his hand.

Anya says, "Well?"

"It all depends on your perspective," he begins in a careful, meditative voice.

Kira snorts. "A coward's answer."

Anya keeps her gaze steady on him. "Are you saying you didn't know what was going on?"

"Tell me, Anya," he continues, grasping at equanimity. "What was going on?"

"For example, in August 1966 —"

"That's going a long way back —"

"— your government bought three used passenger jets —"

"No need to go on. I've heard it before. Five million unaccounted for —"

"Well?" Anya says. "You aren't going to say you don't know where that money went, are you?"

Seepersad shrugs, gestures in helplessness.

Kira says, "You know what they say, Seepersad."

"No, Kira, what do they say?"

"That ignorance is the last refuge of the scoundrel."

"And knowledge?" he asks. "What is knowledge?"

Kira says, "Honesty."

Anya says, "Truth."

Seepersad looks from one to the other, from Kira to Anya, speaks slowly: "There are those who would say that knowledge, the kind you're talking about, is the last doorway to despair."

Kira snorts again.

Anya says, "Ignorance is bliss?" She spices each word with a light sarcasm.

"That's the negative way of looking at it, Anya."

Anya smiles, nods in the way of comprehension but not, Seepersad notes, of conviction.

Kira shakes her head in tolerant dismissal, as of a child's precociousness.

Seepersad is heartened by their responses. They are willing to go beyond question and accusation, will engage in debate. "Next question?" he says.

Kira thinks: How could she have lived with him? How could she have put up with him for over forty years? But then, he couldn't always have been repulsive. In fact, he was quite handsome when he was young, if the photos are to be believed. She must have loved him, though. Even with his reputation for screwing around. Or maybe she'd simply needed him, in some way too personal to be evident. What was curious, of course, was that he had married her. She was not an unattractive woman but had let herself go, her face thickening, her body bloating as if she'd had air pumped into her. And she was apparently no great intellect, either. Air up there, too. Didn't come from a family of any great distinction. Or, more important, wealth. So why'd he, a man dangerous with ambition, marry her? Far as anybody can tell, for everything she was not. For the modesty she would bring to him, by association. The humility.

And then, after a few years, when he'd achieved his goals, when he'd made himself unassailable, she'd withdrawn, or been withdrawn. Gone — like that — from the public eye. To the dark rooms of their home, or to the darker chambers of the madhouse, or, people whispered, to the greatest, most final darkness of all. At the hands of her husband perhaps. But also rumoured to have been exiled, abroad, to Switzerland or Monaco or some obscure corner of London. Somehow, you could see it — the discomfort that would lead to retreat —

in the early photos, the only ones in which she appeared, the solemn bride — as if already doubting her luck — or, for a while, the timid wife retreating into a scowl, her role failing to impress itself on her.

Rumours of mistresses, of prostitutes, of legendary sexual prowess: the genesis of the mystification of Maxim Seepersad that would, at first, in the small place he was from, be like glory; and that would turn only much later, with the whispers of perversions political, economic, and sexual, to infamy.

And somewhere, perhaps, his wife. With a child, it was sometimes said. Perhaps loving him, perhaps hating him. Perhaps only relieved that her public role was over.

But wherever she is — or was — it's not here. Not in this living room well but coldly decorated. Not in this house. You sense no woman's hand. You sense no warmth. It's a room, a house, in which voices echo, in which, on a cold winter's evening, you could shiver half to death from emptiness.

Seepersad says, "I don't think that's any of your business, Kira."

"Is she alive, at least?"

"You're being superficial."

"And you're being elusive."

"But — don't you see? — this has nothing to do with anything."

Anya says, "Doesn't it? Don't you think your private life might help elucidate your public one?"

Kira affects astonishment, soundlessly mouths: *Elucidate?*

"How? This is just a desire for gossip, let's face it. A handful of dirt here, a smear of spit over there. We know everything about John Kennedy's private life, but I don't think the details of his affairs have added anything to our understanding of his public policies, do you?"

"But —" Kira intervenes.

"Let me finish. What do we know about the private lives of Churchill or de Gaulle or Brezhnev? One painted, smoked cigars. The other — I don't know — probably pontificated at the breakfast table. The third couldn't quit smoking. Big deal. Was there a Mrs. Brezhnev? Well, he had kids. And so? How would it help anyone to know the colour of Mrs. Brezhnev's hair or whether she preferred tea to coffee? None of this has anything to do with anything."

"People," Kira says, "wonder what happened to your wife. She seemed to disappear —"

"I've heard the rumours. I'm supposed to have strangled her or poisoned her or some such thing."

"Or exiled her," Anya interjects.

"That one from my supporters, probably," Seepersad says, bitterness lost in a bubble of laughter.

Anya smiles, and even Kira allows a hint of amusement to flit across her tightened features.

"But why," Kira pursues, "won't you even tell us — tell me — if she's alive?" She glances uneasily at Anya.

Anya says, "Maybe you can't tell us, Mr. Seepersad. Maybe you don't know what happened to your wife —"

Seepersad's eyes flit to Anya. She looks at him as if seeking an opening, a way to peek into places he would rather keep closed. "Why begin something that won't go further? What's the point? You won't get more from me. If I tell you she's alive, you'll go looking for her. If I tell you she's dead, you'll go looking for her grave."

"What are you afraid of, Seepersad?" Kira asks. "What are you afraid we'll find?"

"Afraid?" He pauses, thoughtful, as if the word is new to him. "But, Kira, I'm not afraid of anything. Not even —" And he glances from Anya to Kira and back again. " — of you."

Anya thinks: Could it be the room? So large, so clearly designer-decorated, but by a designer with a nineteenth-century sensibility. A room in which things, objects, take precedence: the overbearing lamps, the ornate vases, the ugly oil painting on the far wall. A room meant to diminish people. Even its owner. Surprisingly.

You hear about certain people all your life, but you never see them in the flesh. You always expect they're going to be taller, their reputations stretching them, somehow. And the closer you get to them, the more you stare at their pores and the bags under their eyes, the shorter they become, the more they shrink.

In the stories, he's always tall, he's always looking down, others always looking up. Strange to think that, looking at him now. He could be a country shopkeeper with a weight problem. A harmless old guy getting long in the tooth. It's never occurred to her before, but maybe that's all he really is: an old guy with a big belly getting older and slower day by day. But that would be denying his past, wouldn't it? That would be playing his game. And she has never been very good at playing games. As far as she is concerned, Maxim Seepersad could never be just an old guy growing older.

Anya says, "It has been suggested that your political career stems directly from —"

Seepersad interrupts with a click of regret, says, "I'm disappointed. I'd hoped you two would do something different. Instead, it's the same old song —"

"There are too many unanswered questions, Mr. Seepersad. Lots of ground to cover. Allegations of torture, your CIA connections —"

"You can't have everything, Anya, and there are many more that could be asked. It's been years since anyone's written about me. Except in the history books. And only ideologues are writing history these days."

Kira pulls back, leans back into her chair. "You old bastard." But she speaks softly, a chuckle hacking in her throat. "You just don't want to be judged on your record, do you? You think you can get away with it all."

"But he has," Anya says. "That's the thing."

"Not true," Kira replies softly. "Listen to this house. Feel it. You see? He hasn't got away with a thing. Not a single thing." She fixes Seepersad with a cocked eye. "Do you feel you've got away with it all, Seepersad?" she says, the question stated like a declaration of victory.

Seepersad thinks: What can they know, these young people? They think: Everything. Look at them, so cocksure, so self-possessed, this journalism of theirs just a game, even if a serious game. Experienced in their world. Even hardened in their terms. And yet, apparently so artless, without subtlety. This disarming lack of guile, the charm of it: he fears that maybe it's all just part of their game, that maybe he's underestimating them, falling for their ploy, a victim of their artifice

42

and of his own gullibility before the apparent sincerity of youth.

But he has the upper hand still, doesn't he? It reassures him to recall that he knows their context as well as they know his, possibly even better, with greater accuracy; for while they labour under the heavy braiding of rumour and speculation and ideology and interpretive history that has knotted itself around him and his life, he knows the papers they work for, has read their work, discerned their biases, has even constructed a family past for each: parents who shared an island with him, who knew the same people, attended the same parties, scooped from the same troughs; fled from the growing chaos before he did; and now their daughters, opposite twins born out of the same egg, here in his living room, questioning him as their parents might have done, expressing their contempt for him even as they profited from the opportunities he himself had created. So he knows much about them, Kira and Anya, understands the picture of him their parents would have conveyed, understands the similarities and dissimilarities of their outlooks. Retains, he knows, that all-important upper hand. The thought cheers him, gives him a sensation of buoyancy.

"You know," Seepersad says, "everything you've heard about me, all the lies and half-lies and truths and half-truths, all of that is just because I was doing my job. No one disappeared under my —"

"Sit on it, Seepersad," Kira says.

"That's the oldest excuse in the world for being a louse," Anya says.

Seepersad's body goes cold — this, in his buoyancy, is

not the reaction he hopes for at this point of the debate —
and it is with effort that he controls the irrationality swelling
within him. It's been a long time since he's felt this urge to
lash out, to strike blindly at those who, uncomprehending,
unforgiving, cherishing only their own interests and agendas,
so easily applied to him the labels of other times, other
places, other conditions. He would like to believe the impulse
gone, its disappearance a sign of the maturity — it is the
word he has settled on — that eluded him in the days of
power. But he sees now, with disappointment, that it has only
been submerged in the unchallenged ease in which he has
come, over the years, to live.

Kira says, "You want the list of names from Amnesty
International? Why don't you just come clean for once,
Seepersad."

Seepersad nods gravely at her, concealing his discomfort
with thoughtfulness. "Come," he says, deciding to take control of the agenda. "I want to show you something." He gets
to his feet with less effort than usually required.

Anya and Kira stare suspiciously at him, at each other.

"Out to the backyard," Seepersad says. "I want to show
you my hobby." He gestures disarmingly towards the kitchen.

Kira and Anya reach for their tape recorders, hitch the
straps onto their shoulders, and holding the microphones
carefully before them follow him through the living room,
through the kitchen — brightly remodelled and clean in the
disinfected, untenanted way of a hotel, evidence of infrequent
use and of professional cleaners — to the back door, painted
a plasticized white and with a small square window cut into
it, the pane of old glass opaque with scratches and reflected
illumination.

Seepersad opens the door, leads the way out, the wooden stairs leading down to the lawn swaying under them, seeming to settle under their weight. Out here, in the backyard fenced and shrubbed, in the somnolence of the warm summer afternoon, under the slash of a pigeon against the sky hazy with humidity, it is possible to forget that just streets away the city is rushing about its business in a sizzling of petulance and verve.

"You know," Seepersad says, his voice hushed, "I regret all this."

Kira and Anya look around: at the grass limp and ragged at their feet, at the earth beneath dry and flinty. At the flowerbeds, collapsing in neglect, that line the yard all the way to the back fence, the shrubbery — rose bushes at the sides, tomato plants or something similar at the back — sparse and sickly where still alive, browned into stripped sticks where not, stuck precariously into soil hardened and cracked.

"What exactly?" Anya asks. "The garden?"

"The failure. Of nerve, in a strange way."

"This is hardly new," Kira says. "Nobody ever claimed you had a green thumb. You killed the island's agriculture, after all."

Seepersad cannot suppress a smile: is there anything they won't blame him for? And it occurs to him that, even now, he fulfils a function useful to the island. The convenient scapegoat. Agriculture dead? Blame Seepersad. Treasury empty? Blame Seepersad. Toilet backed up? Blame Seepersad.

"People are starving because of you, Seepersad. You're the one who picked up fat cheques for letting multinationals

45

grab the land from small farmers. You're the one who gave them tax breaks to grow export crops instead of food crops. Or have you forgotten all that?"

He can only shrug at the accusation, move on. But the regret won't leave him, for his dreams have never been of this sterility; have been of cultivation, of a yard landscaped and burgeoning, shaped by hand and mind, nurtured by the combination of selflessness and selfishness finely balanced against one another that seems to him the best of human motivations.

But he has discovered the work — a labour of primeval instinct — to be not one of his talents. The demands of the garden quickly proved less fulfilling than his anticipation of them. All the weeding, pruning, watering, the tedious battles against insects and rodents and disease, the weekly mowings of the lawn that he found particularly debilitating to the soul; the tasks, Sisyphean, claimed ever more of his time and thought and ingenuity, began eating at his patience and at his rapidly fading fantasy. He'd thought of hiring a gardener, but such a tacit admission of his own incapacities would have defeated the purpose. He would do it himself, or it would not be done.

In a vain attempt to make the work more manageable, he trimmed back some of the shrubs, dug up others. And one day in a fit of rage — this incomprehensible, uncontrollable urge to lash out — he thrust the roaring lawnmower at a rose bush, half expecting it to recoil in fear, half disappointed when it failed to do so. With the growl of the machine filling the garden, hammering and reverberating in his head, he reached for his pruning shears. But decided, feeling their weight and balance in his hand, that, no, they were too delicate for his purpose; fetched instead from the house the machete he kept under his bed and slashed, grunting with effort and gratification, at the recalcitrant rose bush. The stalks, thin, thorny, melted before the blade. Then, perspiring, breathless, he turned his back on the wound of severed stalks and petals and sauntered into the house, the machete swinging loosely from his hand, his back turned for good on the garden.

"Nobody can hide in forgetfulness, Kira," he says finally. "There's always too many people to remind you, too many tales to follow you."

Anya says, "Too many memories to haunt you?"

Kira says, "You sleep well at night, Seepersad?"

"Very well, Kira."

"I hear you use sleeping pills."

"And you know about my hemorrhoids, too, I suppose?"

"No. Didn't know you *had* a pain in the ass, too." Kira cackles in amusement, the sound unpleasant and intrusive in the way of theatrical barroom laughter.

Anya looks around, eyes sweeping the yard. "This is your hobby, Mr. Seepersad?" She puts the question in a surprisingly delicate manner.

As if speaking to a person of uncertain mental stability, it occurs to Seepersad. "No-no. That would be sad, wouldn't it?" Or as if maintaining precarious balance on the edge of derision.

"Seeper-sad, you might say," Anya replies deadpan.

"More like super-sad," Kira says, grinning.

Seepersad rewards them with a smile, even though their puns unsettle him. The humour is too easy, he cannot read it. "Come," he says, leading them across the fading lawn to the far end, through a gap in the shrubbery to a gate in the back fence. He undoes the latch, motions them through.

Kira intones: " 'Come in to my parlour, said the spider to the fly.' "

"Nothing so ominous," Seepersad says. "Besides, who's the spider here, and who's the fly?"

Kira and Anya find themselves ushered into what feels like a roofless room, small and crowded, but by what they do not immediately know. It takes them several seconds to discern that what they are seeing is clustered statuary, fanciful figures of grey or alabaster perched on pedestals. Figures of piety and glory, pity and ecstasy. Here the Virgin clasps at the Christ-child, there an angelic herald sucks at a concrete trumpet. Chubby cherubs, winged and scantily clad, hover in arrested ascent, while one of their number hugs the legs of an adult Christ with exposed heart. At the base of an obelisk of black marble, a spray of doves rises in frozen flight from a concrete thicket. The symbols — the Virgins, the Christs, the trumpets, the doves — repeat themselves in minute variation, a tilt of the head here, a spreading of wings there.

Kira says, "Holy shit."

Anya says nothing, just stares as if mesmerized.

"Cemetery statues, Seepersad?" Kira says.

"Funerary statuary," he replies firmly.

"You in the business?"

"I'm a collector."

"Is it a religious thing, or what?"

"Hardly. I"'m not what you or anybody would call a religious man."

"So what's it about, then?"

Seepersad shrugs. "I find them beautiful."

"And?"

"And the rest you'll have to figure out for yourself. This is as clean as I can come, Kira." Seepersad holds back close to the open gate, watches the young women gazing at his collection.

Anya casts a suspicious eye over the statues, approaches them with circumspection. Her teeth, sharp and white, nip at her lower lip.

Kira, he sees, is more distanced, views them with a cooler, less personal eye. Sees them not as statements of piety or art, not as objects of beauty, but as clues to the deeper recesses of his personality.

"Seventeen," Seepersad says.

"Pardon?"

"Seventeen," he repeats. "You were counting them, weren't you?"

She nods almost imperceptibly.

Anya walks slowly past her, up to a statue of Christ crucified in stone. "There's one like this over my grandfather's grave," she says, her voice husky.

Seepersad takes a step forward, but then stops himself. Anya, in her sudden emotion, has claimed the space around her, has drawn a private boundary. "A beauty," he says after a moment. "And that's the thing, you see." He grows more animated as he feels Anya's privacy evaporating at the sound of his voice. "Why should we wait until we're dead to collect them? Why not enjoy them before? It's like life insurance. What's the point? Neither makes any sense."

Kira looks over at him. "Life insurance isn't for you, Seepersad. It's for those you leave behind, to make their lives easier. Assuming you care, of course." Her left hand gestures dismissively at the statues. "But why collect this shit in the first place? Gives me the creeps."

"You're not seeing them," Seepersad says, a touch of condescension creeping into his words. "But Anya — she sees them, don't you, Anya?"

Anya moves on into the thicket of statues, pausing occasionally to let her hand caress a concrete fold or slip along a marble edge. "I used to play in a cemetery when I was a kid," she says quietly, "after we moved here. It was the safest place my mum could think of to turn me loose. No cars, only the occasional bicycle, hardly any people. It was great."

"No wonder you're so weird," Kira says with a pained expression.

"I used to hide behind trees to watch the burials —"

"Jesus!"

"You religious, Kira?" Seepersad asks ingenuously.

Kira snorts in derision. "Haven't been to church since I was six —"

"But are you religious?"

"You kidding?"

"And you, Anya?"

"I —" Anya's hands quickly withdraw from a cherub's foot, become agitated. "No." Grasp tightly at the strap of her tape recorder.

Seepersad and Kira both stare at her, wait.

"Well, maybe. Why not?" Her equanimity refashions itself, visibly, like a shattering glass suddenly arrested, then — magically — reconstituted. "I guess so." She releases the strap, her slim, pretty hands lightly rubbing, squeezing at one another not in distress but in quiet contentment.

Seepersad nods, thinks with regret that he could grow to like Anya. He is comforted by her uncertainty, her confusion. "Good," he says finally. "The world isn't a simple place. There's nothing quite as dangerous as an unquestioning man, a man without doubts."

"Or a woman," Kira says.

"Or a woman," Seepersad acknowledges.

But Anya has not heard their exchange. She is continuing her tour of the statues, reaching up now and then to trace the flare of an extended wing, to explore with her fingertips the details of a sculpted foot.

"So tell me, Seepersad," Kira says, "how does it feel to be a deposed king?"

Seepersad bristles at the question, and the picture comes to him of Kira picking minutely through the bumps and ridges of his brain. And Anya too, he decides after a moment, but with a greater delicacy, even with a touch of distaste. "I've never been a king —"

"Your crown was invisible, but —"

"— that's just what the newspapers called me."

"— it was there."

"Anya," Seepersad calls, his voice thinned. "Anya, do you think I was a king?" And when he hears himself, as he hears the sound of the words forming in the bright and heated air, he realizes what a plaintive question it is.

Anya looks around from the figure she is examining — not one of Seepersad's favourites, a miniature, little more than a foot high, of a cherub flat-footed, earthbound, static in its attitude, as if lost and wondering what to do next — and considers the question for a long moment. Her lips are compressed, her eyes distant and glassy in the way of the drugged. Finally, with the slightest of movements, she nods yes.

Seepersad is disappointed. He sees that his statues speak to Anya as they speak to him; he expects more from her, but accepts with equanimity what he feels to be a betrayal.

Kira turns to him in triumph.

He can only shrug.

"Well?" Kira says. She holds her microphone up to him.

"Well what? No matter what I say you won't believe me. It'll sound like rationalizing after the fact, and that's how you'll write it, am I right? The facts and the details hardly matter any more."

"I don't know, Seepersad. Seems to me it's a question of how you view the facts —"

"Of perspective?"

"No. Of how hard your sense of reality is. The sky is blue, and you must know it's blue even if it looks green or red or yellow through your coloured glasses."

"So I should acknowledge all the epithets about me are right: thieving, corrupt, murderous —"

"It'll be a start."

"Give up the pound of flesh —"

"And the blood."

"So you'll have your scapegoat. Then what?"

"Maybe you could return the money, too."

"What money? I'm not a rich man, Kira."

"And this house?"

"I had a good salary. I led a frugal life. All my savings went into the house. I barely get by now."

52

Kira shakes her head. "Yeah, right."

"I have a question for you, Kira."

"I'm the journalist, Seepersad."

"I'm just wondering what all this has to do with you. You were born here, weren't you?"

She nods, waits for him to go on.

"So what's the point, for you?"

"I'm a journalist."

"That's not enough. I wouldn't exactly call this a professional interview. There's more —"

"Yeah, Seepersad, there's more. There's my parents. They had to leave, they saw what you were doing to the island and they hated you for it. As long as I've known them, they've had this sadness about them, a kind of perpetual homesickness. And they blame you, for everything. I grew up with the name Seepersad as a metaphor for incompetence and monstrosity of every kind."

"So what are you doing here? What are you looking for?"

Kira takes a deep breath, stares up into the white sky. "I just had to see for myself."

"And?"

Spittle bubbles and bursts at the corner of her mouth, sprays glittering when she speaks. "And I'm not convinced that they're wrong, my parents."

"Mr. Seepersad?" Anya calls from among the statuary.

"Yes, Anya." He steps towards her, away from Kira.

"How much is this one?" Her hand is resting on the shoulder of the lost cherub.

"It's not for sale, Anya."

"I'll pay anything you ask."

"It's part of my collection —"

Kira comes up to them. "Everybody has his price, Seepersad. Especially you."

Her words, even though unsurprising in themselves, still bite at him. He reaches out and picks up the off-white figure from its pedestal. It is heftier than it looks, more solid than might be guessed from the tentativeness of the cherub's expression. This is why he has held on to it, why he is reluctant to part with it: there is more to the figure than is apparent. He holds it out to Anya. "Take it," he says. "It's yours. No charge."

Anya takes the statuette in both hands, brings it close to her, cradling it the way the inexperienced would a baby.

Seepersad turns to Kira. He wants to savour the moment, his own sense of triumph; he wants to enjoy her annoyance. But his pleasure evaporates when he sees that she is smirking at him.

Seepersad closes the door behind them.

The house is cool after the backyard, but Kira cannot decide whether it is a relief to be back inside or not, cannot decide whether this is freshness that she feels or chill. Perhaps, she thinks, she is coming down with the flu. After the glare outside, the kitchen no longer seems so bright, so modern, so clean, reveals now traces of an ingrained dinginess in the corners, along the floorboards, in the cracks between the rubber tiles.

Seepersad offers a drink: "Something soft? Something hard? Something in between?" It is an old joke from his university days, but for the first time he feels the power of its vulgarity.

Kira wags her microphone at him. "Can I quote you on that?" She is not amused.

Anya, clutching at her statuette, simply shakes her head in refusal.

Seepersad leads them back into the living room, pauses before the painting — the river, the square, the buildings, the sky — directs their attention towards it by looking at it himself. "Picked it up at a flea market," he says.

"No kidding," Kira responds without hesitation.

"You don't like it?" He can't keep the pain from his voice. It is important to him that she like something of his, if not his statues — that, he knows, is an acquired taste — at least the painting, a work less demanding, more accessible, more — the word coming to him with an aftertaste of contempt — *proletarian*.

"Doesn't do much for me, Seepersad."

"Anya?"

Anya steps closer to the painting, runs the fingers of her free hand along the ridges of hard, dry paint, exploring its texture, as if reading it by touch.

Seepersad notices once more what fine hands she has, and he finds that he must resist an urge to reach out for them, an urge, he notes with curiosity, that holds no sexual thrill.

"I could lose myself in this painting," Anya says.

"If you want my opinion," Kira says to her, not unkindly, "you don't need the painting for that. You're long gone."

Seepersad's anger flares. "D'you mind? I'm talking to Anya."

"I was just —"

"What's your problem? What's eating you?"

Kira is caught unawares by his vehemence, can at first

make no reply. Then she speaks softly: "Cool it, Seepersad, I'm not your wife, you can't talk to me that way."

Seepersad, reassuming control as if shrugging into a coat, turns away from her, says, "Tell me more, Anya."

Her fingertips still wander the surface of the painting: the dark water, the gilded paving, the empty square, hesitating only at the distant buildings — at the darkness of their interiors and their sense of quarantine — and the sky that in its fragility promises a ruthless absorption.

"Anya?"

Her index finger pauses on one of the darkened windows, the nail tracing again and again the squared outline of it.

"Careful," Seepersad whispers. "The canvas is old, it's very brittle."

Her finger pauses, the edge of the nail resting on the darkened square. Then, before Seepersad can protest, even as Kira gasps, she presses the nail forward through the window, her finger swiftly penetrating the canvas to the second knuckle. Then she steps backwards, away from the painting, withdrawing her hand to the statuette.

Seepersad is aghast, his gaze riveted on the hole in the canvas, the window now as if opened to the mysterious interior.

And he does not feel the blow. Just feels himself crumple under the force of it, feels his knees give way. Senses a diminution of his vision in a surging darkness. He feels the wooden floor under him, knows he supports himself now on his hands, his bodily strength concentrated there, *only* there. A dull throb thumps in his head: it is as if his skull is expanding. As if through a tunnel now, he sees the river, the square, the gaping window; watches as the sky takes on a living hue, boils with storm cloud.

He does not feel the second blow. Just knows that his head has been wrenched brutally forward. When he struggles once more to the painting — only with his eyes, his head will not rise — he sees through a black straw nothing but the window, perceives with astonishment a golden illumination materializing in the darkness beyond. A hot, thick liquid floods his mouth, and he smells a familiar sickly-sweet stench.

He does not feel the third blow.

Or the fourth.

Or the fifth.

Kira shepherds Anya out and pulls the front door shut behind them. She carries both their bags and tape recorders. Together they walk to the concrete stairs. Neither speaks, neither has anything to say.

The afternoon is well advanced, the air sultry, the sunlight thickening. Streets away, in a distant rumble, the rush home has begun.

Kira thinks, with awe: But the world has not changed.

They make their way down to the sidewalk.

Anya still clutches the statuette, pressing it tightly to her shoulder, her left hand curled around the head, her right around the legs. There is discoloration on only one edge of the small base.

Kira says, "Can I give you a ride somewhere?" Her car is parked farther down the street.

Anya refuses with a shake of her head. She walks to the garage.

"Did you see the car?" Kira asks. "I asked him about it before you arrived. He said vandals did it. Years ago. 'People who wield clubs instead of questions.' He just left it like that, figured there was no point in getting it fixed." But Anya gives no indication of having heard her, and Kira gets the feeling that her speech is too rapid, that she is babbling, that her suppressed panic is beginning to spurt in pointless prattle.

Anya brushes past the vines, stands just inside the garage. Using both hands, she flings the cherub at the car. It flies into the darkness, crunches through the windshield.

Kira takes her by the arm, pulls her back out into the sunlight.

Anya smiles at her, takes her handbag and tape recorder from Kira's shoulder.

"I see," Kira murmurs after a moment, wondering that she didn't see it before, understanding that she had not been open to the possibility. "I see. You're the real story here, aren't you."

Anya says nothing, blinks back tears.

"So will you tell me about your mother?"

Anya shakes her head: no.

Kira shrugs in resignation. "All right," she says. "I think I understand." And after a moment: "But do you?" She does not expect an answer, gets none.

On impulse Kira leans forward, embraces Anya, presses her lips to hers, lets them linger. Anya's lips are hot and dry, unresponsive. Kira releases her. Without a further word, they go their separate ways.

Smoke

"I WAS LISTENING to the French radio this weekend —"

"En français, s'il-te-plaît, Francis!"

"En français?"

"Ici, dans cette classe, on parle français, Francis. C'est pourquoi vous êtes tous ici."

"Yeah, well —"

"Francis, c'est toi qui paie ce cours ou ta compagnie?"

"Ma company."

"Ahh!"

"So, can I continue?"

"En français?"

"Non en français —"

"Francis, on perd du temps, mer—"

"Just this —"

"Okay, okay, do anybody mind? No? Okay, if you insist, Francis."

59

"Merci. Anyway, as I was saying, I was listening to the
French radio on the weekend —"

"Radio-Canada."

"Oui, right. And two people were talking, a man and a
woman, and to tell you the truth I wasn't getting too much of
the conversation —"

"Question de pratique, Francis, l'oreille —"

"— but I got one sentence loud and clear —"

"Bravo!"

"— well, loud but not so clear."

"Pardon?"

"Yeah, that's what I said."

"Alors, c'était quoi la phrase, Francis?"

"Well, it was either 'Je veux la voir' or 'Je veux l'avoir'.
And I figure there's a pretty significant difference between
the two."

"Oui, d'accord."

"So which is it?"

"Bon, c'est une question de contexte. What was it — you
know — their subject?"

"Je ne sais pas."

"Tu ne sais pas."

"Non."

"B'en. . . ."

"So you don't know either, eh? You see my problem?"

"Non, pas vraiment."

"Well, I mean, if you don't understand, and I don't understand — do you people really understand each other when
you speak?"

It was from the minutes of disbelieving silence following
the question that Francis surmised that his wit had failed.

Lise, with a sigh of exasperation, signalled the break with her usual cryptic "Cinq minutes," which often became dix or even quinze minutes depending, Francis thought, on the number of cigarettes she needed to consume or the number of phone calls she had to return. He knew that she found his questions disruptive, knew that the levity he occasionally attempted to provide — he found the earnestness of the class oppressive — was not always appreciated. But it was the only way he was going to survive.

It was not of his own volition that Francis was the only man in a class of eight. The company he worked for — he peddled bicycle parts all over southern Ontario — had dreams of expansion. The Quebec market beckoned, and because he had declared himself bilingual in his application form, he was chosen to lead the commercial charge. He regretted now not having taken the question on linguistic ability seriously, regretted having said *au revoir* at the conclusion of his interview. So here he was, having convinced his boss that his French had merely rusted, oiling the non-existent on company money. He felt it to be unfair. After all, he knew tons of people who claimed to have a working knowledge of French, some collecting extra salary because of it, most of whom strangled themselves on *bonjour* and sweated bullets through to *au revoir*. But there was nothing to be done. To admit to having lied on his application form would bring immediate retribution. His boss, a born-again Christian, tolerated no untruths but his own.

Francis had gone to the first class, for beginners, not expecting to return for the second. But it had not been as discouraging an experience as he'd feared. He'd remembered many of the basics he'd picked up, almost accidentally considering the effort he'd put into studying, in high school. *Je suis* was no problem, neither was *vous êtes*, and although he was rather cavalier — did it really matter? — about the gender of things, the vocabulary of nouns — *la table, la chaise, le livre* — proved not terribly taxing.

And then, sitting across the round table from him, there was Angelica.

Angelica. The best reason for learning French he'd ever come across. Angelica. The name suited her. Long blonde hair — the dark roots were not difficult to ignore — curled into a billowing cascade. Green eyes of a tantalizing boldness. Lips full and precisely painted, shaped as if for, well . . . speaking French. When, at the break, she strolled out of the classroom, he remained rooted to his seat, only his eyes capable of motion, his mind racing to register all that he saw.

He'd got an inkling he was in trouble when, before the beginning of the second session, he popped into the washroom to check his hair and moustache. He was careful to comb them neat, but the strands of premature grey, prominent in the dead light, distressed him as never before. He let the cold water run to freezing and desperately splashed his face, enjoying the bite as the water stung his skin from the colour of a freshly peeled potato to a spotty ruddiness, an approximation, he thought, of vigorous health. He straightened his tie, hitched up his pants so that the flabbiness around his waist was camouflaged, shined his shoes briefly against his calves, and hurried to the class.

Angelica's was a beauty that disarmed him. A sad and desperate inner voice told him that he could never have a woman like her, could never hope to appeal to her sense of glamour and style. Yet even this despair was delicious; it fed on itself to create a kind of spurious optimism, an aching hope that was more satisfying for the apparent impossibility of its fulfilment.

It was during the break of the third session that he got up the nerve to approach her. He had tried, but failed, to catch her eye during the class. She rarely looked in his direction, appeared to peer right through him when she did, her eyes — curiously blue today — liquid and distant. When he spoke in class, she seemed to concentrate more intently on note-taking, and it was only with effort that he convinced himself that she was not consciously ignoring his interest.

When Lise called the break, he waited for Angelica to leave the classroom, not wanting to appear too eager. After a minute, unable to contain himself any longer, he took a deep breath — it was his way of compensating for the cigarettes he had given up three months before — and, straightening his clothes, followed her out.

She was not, as he had expected, with some of the others at the coffee machine. And she was not in any of the other classrooms or in the administration office. He decided that she must have gone to the washroom. He perched carefully on a chair close to the door, flicked sightlessly through an old magazine — he was more than halfway through it before realizing it was in Italian or Spanish — and waited.

And waited, and waited.

And it was only when the women at the coffee machine began drifting back to the classroom that he realized there was one room, at the very back, that he had neglected to check: the smoking room. But it was too late. The smokers, Angelica among them, were already filing in, all chuckling at a story that Lise was telling — in English, yet. He watched them enter the classroom, took several deep breaths to dispel his exasperation.

And so, before the fourth session the following week and after a weekend spent brooding on social mechanics and the demanding gestures of love, he stopped at a corner store not far from the school and bought a pack of the cigarettes he had smoked for almost twenty years. With it, and through breath wheezing in a chest tight with tension, he purchased a butane lighter of transparent red plastic.

Concentration on language was difficult that evening. His mind, too aware of the extraordinary weight of the purchases in his pocket, would not grasp French numerals beyond *seize*: If seventeen was *dix-sept*, ten plus seven, and eighteen *dix-huit*, ten plus eight, then why weren't the numbers before, fifteen and sixteen, say, *dix-cinq* and *dix-six*? He could count easily enough from *un* to *seize*, but the moment the mathematical switch came his mind collapsed into confusion.

Lise was not unfamiliar with the problem; had seen it often in nervous beginners to whom the simplest concept could easily become a major hurdle. She pointed out that he was being too literal, suggested that he make an effort to distance himself from the English and to simply accept the French. He knew she was right, but the simple problem had taken on, in his mind at least, additional weight: how much more complex it all seemed that his incapacities were revealed before a roomful of women. The embarrassment muddled things even further and his relief was immense when a frustrated Lise called the break early.

The smoking room was small and windowless, with dog-eared travel posters pinned to the walls and chairs stacked in a corner. It was crowded, the smokers of several classes standing around in a mist blued and thickened by the fluorescent lighting.

Francis hesitated at the door, his nose twitching involuntarily at the acrid bite of the air, his eyes blinking at its sting. Looking around for Angelica, he was only dimly aware of the step he was about to take. And it was only when he spotted her in the far corner in animated conversation with Lise that his fingers withdrew the cigarette pack from his pocket and ripped at the cellophane. He edged his way through the crowd towards her.

Neither Angelica nor Lise paid any attention to him when he squeezed in beside them. Their conversation — something to do with the merits of various sportscars — had the intensity of competition, left no room for a graceful entrance. He removed a cigarette from the pack, felt around in his pocket for the lighter. As he brought flame to the tip, he heard himself mumble, "I almost bought a 'vette once."

Lise's eyes flickered at him, momentarily without recognition, her words dying on her lips.

"A 'vette," he repeated.

Angelica frowned. Her eyes, brown today, tightened onto his cigarette.

Then a caustic odour, like that of burning rubber, caused him to gag, and flame flared hot against his nose: he had lit the filter. He snatched the cigarette from his lips, dropped it into the ashtray that Lise held out to him.

He grinned, shrugged, carefully lit another. Was thrilled to see that Angelica, expelling smoke between her funnelled lips, was amused. He took a hearty pull at the cigarette, felt the smoke snake warmly down his throat.

Angelica said, "I don't like Corvettes."

The smoke hit his lungs.

Lise, chuckling, said, "In Quebec we call them — how do you say it? You know, for hemorrhoids?"

His head went light. His stomach did a slow turn.

"Suppositories?" Angelica offered.

"Yes, suppositories."

They both laughed, but Francis was too taken up with the upheaval in his stomach, and the cold flush surging through him, to manage more than a weak smile. He took another puff from the cigarette — what choice did he have? — to try to disguise his discomfort. Was grateful when after a minute his stomach settled down enough that the first wave of a familiar pleasure crept through his body.

Lise said, "And we have a saying: *Grosse Corvette, petite pissette.*"

Francis, eager to return to the conversation, asked what it meant.

Lise, grinning wickedly, repeated the phrase slowly. She winked at Angelica. "You can figure it out, Francis?"

It didn't take him long — he knew it had to be something unpleasant. He chuckled weakly, then concentrated on finishing his cigarette.

Their conversation veered on without him, trading the technical intricacies of Porsche against those of Saab, Jaguar, and Mercedes Benz.

The truth was that Francis knew next to nothing about cars, and cared even less. He would have bought himself something fancy to replace his seven-year-old Honda if he could have afforded it, but he couldn't, and knew he never would be able to.

The break came to an end. They put their cigarettes out and trooped back to the classroom. Lise put the French numerals aside for another day, introduced them to the verb *avoir*.

Afterwards, Francis watched from a distance as Angelica drove out of the parking lot in an old Toyota. He wasn't totally satisfied with the way the evening had gone, but he wasn't unhappy either. He had made contact, however tenuous. On his way home he stopped at the convenience store and picked up a car magazine.

It was not an unpleasant life. It was just not life as he'd pictured it at eighteen or nineteen. The apartment had been larger; the car flashier, sportier, European perhaps; the evenings livelier and less predictable. Who, after all, in the mindless optimism of late adolescence, fantasizes for himself evenings of beer bottles, frozen dinners, cigarettes, and late-night television reruns? His dream of social exuberance had never for a moment included Ricky Ricardo and Sergeant Bilko.

There had been no notion of a wife, either — women, of course, varied and numerous, each of them too desirous of his company to be jealous — yet he'd acquired one of those, too. For a few years, at least. How, he knew. Why, he was less certain. It had something to do with his Bachelor of Commerce degree, now framed and hanging in his parents' living room beside his graduation photograph. And something to do with the pride of settling into his estimator's desk at a transport company. And, in some unfathomable way, with the pictures that came to him of friends and acquaintances, fellow graduates with more impressive résumés, ushered into carpeted offices of plush grey and chrome. But, most of all, it had to do with his parents, and the choices they made so easily for him towards their own vision of the good life.

His life, as he looked back on it, had followed a simply plotted path through a map of conventionality. Kindergarten and primary school. Sunday school and then, with adulthood, church. University downtown, living first in a college dormitory, later sharing a house with other students — with the requisite all-night parties of alcoholic ingestion and regurgitative indigestion. His parents, living seamless lives in the newly urban periphery, were a convenient refuge through all this, providing the occasional infusion of fresh cash and fresh food, and retreat from the echoing loneliness of emptied halls at Thanksgiving, Christmas, and reading week. Only once were there sufficient funds to head south, a few days of pre-planned adventure on an overcrowded Bahamas beach, days discouraging in sunburn and the peculiar wrenching of rum-induced hangovers.

Francis hadn't particularly wished to study commerce at university. He had, in high school, developed a passion for theatre, and in his most whimsical moments saw himself in Shakespearean costume. He had preserved a picture of himself from his high school drama club's production of *A Midsummer Night's Dream*: himself as Bottom, the ass's head tilted back to reveal his grin, sincere despite the theatrical whispers of "Hey, jackass! Yo, asshole!" that followed him down the corridors during the weeks of rehearsal. The applause at the end of the performance, the congratulations of teachers and fellow performers, even the crystalline scream of obscenity from the back of the darkened hall — it all remained with him through the years: the magic of triumph, the sound of reward recollected and unquantifiable. But it was never repeated, save in feverish retellings in his mind.

Francis remembered his father's reaction when, one evening at dinner, he broached the topic of the fine arts and, even more tentatively, a theatrical career. His father's eyes never left his plate, flickered as if in search of response at the slices of gravied roast beef, the mashed potatoes, the too-green peas. His mother, uneasy when she could not be jolly, withdrawing into an absorbed silence at the merest intimation of familial tension, lost her appetite, busied herself spooning the leftover potato into a ball.

"Fine arts," his father said. "Hmmm. Painting, dancing, stuff like that. Fine hobbies, I suppose, eh?"

"Fine professions, too," Francis ventured. "A painter, an act —"

"You need a real profession, Francis." His father chewed as he spoke, the crunching of gristle lending bite to his words. "You can always do some play-acting on the side. There's lots of community theatre, weekend stuff."

"But I —"

"But you've got to have a financial base in life, son. It's called security. And you don't get that by putting on a pretty costume and reciting some other guy's words on a stage."

Francis was tempted to argue back, but the determined scraping of the serving spoon in the potato bowl — the sound like that of a dentist's pick screeching at teeth — drew his attention to his mother.

There was a peculiar set to her face, a distress unreadable in that it was impossible to say whose side she was on, his or his father's. Francis had seen the look only once, two years before, when his sister, a full five years his senior and

69

accepted with bemused resignation by their parents as a "hippie", revealed to the family that her new live-in lover was named Cheryl. "Cheryl?" their father had said. "He must have had a time in sch—" His sister, without breaking stride, pointed out that Cheryl was a woman's name. And it was at that moment that their mother's face assumed its unreadability. She spoke not a word; his sister left a few minutes later. Parents and daughter hadn't spoken since, although Francis secretly made occasional calls to his sister to check up on her.

Francis never forgot his mother's expression. He saw shadows of it flit across her face when television news images grew too graphic; saw hints of it, too, when their church discussion group split venomously over abortion. And when he saw it once more in this discussion of his future, he curbed his tongue, agreed without further argument that some kind of business degree would stand him in best stead.

It was only later, in bed, that he raged and mourned for his surrendered dreams.

Classes, examinations, graduation, job. To his parents, distrustful of flash and sensing danger in exposure, his was a familiar and comforting path. They took pleasure in pointing out the unflagging conventionality of it. And when Judy, a secretary at the transport company, entered the picture, their pleasure was unabashed.

They went out fairly often, he and Judy. Movies, dinners, a wine bar. They necked in his car, petted in his apartment. She would not sleep with him, though, always pulling back when simple arousal verged on physical passion. He was patient, even on the day that she, in tight slacks, tripped breathily over into orgasm with his thigh clutched between

70

hers and then, unmindful of his desire, declared herself hungry. Eventually, out of simple circumstance, he introduced her to his parents. Wedding plans were formed. Francis, not in love but not not in love either, did not object, didn't even really want to. It all seemed of a piece with his parents' acceptance of his newly acquired adulthood, the logical extension of the security they so highly valued. Of a piece, too, with the first real job, and with a sense of his generation's getting on with life. The setting of the date was the first time his father let him open a bottle of wine, the first time he let him pour. Francis had the sense they were all playing a game, but one in which he had a new and unaccustomed status. He decided, quickly, that he enjoyed it.

The convenience store beckoned once more before the next session. He hadn't intended to, but he had somehow succeeded in emptying the cigarette pack. He thought briefly of the three months of effort he had been through: of the weeks of agony when will-power wavered and tobacco seduced even his dreams; of the moments of thrill later on when he relished his freedom. He had been careful not to become judgemental about smokers, not so much because he detested the self-righteousness that came so easily to the reformed, but because he was aware of how simple it would be to revert to old and comfortable habits.

And now here he was, the convert reverted. It was, he had to admit, a relief. He felt only a vague disappointment in himself, one leavened by the knowledge that his return to tobacco had not been mindless, had been a conscious decision in pursuit of a defined goal. He could almost detect a certain nobility in it — sacrifice made in the name of a higher ideal and all that — despite the twinge of unease that came to him when he asked for the new package.

The class began well. He had made an effort to memorize the French numerals, and when he showed off the results of his frantic labour there was a round of only slightly sarcastic applause. Lise, in obvious relief, cried, "Bravo! Bravo!" Angelica, head bowed, scribbled on her worksheet.

At break, emboldened by his success, he accompanied Angelica to the smoking room. He sought to avoid the topic of cars — the magazine, in its assumption of technical knowledge, had proved confusing — and led her instead to speak of herself.

He learned that she was taking French — was there any other reason? — for work. She described herself as an account executive at an advertising agency he'd never heard of; and a woman in a man's profession, she said, needed every edge she could get.

Francis envied her the title. He'd tried to get his boss to use it on his business cards, but the man's zealousness for the plain truth led him to insist that "salesman" was as elaborate as he was going to get. Nevertheless, in describing his job to Angelica he appropriated the title; it seemed hardly a lie, was silently justified as simply a glamorized truth, like the cars he had once sold that were not "used" but "pre-owned", or the fetuses which, in his mother's anti-abortion vocabulary, had become "pre-born children". A harmless beautification of reality in the name of a self-defined greater good.

They smoked as they spoke, Francis gleefully lighting Angelica's long, slim cigarette. Conversation faltered a bit after they had exchanged the details of their résumés. Breaking the uneasy silence at one point, he ventured the possibility that maybe they could get together between sessions to practise, but the suggestion was ignored and he dared not bring it up again.

He managed to join her once more during the break in the next session, only a little put off that Angelica, enjoying her cigarettes, seemed always to be looking beyond his shoulder. She made no effort to maintain the conversation, and Francis, by simply babbling on, soon found himself telling her about his failed marriage. It was not, he knew, the best way to attract her romantic attention, but once started he could find no way of stopping, even though a certain discretion grew of itself. Not once did he use Judy's name, nor did he explain that his passion for her — as he understood with a growing horror not months after the ceremony — had been simply that of denial, a thirst quickly quenched; to reveal this would be to admit to a kind of failure, his pride would not allow it.

So, despite his sense that his words were cutting his own throat more effectively than a razor, he related the entire miserable story, somehow unable to keep from her even the fact of his affairs — he had the perverse thought, in the midst of a rising panic, that his adventures might cause her to see him in a more dangerous, and so more attractive, light. Even as he knew he was talking too much, even as he wondered whether women other than his wife saw mystery in the illicit, he was caught by the fact that he had Angelica's attention. Her listening to him was more than a novelty, was like a drug further loosening his tongue. So on he went in a torrent of words, relating, revealing. Besides, he silently assured himself in the fragile optimism of his helplessness, she would have to know it all sooner or later anyway.

He told her, in a voice just barely restrained, about the ignoble end of the marriage. About how his girlfriend stayed too long and, in her hurry to leave before his wife came home from work, forgot her handbag; how he noticed it on the sofa a couple of minutes later and, desperate to get rid of it, dashed out of the house after her, the bag in hand; only, seconds into his sprint, to be pulled over by a police cruiser, the cops skeptical of the story from this dishevelled, half-dressed man they'd seen scuttling along the street clutching a woman's handbag. . . .

He was sitting handcuffed in the back of the cruiser when his wife walked by on her way home. His initial reaction when she idly glanced in and, with horror, recognized him, was a feeling of foolishness. The entire episode just seemed so silly, so absurd; things like this only happened on television, they weren't supposed to happen in real life.

At least, he said to a nodding Angelica, eager to stress the only comfort that remained, at least there were no children.

Angelica squashed out her cigarette, began moving towards the door. "How many?" she asked.

"Pardon?"

"How many kids did you say you had?"

Francis, at a loss, just watched her go.

Francis' attempts to monopolize Angelica's break time met with only intermittent success. She and Lise seemed to have developed a friendship of sorts, the communality of smoking that Francis had missed during his months of abstinence. Standing a little off to the side with coffee and a cigarette, he often eavesdropped on their conversations, listening for any hint of romantic involvement, any indication of boyfriend or husband or commitment beyond the casual. But they seemed always to dwell on cars or clothes or holiday destinations, still in the outer reaches of amicable intimacy. He found no direction there.

It was two or three sessions later, after he had ventured to compliment her on her name in a voice quickened by hastily consolidated courage, that he found out that she had not been baptized Angelica, she just called herself that. It was a name, she said, that she was trying out. She wouldn't divulge her given name — she objected to his use of the word "real" — but let on that she had been known for several months as Robin and that, growing tired of Angelica, she was toying with either Charlotte or Anita.

Francis took the revelation as a confidence, let on that his middle name — it was the best he could do — was Wolfgang. "You can imagine," he said, "I had to keep that quiet in high school." She nodded absently, asked which name he thought she should go with next. He was, once more, at a loss for an answer.

His smoking had picked up, a pack a day on good days, a pack and a half on bad. It was only in the mornings when he awoke to a bitter taste in his mouth and the stench of stale smoke that he regretted his return to the habit. Struggling to the shower, washing the sleep away, he quietly berated himself for his weakness. But the smell of his first coffee evoked, with a gentle thrill, the indescribable pleasure of the first cigarette. Lighting up, he thought only of Angelica, of the sensuous way she tapped a cigarette from the soft pack, placed it delicately between her lips, and lit it with a sigh at the first smoke. And feeling himself stirred, his senses sharpened, he relaxed and enjoyed the quiet of the morning.

It was halfway through the course, as a break-time conversation with Angelica and Lise veered towards the slowness of his progress, that he told them about his father. Francis Sr. had been born in the Gaspé and had spent the first twenty-five years of his life there before moving to a job in Montreal, then later in Toronto. He had died five years before, an electrician of comfortable achievement who, as age distilled his life to a few treasured boasts, responded to the French fact by telling all within earshot that he had never let a word of *that* language pass his lips. Any question or comment directed to him about Quebec met with a gruff "I am English, thank you!" followed by a charged silence. He would have been horrified at his son's attendance at French classes, would have disinherited him, as he had his daughter, without a second thought.

Francis looked from Angelica to Lise, from Lise to Angelica, their faces noncommittal, and wondered aloud whether this little betrayal of his father — was the word too strong? he asked, but they had no opinion — might be retarding his progress.

Angelica and Lise looked quizzically at each other. Angelica lit a cigarette. Lise shrugged. "And your mother?" Lise said finally.

"My mother —" But, of course, that was where it broke down: she had grown up bilingual in Montreal. "My mother," he said. "Yes, well. Yes, my mother speaks French. At least, she used to. But you see, my father, well, he was the one who, you know, who set the tone."

But even as he spoke to Lise's skeptical grimace, his eyes were following Angelica's unsympathetic back out the door.

Francis tried, in moments of mental drift, to picture Angelica in her life beyond the classroom. As he ate, he saw her eating. As he showered, he saw her showering. As he drove, he saw her driving. But when he watched television, he couldn't quite imagine her slouching on a sofa in front of a television set, a bowl of chips or popcorn balanced in her lap, a Coke or a beer clutched in one hand and the channel-changer in the other. Did she too, seeking relief and a little physical pleasure, sometimes idly touch herself in auto-erotic intimacy? He forced himself to picture her at the less glamorous tasks of life: washing the toilet, doing the dishes, cutting her toenails. But in each mental image, she retained her cool detachment; her hair retained its perfection, her gestures their grace, her thoughts their calculation: there seemed no time when she got beyond herself. This picture, this perfection: it was part of Francis' thrill, and it was, he knew, part of his deception.

"No," he said, for the first time uncomfortable at the admission. "I don't cycle myself."

"I've always believed," Angelica said, "that salesmen —"

Francis winced at the word.

"— or at least the good ones, should know their products inside out. They should know how they work and how to use them."

"The theory and the practice," Lise said with a laugh. "Like the good lover."

"So," Francis said defensively, "if I sold sewing machines I should know how to sew?"

"And what's wrong with that?" Angelica challenged.

"If I sold encyclopedias —"

"Then you should know them from back to front," Lise said with mock seriousness.

"You're kidding, right?"

"I," said Angelica, puffing dramatically at her cigarette, "never kid."

Lise, with a touch of the theatrical, restrained a smile.

What, more than anything else, drove Francis to distraction was his inability to wring the personal from Angelica. He knew that she had moved to the city from elsewhere, but the when and the whence she would not divulge. He knew, too, that she lived in a midtown apartment — she had once said to Lise that if she had to live in the city, then let it be in the city, not on the edge of it — but exactly where she gave no indication. If he had had to guess, he would have picked Yonge and Eglinton; she seemed a creature of its trendy restaurants and singles' bars.

Francis himself lived in what he liked to think of as a less earnest area of the city, an area less self-conscious because undefined in its smatterings of Ukrainians, Poles, Italians, Koreans, and Portuguese, not exactly downtown but not that far from it either. From his fifteenth-floor balcony — a rectangle of bare, metal-wrapped concrete large enough for two garden chairs and a picnic cooler of beer — he could see east across a carpet of trees and low red-brick buildings to the distant conglomerations of midtown apartment towers and downtown office towers.

To his right, he could follow the coastline of Lake Ontario. He liked, when storms moved in, to turn off the apartment lights and watch through the balcony window the violence of the display: heavy clouds, graceful in their lumbering, spitting rain and lightning into the lake, the ethereal light flicking from time to time at the lightning rods atop the tallest buildings. There was a lonely beauty in it all, a scintillating brevity that rarely failed to put him in mind of explosive applause and klieg lights.

On summer days, the lake was blue and sail-dotted. It was from there, he suspected, from the deck of a sailboat perhaps, that Angelica would get her only view of where he lived. This distance between his apartment and the lake seemed the measure of the gulf separating him from her.

"Francis," Lise said, her eyes alighting on him. "Manges-tu des pommes?" She had already drilled everyone else in the class and Francis knew, with rising tension, that he would be the last before the break.

"Oui," he said. "Je mange des pommes." That was easy.

"As-tu mangé des pommes hier?"

"Oui." Past tense, he thought. "J'ai mangé des pommes hier."

"As-tu mangé vingt-cinq pommes hier?"

"Oui, j'ai mangé vingt- . . . ahh, pommes hier."

" — Vingt-cinq —"

" — Vingt-cinq pommes hier."

"Et mangeras-tu des pommes demain?"

Ahh, yes, the future tense. "Oui, je mangeras des pommes hier."

"Je manger*ai* des pommes *demain*." She gestured forward with her hand, to indicate the future.

"Ahh, oui." Francis chuckled. "Je manger*ai* des pommes *demain*."

"Et combien de pommes mangeras-tu demain?"

"Je mangerai vingt-cinq pommes demain."

"Vingt-cinq!"

Francis grinned. "Oui, j'aime les pommes. Beaucoup!"

Lise theatrically narrowed her eyes at him. Thin smiles broke out around the table — except Angelica, of course, who, fingers interlaced on the table before her, seemed absorbed. Lise closed her instruction book, called the break.

Francis hurried to the smoking room. He was pleased with himself. Sales were going well, the French was coming along, he had even lost a little bit of weight. The rush of nicotine from his cigarette topped off his sense of well-being. He felt so good, in fact, that he thought this might be the evening to ask Angelica for a date — he would be casual, would suggest dinner almost as an afterthought — and made a mental note to pick up a restaurant guide at the convenience store after the class.

It was when, his cigarette more than half gone, Lise entered the smoking room alone that Francis began wondering where Angelica was. Lise approached him, said she was out of cigarettes, and asked for one. Lighting it for her, he resisted asking about Angelica's whereabouts: the question could not be asked casually, would be too revealing.

He lit another cigarette for himself, chatted with Lise, his impatience barely restrained, his eyes straying often over her shoulder to the door. Lise talked about her family in the Beauce, about coming to Toronto to improve her English, and her longterm dream — she had a degree from Laval — of owning her own communications company, in Montreal if things worked out.

Francis was as polite as he could be, listened enough to ask the right questions, hummed and ahhed at the appropriate times. But he couldn't stop wondering why Angelica wasn't there.

Had Francis ever been to Montreal? No? *Dommage*. The joie de vivre. . . . But of course, Toronto had joie de vivre too, only it was different. But he had been to Quebec City, though. For the winter carnival? He could tell she was disappointed. When she said it was only for tourists and drunken young people, he just nodded sagely.

When they returned to the classroom, Angelica was there in her seat poring over her notes. Francis tried unsuccessfully to catch her eye: maybe she wasn't well? She looked tense, her lips were tightly set.

Francis' concentration faltered in the second half of the class. But he was surprised to note, as if from a distance, that the French none the less flowed easily from him; he simply reacted when questioned, and his reactions, unexamined in his distraction, proved accurate.

Lise was ecstatic, the other students — except Angelica — nodding and smiling in relieved congratulation.

Francis hung back at the coatroom after the class, waiting for Angelica to come for her coat.

"Not smoking today?" he said when she appeared clutching her purse and notebook.

"Not smoking," she replied seriously. "I quit."

A rumble of despair roiled through Francis' stomach. "You what?"

"I've been following a program. Today's quitting day."

"But —" He stopped himself. He wanted to protest, he wanted to tell her she couldn't do this to him, he'd begun smoking again just to be with her, after all, and now — now that he needed the nicotine, now that he was once more well and truly hooked — she was abandoning him. "Angelica —"

"Toby," she said. "Cute, don't you think?"

"Toby. . . ." The next tack, he thought, would be to ask about the program she'd taken, get the details, ask how it had been, was it hard, show an interest he didn't feel. But — Toby? His hurt was inseparable from his exasperation, was inseparable from his. . .what? From his sense, for both of them, of farce. He felt simply foolish; saw her, too, as foolish.

"So what d'you think? Don't like it?"

"Pardon?"

"The name. Toby. What d'you think?"

He nodded. "It's fine," he mumbled, off-handed. "It's just fine."

"Y'know," she said, shrugging into her coat and making for the door, "so's your French, who would've thought it at the beginning?"

Then the door slammed shut and she was gone.

Francis crumpled into a chair, his throat uncertain with either a sob or a laugh — he didn't know which, thought each appropriate. He extracted a cigarette from the pack, sought out the lighter, lit up. As he sat there, puffing, running through the recollected images of his absurd chase, Lise emerged from the administration office. She had put on a hat, was buttoning up her coat.

"Something wrong?" she said, pulling on her gloves.

"Wrong? No-no. Just. . . ."

"Tired?"

"A little."

"You want a beer?"

"Pardon?"

"You feel like having a beer?"

He shrugged. Why not? Stubbed out the cigarette, stood up.

Lise waited for him at the door as he pulled on his coat, threw his scarf around his neck. She was not bad-looking, he thought, then realized, with a little jolt, that he'd never really looked at her. No, she wasn't bad-looking at all, was quite attractive actually, in an unadorned sort of way.

As they made their way along the sidewalk towards the pub at the end of the block, she slipped her arm through his. It was an easy, familiar movement, a comfortable joining. Neither spoke until they had descended the stairs to the pub. Then Francis said, "Did I ever tell you how much I like the theatre?"

Security

ALISTAIR RAMGOOLAM stretched carefully out on the sofa in the living room, the cushion under his head giving off a newness powerful enough to efface, at least momentarily, the thicker, sweeter scents of the incense sticks he had lit in the corner behind him. He clasped his hands on his paunch — the stomach medicine hadn't yet taken effect on his ulcer — and sighed. The sofa's smell, of factory plastic wrap and newly milled material, distressed him; it conjured up an unfamiliarity and a sense of dislocation he had never expected to experience. His children and his grandchildren, yes, but not he or his wife of so many years. He mumbled, in a voice of grumbling complaint, "I knew we were insecure on that damned island."

But only the television responded: *Althea Wilson, come on down!* And Althea Wilson bounded convulsively from the audience, careered down the stairs, her heavy breasts leaping

85

and swaying as if alive under her blouse, to the podium on the stage.

Mr. Ramgoolam thought: Fool, why are you making such a spectacle of yourself? On national television, to boot? But a part of him envied her, coveted this opportunity for wealth that had so easily bartered itself for her dignity.

Althea Wilson squealed and squirmed before the microphone, as if called by nature and not permitted to answer. The television audience applauded, roared its approval of Althea Wilson, of her fellow competitors, of the silver-haired host recoiling with a febrile guardedness. Mr. Ramgoolam could not push away the man's silver hair, his wrinkled face, the plasticized smile, and the eyes appalled by, disbelieving of, the thirsts he had unleashed.

Mr. Ramgoolam shifted onto his side, away from the bright television, banishing from sight this vision of himself as he might be, as — he was uncomfortably aware — he had partly become. But he could not fully escape Althea Wilson, knew too well the dynamics of the emotion and the manipulated greed, needed too deeply the vicarious thrill of her excitement. His gaze drifted to the balcony doors, rectangles of black aluminum frame and double-glazed panes and wire-mesh screens. He could see the narrow balcony, his backyard now, and the sky grey and unfriendly beyond. These clouds, this deepening greyness: the sky seemed to weigh on him, encasing him like the heavy blankets he'd left behind on the bed not long before.

His wife had removed the drapes before going to work that morning, lifting with them a sense of cloister, baring the living room to the sky and the clouds and the tops of taller buildings. Earlier that morning, peering through the dusty

panes and squared wire-mesh, he had been able to see, as
if for the first time because so long unseen, the solid, upward
rush of the dense downtown, the trees still stripped to forlorn
brown in the fading winter, the distant lake a grey horizontal
smudge almost indistinct from the sky. It had been an enervating sight, and he could not prevent a rush of resentment
against his wife, against the missing drapes, against the city
itself.

Mr. Ramgoolam thought with unease of the hours of television that lay ahead, the game shows and the movies and the
discussions of beauty and sex. The weekdays were long for
him. He had not, even after many months, grown accustomed
to the endless stretches of being alone. On the island, someone had always been there: his mother, his wife, a maid. But
now — curious thought — his wife went out to work. His
eldest son — after years of residence here, Canadian to the
point of strangeness — was at his desk in a big, black office
tower downtown, a telephone receiver plastered to one ear,
a computer terminal sitting luminescent on his desk. Vijay,
his second son, having taken to life in the new country
more avidly than his father would have guessed after the
unhappiness of his university years, was out there somewhere, working on the deals that he mentioned only vaguely,
keeping details to himself with a calculated display of irritation. His youngest son was at the university, studying a
subject — something to do with electrical impulses in crab
legs — that Mr. Ramgoolam would have thought foolish were
it not for the lucrative job offers his son, not even close to
graduation, was already receiving.

Lately Mr. Ramgoolam had begun dreaming his own fantasies of easy money, of untold, unearned riches. Every week

he threw out handfuls of lottery tickets and horse-race stubs, stepping back from the sense of hope evaporated to the renewed possibilities of fresh numbers and fresh horses. Yet he had earned the right, he thought, had worked hard all his life and did not deserve to find himself returned, in the twilight of his life, to the moneyless uncertainties of his youth.

He closed his eyes, felt consciousness slip. A deep male voice boomed orgasmically over a set of new luggage. His awareness grew listless, and he sensed with nebulous pleasure the tentative encroachment of submerged images.

Images of bustle and fear. Of darkness buzzing with a confusion of rumours. Of shortened breath and the acidic seething of his ulcer.

Vijay, grown mysteriously from a wild-eyed teenager into a gloomy young man, a little extra skin on him now — he looked no longer simply like a rake, but like a rake draped loosely in a flesh-coloured garment — had quietly taken charge. Vijay had surprised his father with his cool efficiency, the effect, Mr. Ramgoolam speculated, of the business degree he had paid so dearly for and which had seemed, in the years following Vijay's return to the island from Toronto, to have been utterly useless. But the boy had done well in the multiplying chaos. Had somehow, through whispered telephone calls and furtive car trips into the night, made what he called "arrangements".

"Arrangements?" Mr Ramgoolam had said. "Arrangements for what?"

And he had put it well, the boy, with a subtlety Mr. Ramgoolam appreciated even at the time, even as his wife crumpled tearfully into her handkerchief. Vijay had said, "To go, Pa. To Toronto." Not, Mr. Ramgoolam noted, to *leave* but *to go:* the boy was forward-looking.

"When?"

"In two hours."

"Two hours!"

"Two hours or nothing."

"How?"

"By plane."

"What plane? No planes comin' in these days."

But Vijay had not replied, had simply gazed back at him with a look that was tired of questions.

Mrs. Ramgoolam had said, "Two hours? But, son, is not enough time to pack, we have too much —"

"Ma." Vijay's voice was merciless. "One person, one suitcase."

Her mouth fell slowly open. "One person, one suitcase?"

"But you jokin', son." Mr. Ramgoolam reached out a hand to support his wife. "We live here all our lives, Vijay. How we going to put a lifetime in one suitcase?"

"Pack tight." Vijay spun on his heel, headed for his bedroom.

Mr. Ramgoolam was stunned. But he was, at the same time, pleased to note that his son had made his "arrangements" as he himself had always conducted his business, deftly, with skill but without fanfare, knowing through experience slyly acquired which string to pull, which button to press. And presenting, then, a *fait accompli.* For the first time, he felt pride in Vijay, felt him to be his son in ways beyond the physical. It made the packing — a discarding of the senti-mental in favour of the financial — easier.

Vijay, silent, tension channelled into activity of quiet bustle, loaded family and baggage into his Mercedes convertible.
He remained indifferent to his mother's sobbing, seemed
himself unmoved by considerations other than those of flight:
so what if this was the house he'd grown up in? So what if his
parents were leaving behind significant parts of themselves?
Vijay's gloominess had nothing nostalgic about it. Mr. Ramgoolam knew this about his son, appreciated it, understood
that much of his strength — the strength here displayed —
came from this bloodless practicality. But it disturbed him,
nevertheless. He wished he could have seen in his son the
merest hint of regret, the briefest glance backwards. But
Vijay would make no concession, concentrated on the task
at hand: the easing of the car from the driveway, the chaining
of the gate that had to it the feel of ritual, senseless but
comforting.

They seemed such a little group, Mr. Ramgoolam thought,
feeling suddenly vulnerable as they rushed through the quiet
night, through its deceptions and its camouflaged perils. He
sat in the front seat beside his son while his wife sat sniffling
in the back seat beside their hand luggage, Vijay driving in
his usual anarchic way, the darkness a spur to his reckless-
ness. Mr. Ramgoolam shut his eyes, the lids heavy and
stinging against the lower rims.

Vijay had not put on the headlights. He didn't want to draw
attention, pointed out he would spot the lights of oncoming
vehicles before they saw him, would be able to avoid them
with ease. Mr. Ramgoolam wondered what would happen if
the other driver had had the same idea as his son, but he
said nothing — Vijay was in charge — and settled for not
staring into the nocturnal void ahead. He opened his eyes

90

only occasionally during the drive through the deserted streets, and the sight of blackened vehicles and smouldering ruins, the frantic dishevelment of wilful urban disorder, caused his ulcer to seethe. Only then did he realize that, in the haste of departure, he had neglected to bring along his bottle of stomach medicine.

The airplane flight, offering in its first minutes a distant glimpse of the city below aglow with dim electricity and angry flame, was an agony of pain and uncertainty. Mr. Ramgoolam writhed in discomfort and Vijay, function fulfilled, responsibility relieved, lapsed into a reverie of alcohol and pills furtively consumed, while Mrs. Ramgoolam seemed suddenly seized by a vein of energy her husband had thought long exhausted. A clearness appeared in her eyes, a sureness in her touch and her words, that made him think of youth. But it took him a while, days, weeks even, to realize that the change in her went much deeper; that she had shucked off a timidity he had always believed innate, as if leaving the island had unclipped her constraints and revealed a self concealed by the demands and expectations of family and of an island small enough to gossip into scandal the slightest deviation from the social code. And it was there, on the airplane, even as she did what little she could to ease his discomfort, that he sensed the shuffling of intangibles that was her taking possession of herself. That was, he saw later, her taking leave of him.

Their two other sons were waiting for them at the airport, smiles creasing through the strain on their faces. The eldest — thoughtful boy! — held a bottle of stomach medicine in his hand. It wasn't Mr. Ramgoolam's usual brand, that wasn't available here, but a couple of quick gulps told him it was an effective one none the less. After the embraces and the tears and the murmurs of reassurance, he noticed that his sons had failed to bring coats and, having visited Toronto only in winter, having last seen the city in the aftermath of a blizzard, he began upbraiding them for the oversight: why, they would freeze to death without coats in this devil of a country, they should think of their poor mother, their brother, not to mention their long-suffering father, and — What's this? Laughing? Such insolence! You too, Vijay? You going to freeze, too, you know —

But it was the middle of July and outside, away from the air-conditioned comfort of the terminal, the day was as hot and as humid as the island they'd just left. Even his wife, patting at her forehead and neck with a perfumed handkerchief, twittered at him as they wended their way through the parking garage, the air seeming to suck perspiration from their pores.

When Vijay saw his elder brother's car, he was horrified. A Honda? Didn't he have any shame? Top of the line? So what? It wasn't a Mercedes, was it? He got in the front seat, with an unbecoming delicacy, while his younger brother squeezed into the back between their parents. Mr. Ramgoolam, ulcer going dormant, suddenly felt like kicking Vijay. Mercedes? What nonsense was the boy talking? All that was gone now, didn't he realize? But he said nothing. He, too, had his regrets to deal with, his losses to mourn. They all did.

Applause exploded. The blonde assistant, smiling through heavy makeup, held a camera up to the contestants. Althea

Wilson stared hard. Thirty-five millimetre. Automatic focus. Automatic flash. Black, solid, compact. Great for those vacation shots! How much was it worth? Her brow crinkled into thick parallel cords; perspiration, bright and fresh in the television lights, laminated her skin.

"Two-fifty, you chupid woman," Mr. Ramgoolam muttered. "Anybody know that."

Althea Wilson hazarded five hundred.

Mr. Ramgoolam sucked his teeth in disgust: Point a television camera at people and they go *bazody*, as if the lens suck out their brains.

A brace of pigeons fluttered onto the balcony railing. Mr. Ramgoolam knew he should get up and shoo them away — given half a chance, they would cake the balcony in excrement that dried to the consistency of cement — but he couldn't, just then, be bothered. Pigeons, pigeon feathers, pigeon shit. His eldest son got very exercised over them, running onto the balcony flapping his arms and shouting when they threatened to alight; but Mr. Ramgoolam figured that everybody — even birds — needed a safe place to land. Surely their wings would tire, he thought. Surely even pigeons, with their innate sense of direction, occasionally needed a point of reference from which they could reassure themselves of their place in the world.

He watched as the pigeons strutted stiffly on the rail, their round, red-rimmed, manic eyes darting around, oriented themselves, then one after the other plunged off as if diving to the earth. He sighed, noticing only then that he had held his breath throughout their presence, that he had managed in the tension of the long moment — looking for the little shot of excrement that he would have to clean up or risk the wrath of his eldest son — to ignore the abrasive fretting of his ulcer.

The bare windows open to a great barrenness: it was, he knew, his fault in the end. He was the one who had insisted on celebrating *Divali* in as traditional a manner as possible. He was the one who had ignored the infidel groans of his youngest son, the weary pleas of his wife, the cautions of his eldest son. He was the one who had appealed to an unresponsive Vijay and interpreted his silence as support. He, too, who had gone yesterday to the supermarket to buy the two dozen aluminum muffin cups. (In this pagan society you couldn't find *deeya*s, the little earthenware oil lamps that flickered an air of mystery over the altar.) It was he who had rolled the cottonwool wicks; who had distributed the cups filled with *ghee* around the living room, making sure that the wicks were adequately soaked and well placed.

While his wife stirred and fried at various pots in the small kitchen; while his youngest son picked at the plates of sweets and appetizers laid out on the table; while Vijay sat hunched in a corner of the sofa smoking a cigarette of vaguely familiar scent; while his eldest son — deliberately, the father thought — worked late at the office, Mr. Ramgoolam girded his loins in a *dhoti* and meandered around the living room with a box of matches lighting his modern *deeya*s. The room blazed in the brilliance of the two dozen little flames. Mr. Ramgoolam was pleased, was put in mind of his parents' house on *Divali* evening when much of their meagre financial solvency was dissolved in hundreds of the little lights, unbroken lines of them on windowsills, beside pathways, throughout the yard of hardened clay, even along the branches of the mango tree. Spectacle for the gods: the way lit, the house exalted.

Mr. Ramgoolam stuck twenty incense sticks into a brass cuspidor filled with potting soil and lit them. "Ma! Ma!" he called to his wife. "Come look."

Mrs. Ramgoolam emerged from the kitchen, perspiring, eyes dull with fatigue, wringing her hands in a towel. She looked around, smiled thinly, said, "It nice, Pa. Very nice. They lookin' like the real thing." Then she paused, her eyes blinking. "But —"

Mr. Ramgoolam's glow of achievement converted to irritation. "But what?" he demanded.

But she didn't have to tell him: already the living room was hazy with the smoke of the burning *ghee*.

His youngest son suggested opening the balcony door to let out some of the smoke. Vijay remarked dreamily that it was a cold night. Instead, Mr. Ramgoolam opened the door to the corridor.

His eldest son arrived not two minutes later. He was alarmed. "What's going on here? The corridor's thick with smoke —"

"We just airin' out the place, son," Mr. Ramgoolam said. "Look at the *deeya*s, you don't find they pretty —"

"Jesus Christ, Pa, you can hardly breathe in here."

"Is just temporary, son —"

His son, dropping his briefcase to the floor, swept his hands around the living room. "We've got to put some of these lights out, Pa. Before someone calls the fire department."

Mrs. Ramgoolam, suppressing a smile of relief, moved to the closest *deeya*.

"No, no!" Mr Ramgoolam snatched at his wife's reaching arm. "Is bad luck to out a *deeya*, Ma, you don't know that? Don't —"

But he couldn't finish. His words were cut off by the hammering wail of the fire alarm.

His eldest son covered his face with his hands.

His wife and youngest son whipped around the room extinguishing the little fires.

Vijay, smiling benignly, remained where he was.

When the *deeya*s were all out, when the alarm had been turned off and the firemen sent away with apologies, when the neighbours had returned to their dinners and their television sets, Mr. Ramgoolam stood in the middle of the living room surveying the damage. The incense sticks continued their slow burn in the cuspidor, but his aluminum *deeya*s had gone cold and dark. The bad luck acquired was incalculable. And in the air cleared of smoke, he saw that the white walls and ceiling now swirled with elegant grey patterns; saw that the white drapes and his shirt and *dhoti*, and his wife's skirt, had greyed. Tissues were splattered black when he blew his nose, the water in the basin ran grey when he washed his face.

So it had been his fault when, this morning, his wife stood on a chair and unhooked the drapes for washing, when she unwittingly revealed this world to him, and him to this world. But still, he couldn't help feeling that she should have known better, that she should have had a bit more consideration for his bruised feelings and the imminence of their bad luck. He couldn't, despite himself and because of himself, restrain his resentment.

On the television, Althea Wilson pondered a trade: the camera for a hatbox.

"Take the box," Mr. Ramgoolam muttered. "Take the box, you chupid woman."

Mr. Ramgoolam had wasted no time in attempting to create gainful employment, but he was hindered by the way in which his plans, so well laid, had failed to materialize. It had begun years before, with his eldest son's insistence on spending the Toronto nest-egg on a house. The healthy bank account, to Mr. Ramgoolam's distress, had gone suddenly anorexic. He had had to become doubly creative in finding ways of smuggling money out of the island to make the monthly mortgage payments. His son, still at school at the time, had been too busy being independent, going to plays and operas and European films, to find a part-time job.

As the years passed, the value of the house rose almost madly, leaping and jumping for no apparent reason except greed in an overheated market. Mr. Ramgoolam's initial anxiety eased, his confidence in his eldest son rising with each new quote received, with each new unsolicited offer to buy the house. Then one day, out of the blue, his son decided to sell the house, informing his father only after the deal had been finalized. Mr. Ramgoolam would have preferred to hold on to it — the property not only seemed a phenomenal investment, but also reflected the traditional virtues of independence, stability, and self-reliance that Mr. Ramgoolam had learned from his father — but his son had declared it too much trouble; the house was not new, there was always something that needed repairing, it claimed too much of his time. So he'd sold it to a Yuppie — he had to explain the word to his father as someone young, rich, and foolish, someone, his father thought, rather like his son himself — and immediately rolled most of the substantial profit into a condominium, less room but less trouble, he'd explained, paying for it in cash.

So when the family arrived unexpectedly, little planning possible in the sudden cartwheeling of politics and fear, there was a place for them to go to, but little money available for them to live on. Mr. Ramgoolam had hoped to use the excess from the sale to begin a humble business along the lines he knew best, import-export. But the money, a modest if not insignificant sum, was locked into a term deposit. There was nothing for him to work with.

He turned to the newspapers, discovering there, for the first time in his life, his lack of qualifications and the limitations of a high school education that had ended almost half a century before. The employment requirements, long lines of incomprehensible terms linked by strings of undefined letters, bewildered him. He gravitated to the simpler jobs, to salaries progressively more modest.

His first job had promised *Progressive Working Conditions. Friendly Supportive Environment. Five Hundred to a Thousand Dollars a Week.* "Canadians are thirsting for education!" the advertisement had assured him, painting a picture of millions of Canadians, crazed by educational deprivation, scrambling and fighting to place encyclopedia orders. He had trudged from door to unfriendly door for a week, encountering not a single person who lit up with relief and delight at his well-rehearsed opening gambit. Just one woman had invited him in, and only because she had mistaken him for a fellow Jehovah's Witness.

His second job — *Join Our Family! Generous Commissions! Twelve Hundred to Fifteen Hundred Dollars per Week! Free Transportation!* — had lasted for two weeks. Few people, he quickly discovered, were interested in owning an industrial strength vacuum cleaner, especially once he had washed and groomed their rugs in demonstration. Surprising himself, he actually managed to sell one to a retired janitor, but it quickly became clear to him that most of the people who made demonstration appointments did so because they were old and retired and craved company; they usually could not afford the machine, or had failed to understand that this was a sales demonstration and resented learning the sad truth. And, yes, the company provided free transportation — the machine was heavy, and none of the salespeople he had met earned enough to acquire a car — but there were long waits for pickup, anywhere from a half-hour to two hours. Sometimes he was served coffee and cookies by sympathetic, always talkative clients; more often than not he was politely but firmly ushered out to wait on the sidewalk. He quit in a huff the day the company van was an hour late, giving enough time for a storm to break, the rain soaking through his suit and through the box of his demonstration machine. The driver, a young man, himself a salesman, a believer in the school of hard sell and irritated by his own recent failures, had greeted Mr. Ramgoolam's complaints with a distinct lack of sympathy.

At home later that evening, having changed out of his wet clothes and into his pyjamas, Mr. Ramgoolam ran his hands through his damp hair, long silvered and now thinning as his father's had done in his final years, and told himself he was too old for such nonsense. He deserved a position of greater dignity and ease, had earned the right to be treated with respect, especially by pushy, half-educated, foul-mouthed puppies like the van driver.

He was up half the night nursing his burning ulcer, while his wife, solicitous but somehow too methodical, her touch and her words governed by a curious dispatch, ministered to him. When, in the silent hours of the early morning, he bemoaned their losses, when he spoke with pain of their jettisoned houses and cars, she sucked her teeth softly, brushed his hair back from his sweat-slicked forehead with her hand, and said, "Shh, shh, is not a time to cry, we ain't have time to cry, we have to think 'bout tomorrow."

And it was the next day, as he remained in bed with a raw throat and soaring temperature, that she went out without saying a word to him and applied for a job as a cook at the Indian restaurant on Bloor Street.

Mr. Ramgoolam was infuriated and ashamed at the thought of his wife's working. She had never held a job before, had depended on him for money, she the homemaker, he the provider. And now suddenly, he was the one who remained at home, she the one who dressed and went out. Left to his own devices, he could not deal with the ensuing silence, could not fill the empty spaces by himself. He was grateful for the raucous intervention of the television. It offered company of a sort, helped hold back the deeper silence. And it provided, too, the soothing, if ephemeral and vicarious, fantasies of easy answers.

"A brand-new . . . washing machine!"

Althea Wilson was stunned.

Mr. Ramgoolam was disappointed. A washing machine: it was like finding jockey shorts under the tree on Christmas morning, or unwrapping a bottle of aftershave lotion on your birthday.

Oh well, he thought, at least she could sell it, pocket the cash. But he found her reaction overdone. It was embarrassing. The sum involved — a few hundred dollars, no more — was barely significant, it hardly justified a further diminution of dignity. He would have shown greater coolness, an I-can-take-it-or-leave-it attitude. But then, he realized, he had never done the wash; that had always been his wife's responsibility. He had no idea of the passion — yes, that was the word, judging by Althea Wilson's reaction — that a washing machine could arouse in a woman. He was pleased for her when, with a flashing of lights and a clanging of bells, the machine was hers.

Outside, the day remained unfriendly. The thickening clouds had lost luminosity. From time to time, flurries, crazed by unexpected gusts of wind, hurtled down. A clutch of children's balloons lurched drunkenly across the sky.

Mr. Ramgoolam thought, with distress, of his wife's going out into this day, into this weather that battered in subtle ways at her body, evoking aches and pains and new abrasions of rheumatism. He thought of her wrapped in a white apron, cutting and chopping and stirring pots not her own. This vision of her, and of the exhaustion she brought home every evening, ripped at him, confronted him with failures and inadequacies he had always attributed only to other people.

She had never complained, his wife, had not once accused him of dereliction of husbandly duty. But she didn't have to. His silent self-accusation sufficed.

Althea Wilson stared glassy-eyed at a projected slide of a blue sea and a crescent of white sand dwarfed by a hotel of mammoth proportions. It was a beach such as Mr. Ramgoolam had never seen: built up, industrialized. The male voice tripped over exotic foreign names. The audience caught its collective breath on cue.

Mr. Ramgoolam thought of the beaches left behind, thought of plunging into warm, salty water, of playing cricket on the sand with his three sons, these boys whose lives he had so carefully nurtured, whose well-being he had so intensely fretted over. He had long known his sons to be distant from him, the major consequence of travel and education and lives led in foreign lands. The discovery years before had been a blow — his ulcer had grated for days, he had sipped at bottles of stomach medicine as at bottles of soft drink — but he had gradually grown to accept the distancing, even in his mellower moments to view it as a sign, distressing though it may have been, of his success as a father.

Now his wife too had grown remote, not through her own fault but through force of circumstance. Yet he could learn to live with even that.

Most frightening of all, though, was the realization that he too had grown away, not just from his sons, not just from his wife, but from himself. He no longer recognized himself, no longer knew who Alistair Ramgoolam was. Was he the independent businessman, proud of his self-sufficiency and success? No, not any more. Was he this man who spent more time than was healthy in front of a television set while his wife and sons went out to earn a living? No, he would not accept that, refused to believe it. But if he was neither of these, then just who was he? More and more, it seemed, he was the Alistair Ramgoolam of the sofa, the Alistair Ramgoolam who found haven in televised thrills of effortless acquisition and in childhood memories, ever sharper, cleansed of ringworm and scorpion stings and vicious parental beatings. It was an Alistair Ramgoolam he did not like. He was becoming the kind of man he had spent much of his life railing against, a man for whom he would have once used the word parasitic. Now, watching Althea Wilson sweat under the television lights, seeing her screw up her face in concentrated thought, acknowledging his own longing to be in her place, he thought it an odious word.

His luck, it had occurred to him, required a measure of divine intervention. He set about erecting, in the tiny den of the condominium apartment, an altar for his morning devotions. He hung various pictures of deities on the wall — the females fair and pink-cheeked, the males black to the point of blueness — constructing below them an altar of stacked milk crates smothered in a length of heavy drapery material.

He located most of the necessary implements in the little Indian-owned stores on Yonge Street, crowded enterprises of glutinous atmosphere and ingratiating service. He had not lingered. The turbanned men and saried women, people so obviously of India in their dress, in their smells, had unsettled him, for while he resembled them, was welcomed as one of them in Hindi, a language familiar to him only in a religious context, he felt himself to be different, found himself distrustful of them and wishing to flee.

But he had acquired enough of the brass vases and plates and idols and muffin cups to suit his needs, to more or less reconstruct the altar he had had at home. The result, a delicate blending of piety and paraphernalia necessary to the full exercise of his devotion, pleased him. There was no longer a dew-smothered garden in which to pick fresh flowers, but a daily trip to the convenience store provided the necessary. There was no longer a large yard in which to plant the *jhandi*, the little flags that fluttered at the top of towering bamboo stalks signalling the completion of devotional duty, but he had found an acceptable compromise in a package of wooden chopsticks and a plant-pot of soil tucked into a corner of the balcony.

Mr. Ramgoolam thought of himself as a religious man, but not as a philosophical one. He was punctilious in his performance of ritual, but in obedience only to the talismanic, "whatif" school of thought: whatif they — and *they* could be anyone with anything to say on religion, even contradictory information finding a home in his fears and uncertainties and still-powerful childhood sense of mystery — whatif they were right? Whatif opening an umbrella in the house really brought bad luck? Whatif failure to propitiate the gods really attracted their anger? Whatif moving into a house on the astrologically wrong date really led to collapse and personal ruin, even death? Why take the chance? Why not do it all? Why not fulfil all the requirements, only occasionally onerous, and assure a maximum of protection?

He made little adjustments in his life. Beef was banned from the condominium, as was pork. No flesh — no fish, no chicken — was eaten on Fridays. Footwear was left at the door, incense sticks burnt every morning.

His wife paid little attention to his deepening devotions. She was just pleased that he was keeping himself occupied. His sons, less tolerant, protested mildly, but backed down before his adamant rules.

"You always did your *pooja*, Pa," his youngest son said to him one evening after being upbraided for wearing his shoes in the living room, "but how come you never get into this incense and beef-banning and all this other shit before? How come now, here, of all places?"

But that was the point, Mr. Ramgoolam pointed out with glee, wondering in an aside to his wife what all this education was doing to their children's brains. If they were all here now, in this foreign land, with insufficient money, with his mother slaving away in the kitchen of a Bloor Street restaurant, with his father having to put up with indignity after indignity in the little jobs he had tried, it was because they had led improper lives before. They had not prayed enough, they had eaten beef and pork, they had failed to consult the gods adequately. This — and Mr. Ramgoolam strode to the window, gestured grandiloquently at the sweep of the city, at the soaring buildings, the dense greenery, the placid blue of the distant lake — this, all this, was their punishment.

His son grinned mischievously. "If that's so, beat me more," he said.

Mr. Ramgoolam was not amused.

In bed that night, he lamented the inadequate upbringing his sons had received. "We didn't bring them up as good Hindus, Ma, we didn't give them no culture. And now we payin' for it. Look at them, Ma, look at our sons. Barbarians, every one of them. Stuffin' themselves in restaurants with steak and hotdogs and hamburgers and —" But she was already asleep, head turned away from him, mouth opened in a gentle, riffling snore.

It was once more his youngest son — the scientist, as Mr. Ramgoolam began sarcastically calling him — who precipitated a minor theological crisis by pointing out that all of his father's shoes and belts were made of leather: *dead cow skin*. An hour of meditation brought the answer, however: plastic around his waist and running shoes, leatherless, on his feet. His attempt to discard his wife's shoes — she had discovered him in the garbage room attempting to stuff a bag of her footwear into the chute — had met with a hard-eyed rejection.

And she had been less than sympathetic — her response was to twirl her index finger at her temple — when he admitted his growing resentment of the vacuum cleaner and the broom. He objected to the noise of the one, to the stiff man-made fibres of the other. He wished he could lay his hands on a *cocoyea* broom instead, he said, the implement made from the leaves of a dried coconut-tree branch, spines stripped and bound into a crude broom. It made a sweet, soft sound, a soothing swish that evoked in its trail the clucking of chickens and the distant bleat of a grazing goat. And, he claimed, it did a far better job than either vacuum cleaners or these unnatural, new-fangled gizmos. His wife was somewhat less than convinced, reminding him that his mother had used the *cocoyea* broom only to sweep the yard. Inside, she had used a regular, modern broom. Displeased, Mr. Ramgoolam resorted in his irritation to sullying his mother's memory by declaring that her house had never really sparkled. "And the yard was shinin' bright, I suppose?" his wife retorted.

"You coulda eat off it!" he hissed, locking himself away in the bathroom with his sense of his own foolishness.

Mr. Ramgoolam began feeling, after a while, that in this unexpected deprivation he was singlehandedly fighting a war of domestic skirmishes to uphold traditions which, he acknowledged, had meant little to him before but which suddenly, inexplicably, loomed in importance. Challenged by his sons, he could not explain their new value; could not, when confronted by his wife's weary hesitation, justify his renewed reliance on them; just knew that in this alien land, far from all that had created him, far from all that he had created, they were vital.

On Saturday mornings, Mr. Ramgoolam would tune the radio to a program of popular Indian music, turning the volume up until the strains reached into every corner of the apartment. Sunday mornings brought a program of popular music and dance on the television, the saried hostess chattering in Hindi between numbers. Mr. Ramgoolam would sit in the living room, paying full attention to the programs, not understanding a word that was said or sung, not even really wishing to, simply letting the sounds wash over him, honing his sense of self, taking him back decades to the mystery and hubbub of his parents' religious gatherings: to huge cauldrons of food bubbling spicy aromas at blazing fires, to toothless old women singing and chattering as they stirred and sweated in the flickering light, to grizzled men drinking and arguing as they played cards and smoked marijuana cigarettes late into the night. It was always a disappointment when the programs ended and reality came full-force back at him in the form of a jingled advertisement for a hamburger chain or an unfamiliar airline. Then he would feel an ache just under his ribcage, and his ulcer would begin a gentle burn.

And he felt battered the Saturday morning that his eldest son awoke with a hangover to the insistent strains of Bombay film music. Indian female singers, his son had once remarked, all sounded as if they suffered from permanent nasal congestion. He propelled his father out to the balcony, pointed to the slash of blue lake in the distance, and said in a voice rasping with anger, "You see that, Pa? That is not the Caribbean. You understand? That is *not* the Caribbean you're seeing there."

It was from this loneliness, this sense of abandonment, that emerged Mr. Ramgoolam's deepest worry: would his sons do for him after his death all that he had done for his parents after theirs? Would they — and, beyond this, *could* they, in this country — fulfil their cremation duties, feed his hungry and wandering soul, have themselves ritually shaved beside a river, dispatch his soul to wherever with the final farewell ceremony? He feared they would not, feared they had grown too far from him and from the past that was his. That they knew none of the reasons the ceremonies had to be performed did not disturb him — neither, after all, did he — but their remaining almost wilfully ignorant of even the simplest of the protective and supplicatory gestures conjured up paralysing visions of his soul left to the vagaries of an alien and forbidding void.

Mr. Ramgoolam had never credited his imagination with much power; movies, whether in the cinema or on television, had never engaged him, usually lulled him into somnolence after ten or fifteen minutes; books could never hold his attention past the first four or five pages. The images sat dull in his mind, his imagination incapable of sharpening their vagueness into a reality deserving of serious consideration. But now, for the first time in his life, he could imagine only too well the fate that he feared awaited him: could feel himself floating free, out of control in a chilled darkness; could feel his mouth opening and closing in soundless appeals for rescue.

Althea Wilson and a friend would be going to Hawaii. And she was going to have a new camera to take her photographs with. And a set of new luggage to put her new designer wardrobe into. And a thousand dollars spending money. U.S., Mr. Ramgoolam thought, quickly and automatically working out the exchange into Canadian dollars.

His ulcer crabbed at him, its heated pinch spreading and tightening from his belly to under his ribcage and beyond.

Althea Wilson jumped and jumped. She hugged the host, never noticing the momentary look of distaste that crossed his smiling face.

Mr. Ramgoolam felt the vice-like grip of Althea Wilson fasten itself around his chest.

The host extricated himself, self-consciously straightening his jacket and tie.

Althea Wilson flung herself into the arms of a beaming relative.

Mr. Ramgoolam was puzzled when he felt his breath leave him.

The television screen glowed brightly. The images grew indistinct, edges erasing themselves, light eating rapidly into Althea Wilson, the relatives who had run to join her, the host.

Mr. Ramgoolam thought: The tube has blown. Tried to sit up on the sofa. Couldn't. His arms would not rise. Legs would not obey. Lungs would not expand.

Applause filled his head.

Alistair Ramgoolam, come on down!

He thought: But I'm not going down, it's up, I'm going up. And he was blinded by the lights.

The Arctic Landscape
High above the Equator

HE REMEMBERS an endless field of shadow-dappled cloud. An arctic landscape high above the equator.

It should have told him something.

Her breathing, light and regular, soothes the darkness of the room. She lies languid on the disarrayed bed, her long legs striped zebra-like by the light coming in through the venetian blind.

Rance fingers an unfiltered cigarette from the stiff pack, lights it. Flecks of tobacco and the rush of hot smoke mingle with the aftertaste of the wine they've been drinking, a bitter local red given to him by one of his informants. *Un regalo*, the man said apologetically. *Un regalo:* the man had nothing else to give him. He paid anyway.

The night is quiet, as is every night here, as befits a capital in ruins in a country at war. Only the occasional police patrol animates the street outside, the silence unnatural, the stillness a mark of the discontent he has helped create. Public utilities are no longer reliable: streetlamps are burnt out, water supplies unpredictable. It is as if he and those with whom and for whom he works have the power to change the very personality of a people.

Rance knows he should take satisfaction from this influence: it is, in the end, the ultimate goal of consular activities. But he never anticipated that the achievement would be of darkness, a retreat of the light to a small, hard circle. Disruption of lives is not what he set out to create.

Rance sucks at the cigarette. He keeps these thoughts to himself. They are, he is aware, a sign of conscience ill-directed; are, in bureaucratic eyes, threat; in ideological eyes, treason.

Her breath catches in her throat, rattles, settles down. Rance shivers at how fragile the drawing of breath seems in the darkness.

Somewhere out there, dominating the ruined city, the embassy sits pulsing in its spotlights, as secure as knowledge unchallenged in its authority.

She stirs in the bed, his name, sighed, a question. Sits up, drawing in her legs and hugging them with her slim arms. Her feet, shapely and cared for, nestled together in a strip of light. There is a tension to them — in the ankles, in the slope towards the painted toes — that captivates him, once more stirs his desire.

The room is hot, the air exhausted. The air conditioner hangs burnt out in the far wall.

She asks, her voice a whisper, tender with a lover's concern, if he is all right.

He is touched, hungry now for her. Squashes the cigarette in an ashtray, pads softly over to the foot of the bed. He hesitates, lost for a moment in the surge of his desire. Then he kneels, reaches for her left foot, cups her heel in the palm of his hand. He lowers his head, sucks gently, one by one, on her toes. They taste lightly of perspiration, the skin rough and dry. She giggles, laughs her throaty laugh. But when next she whispers his name, it is in a voice gritty with quiet passion.

The entire hill belonged to them, purchased decades before for five hundred rifles, a thousand pairs of combat boots, and a couple of "advisers".

They had carved what they needed from its heavy forest, surrounding the perimeter of cleared land with double fences of chainlink and razor wire, illuminating the security strips between and beyond with spotlights. The cameras, hooded eyes mounted on poles, came only later, with the growth in urban insurgency.

The buildings went up, imposing and whitewashed, dwarfing even the presidential palace. Word spread in mysterious whispers that the remaining forest was heavily mined. A few years later, a bored Marine spotted a dog sniffing around at the edge of the vegetation. He tossed a grenade, the blast bringing the curious to the gates of the compound. They were given a tour. A cheap goodwill gesture. Were shown the destroyed vegetation, the smatterings of bloody flesh.

Rance, rolling through the microfilm, had seen indignant reports of the incident in the local newspaper: "An explosion was heard. . . . The dog was no more. . . . The ambassador would neither confirm nor deny the rumours of minefields. . . . Citizens should be wary. . . ." Rumour was lent credence. The journalist, a man named Grimaldi, had survived through the years, had gone on to become publisher of *Cuaderno*.

From down there, in the destroyed city, the compound glowed in a splendid, spotlit isolation, what the last ambassador — recently recalled and unlikely to be replaced — liked to call in his rare public speeches a shining beacon, but he never explained for whom. For State, probably, for Langley, the glow lovingly viewed from D.C. — but Rance didn't like the lights, never had. They made him feel targeted. Living in the Bull's Eye, he called it.

His office, on the third floor at the rear of the building, looked out onto the extensive back lawn, treeless, shrubless, a manicured field of fire. In his increasingly lengthy hours of idleness, Rance would find himself fantasizing gunmen lying on the lawn, assault rifles trained on the building, the fences behind them sliced open. From his window, he picked them off with a cool, unhurried calculation.

It was the evening of his second day in the new post. A reception in the main ballroom. She walked in on Grimaldi's arm, tall and slim, young enough to be his daughter; mistresses, Rance thought, are getting younger and younger. But she was simply dressed, a silver bracelet her only adornment — the other mistresses in the room proclaimed their status in excess — and she carried herself with an assuredness that he liked. Her self-possession declared itself all hers; it had nothing to do with the man she accompanied.

Rance made his way through the crowd, introduced himself to Grimaldi.

"Ahh," Grimaldi said, extending a plump hand. "The new spook."

"My field is culture, *señor*."

Grimaldi gazed amused at him, his eyes ironic beneath bushy eyebrows. "Yes, well . . . there's culture and there's culture, isn't there?" Then, without a blink, he introduced Rance to Isabel. "His field is culture," he said with a gentle bite.

"Yes," she said. "I heard." Her grip surprised him with its strength, the other mistresses having offered only a brief flirtation with the fingertips, and she gazed frankly at him, a hint of haughtiness making her appear for a moment taller than he was.

It was probably this — the unexpected sting of her gaze — that caused Rance to turn back to Grimaldi and say, "You have exquisite taste in women, Señor Grimaldi."

Grimaldi was silent for a moment, one fleshy lip pursed against the other. "Señor Rance," he said finally, almost whispering, "you must beware stereotypes."

"Señor?"

"Let me introduce you again, Señor Rance." He gestured at Isabel. "May I present Isabel Grimaldi, my daughter."

Rance's control faltered, blood surged to his face. "I —" He couldn't suppress a smile he knew to be idiotic. "Señorita Grimaldi —"

Her expression changed little, and Rance thought of the word unforgiving. His mind raced to the byline — I. Grimaldi — he'd seen in the microfilm rolls of *Cuaderno*. It wasn't the old man — he was Antonio — and he knew

Grimaldi had no son. A cousin or a nephew then, he'd assumed. The reporting was tough, fearlessly opinionated. And he remembered the picture he'd formed of the writer: a man slightly manic in a political way, unhappy with everyone, every program. The kind of man who, working on the basis of an unstated political agenda, made enemies everywhere.

"— so you're I. Grimaldi."

"I see you've done your homework."

"I had no idea —" Hers was not an immediately arresting face; yet the imperfections — the ripple in the middle of her nose, the glittery narrow-set eyes — created an unusual attractiveness against the field of her thin face. Her cheekbones, starting high and sloping downwards to the edges of her lips, suggested the soft features of an antelope.

"I always escort my father to public functions."

"Yes, I know." Her mother, Grimaldi's wife, had been bedridden for years.

"You know? You think you know everything, don't you, Señor Rance?"

"Not everything, Señorita Grimaldi —" They each took a glass of wine from the platter of a passing waiter. "— but maybe more than you think." He noticed her hands: fingers long and slim, with well-filed, unpainted nails. Serious, sensuous fingers.

"Or maybe not." She smiled, her look softening, losing its combativeness.

"Or maybe not."

"Truce?"

"Truce."

She raised her glass to his. "*Salud*, then."

116

It had seemed, eighteen months ago, like a plum posting, enough going on overtly and covertly to assure the rewarding of initiative. But a little unravelling had occurred not long after his arrival, enthusiasm leading to carelessness to revelation to stalemate.

The government, of men and women dressed in combat fatigues, proclaimed another revolutionary victory, organized spontaneous demonstrations, ordered out — in prudent enthusiasm — a few lower-level members of the embassy staff.

At home, there were newspaper revelations, internal investigations, public hearings.

Funds froze, careers stalled.

The ambassador and his senior people departed, normal rotations ended, and those remaining behind had only the flag left to tend.

It was a small country, much of it inaccessible. Coffee plantations, banana plantations, stretches of jungle impenetrable except to the obsessed. The roads away from the capital were bad, unpaved and rutted, narrowing at times to overgrown lanes. He had nevertheless managed, in a series of daylong car trips before travel restrictions were imposed, to see much of it.

The coasts, untouched, were a surprise; he had somehow failed to anticipate beauty in what he understood to be a land of dangers. And the interior, except for the frequent army roadblocks — fuzz-faced teenagers casual with AK-47s — and rifle-toting peasants, was almost somnolent. It was hardly a country seething with military activity, hardly a hotbed of revolutionary enthusiasm. There were crates of military equipment mildewing on the docks, and the embassy was wild about the number of weapons openly displayed — anyone strong enough to carry a gun seemed to have one — but Rance suspected that if his own country found itself under siege and all the weapons in private hands were brought out, the sight would be not much different. Only there would be less discipline, a greater threat to the public peace. He stopped in at collective farms, housing projects, literacy classes. And the more he saw of the smaller picture, the harder it became to entertain the larger one.

Driving back to the capital late one night after an evening with the priests and lay workers at a Catholic mission, Rance couldn't help thinking of his father, a wiry man with silvered hair, physically tough, prickly with the pride of the immigrant who had made good. In the suburban house comfortably crowded with department store furniture his father read newsmagazines, listened to the radio, watched television. And fears fostered in the larger picture fashioned nightmares in the smaller. Through his father's head and night-time disquisitions trekked "the marching millions", hordes of Spanish-speaking communists tramping north (the only time his father saw Latin Americans as anything but lazy and shiftless was when he saw them as hell-bent for invasion), Chinese-speaking communists plunging from the sky, Russian-speaking communists swooping up the beaches.

His father was a good man. A touch jealous of his own possessions, a bit rigid in his judgements, but a good man, nevertheless. He prided himself on what Rance recognized as acute immigrant obsessions: success, provision, a gentle invisibility. Like his neighbours, he belonged to various service clubs, owned a couple of hunting rifles, took in the occasional baseball or football game. There were summer barbecues, New Year's Eve dances, summer car trips to distant points. He mowed the lawn, paid the bills, played poker. In fact, his father differed from other fathers in only one appreciable way: he awoke every morning at five for an hour-long workout, various callisthenics followed by barbells, ending with a twenty-minute jog around the neighbourhood. His breakfast never varied: a grapefruit, bacon and eggs, a vile-smelling protein drink concocted in a blender with various powders and milk, a series of vitamin and mineral pills. His father was always in good humour in the morning, his mood darkening only at night when, after dinner, he'd worked his way through the newspaper. He watched television news, he said, only for its entertainment value.

His mother was the starkest reminder that they, his parents, had once had a different life. She was to Rance a mother like any other: she cooked, she cleaned, she tended his wounds. But there was a part of her that was inaccessible, the part that retreated every weekday afternoon to her bedroom and her books, obscure novels in her native German or, often, in translation from Swedish, Romanian, Bulgarian, or some similarly remote language. The part that glittered in her watery brown eyes when she listened, with only nods and the occasional hum, to his father's excited political dissections. While upheaval and displacement — their story, his mother always said, wasn't so special that he couldn't find the grand lines of it in the history books — had simplified much for his father, his mother's manner suggested that she had come to different conclusions. It was one of the many things Rance planned to ask his mother about, some day.

It said a lot to Rance that, while his mother had retained

the German edge to her accent, his father had long ago lost his in the wilful acquisition of a new identity. Rance remembered the curious sight, when he was six or seven, of his father standing before the bathroom mirror, his lips twisting into funny shapes, quietly working on his pronunciation of *with* — "vis, vis, vit, vith, ou-iss, ou-ith" — repeating it over and over again until the sounds came out to his satisfaction. Rance had long suspected that his father was secretly a little ashamed of his mother, and this prompted in him a certain shyness towards her in public. She carried with her an old-world mustiness, while his father had fully committed himself to the new. Yet his mother suggested complexities, satisfying to her, he suspected, where his father offered the reassurance of simplicities. It was what tinged his mother with an understated fragility, what made his father seem so solid.

But it was this apparent solidity that explained his father's fears. He was a man who had lost and gained — and had no intention of losing again. His fear of the marching millions was merely a sign of his insecurities, legitimate or not, a sign of his laying of a minefield. It was what made him proud of Rance and the work he did; yet his work, Rance felt, also prompted the disappointment he thought he sometimes detected in his mother's watery eyes. He would, one day, have to ask her about that, too.

Tweedledum and Tweedledee remained outside, failing to look casual on the other side of the street. Rance supposed that the lack of subtlety in their shadowing of him — of anyone who left the embassy — was part of the game, a kind of attempted intimidation. But he had — they all had —

grown accustomed to them, the four two-man teams assigned to keep watch on the embassy. Tweedledum and Tweedledee, especially, had grown on him; they were a chunky pair who spent their idle time outside the gates arguing over card games. He would worry if, one day, they suddenly weren't there.

The supermarket barely justified its name. A little place, shabby on the outside, webby on the inside. After the burning sunlight, it was several seconds before his eyes — most of the fluorescent tubes were burnt out — accustomed themselves to the gloom.

A group of neighbourhood women sat in a corner muttering among themselves, gossiping, perhaps, or exchanging complaints about the state of things. Several children, half-naked and brown-skinned, played beside them on the grimy floor. Two or three of the women cast suspicious glances at Rance: Cuban? Russian? American? One of the foreign "volunteers" — Swedes, Danes, Australians, Canadians — who'd flooded into the country to help build the revolution? It didn't really matter: none of them was of the country, all of them were suspect. The women's conversation subsided to sighs and an uneasy patting at hair, a straightening of ragged clothes.

It was a new suspiciousness, and one Rance was not used to. The eyes, the whispers, the willed reticence: they made him feel conspicuous. He turned his gaze from them and walked with uneasy confidence farther into the gloom. The wooden shelves were mostly bare, merchandise scarce in the economic blockade, food a subtle and unacknowledged weapon. A few cans of sardines, a couple of bags of mouldy potatoes, Cuban sugar, local coffee, beer, odds and ends.

Some local fruit — bananas, oranges, grapefruit — but even that was becoming difficult to obtain, the lack of Eastern-bloc tractor parts and Western fertilizer playing havoc with agriculture. This was what Rance, with nothing else to do, had come to check: the blatant effectiveness of policy. Success was bare shelves. Success was photos of breadlines, footage of public discontent.

He picked up a hand of bruised bananas, a couple of hard oranges, took them to the counter at the front.

The shopkeeper, a middle-aged man of grave demeanour leaning tired against the wall, yawned into his clenched fist.

Rance nodded at him.

The man, red eyes watering, made no move, scratched absently at his neck.

"Bueno?" Rance said, peeling a bill from his wallet.

The man yawned again, scratched his crotch. "Yanqui?" he said.

It was not a question of friendly curiosity, was said with an unmistakable edge of distaste. "No," Rance said, the word too quick, too defensive to his own ears.

The man snorted, clearly disbelieving. "Pues, tu pais, tu nacionalidad —"

"Canadiense," Rance said.

"Ah, si!" The man's face grew animated. "Toronto! Montreal!"

How often had Rance seen this, not here but, younger, in Europe. He hadn't, like so many, sewn a maple leaf flag to his backpack — he avoided overt displays of nationality — but he had, at times judged opportune, claimed Canadian citizenship. This assumption of a mask, this denial of self, led invariably to a lowering of suspicion. And it led to what

122

he came eventually to do with his life; led to a desire to set things right to alter the image.

". . . un hermano en Toronto, dos primos en. . . ."

But life, he had since discovered, was a great deal more complex. The balancing of right and wrong, of the desirable and the undesirable, required compromise and a recognition of uncertainties, his role — of pursuing specific interests — demanded an acceptance of unchallenged certainties. Rance understood eventually that he could not devote his life to ideological truths, could not deny his distrust of successes. Seeking to avoid one discomfort, he had come upon another — and he still judged it prudent, at times, to disguise himself.

He paid for the fruit, turned — and found himself facing Isabel. She was standing there, just a few feet behind him, and the grin she was suppressing by biting at her lower lip told him she'd been there long enough to overhear his subterfuge. "Hola," he said automatically. "Qué tal?"

"Señor Rance." She stepped past him, paid for her soft drink.

He waited for her at the door.

"Canadian now, eh?" she said in English as they stepped out into the sunshine.

"Es un mundo —"

"Let's speak English. I don't get enough chance to practise."

"I was going to say —"

"You don't have to explain."

They walked in silence, the sunlight digging under the skin into the flesh. Isabel sipped from the bottle. Tweedledum and Tweedledee followed at an indiscreet distance.

"Where'd you learn English?" Rance asked after a few minutes.

"In your country."

"Miami?"

She chuckled. "Toronto." Offered a sip of her soft drink. It was a local cola, sugary, without fizz.

A stray dog paused in its foraging to growl at them; then, as if drained by the effort, slunk away in search of shade.

Isabel gestured behind them with her thumb. "They go with you everywhere?"

"They're harmless."

"Your activities must be more difficult?"

Rance thought of saying, I have my ways; said instead, "Not really. Besides, there aren't too many cultural festivals around these days."

"You were not just buying fruit in the supermarket."

"Checking on general conditions. I still have to file reports."

"Cultural intelligence?"

"Everything helps."

"You're going to send the fruit in the diplomatic bag?"

Rance chuckled. "That's an idea."

She did not even smile "You're different," she said after a minute. "Not your typical spy."

"I'm not a spy."

"Information officer, then."

"That's closer to what I do."

She finished the cola, put the empty can into her purse. "You know, Señor Rance —"

"Just Rance."

"— Rance. I believe you."

He didn't know why, but her admission was a relief to him. All he could think to say was, "Thank you."

The moment she stepped into his office, he tagged her a revolution groupie. She had the face, thin and unadorned, chalky white even with a tan, with scraggly blonde hair. And she dressed the part, in sombre, baggy clothing, with earth-mother sandals — clumps of scuffed suede famous for comfort, unsurpassed for ugliness — encasing her feet. There was a frailty to her that suggested to Rance an overweening vegetarianism.

She said, sitting on the edge of the chair in front of his desk, that she had lost her passport.

Lost or sold, he wondered, but it wasn't worth asking.

She watched, wordless and nervous, as he took out the requisite forms, selected a pen from a desk drawer. He was not accustomed to performing pedestrian embassy services, but the shrunken staff had parcelled out duties. Besides, it was a way of filling the time.

He asked for details — when, where, how — and spent several quiet minutes taking down the information, her occasional sighs punctuating the scratching of pen on paper. He lit a cigarette, never taking his eyes off the forms, ignored her theatrical snort of displeasure.

People like this — people who claimed patriotism from a different angle — unsettled him. Sitting there with an ineffable air of self-righteousness, she was the antithesis of his professional personality, the magnified refraction of his private one. She, and those like her, had elevated to a way of life the unease he felt at his successes; they had embraced that unease, formed a philosophy of it, taken it to areas of the world where they saw wrongs to be righted. It was as if, by their presence and their efforts, they were apologizing for their country, and for the actions of Rance and people like him. They were not dangerous people, he knew. They lacked deceit, lived by a naive honesty. Were, as a result, powerless in a grand sense. They were not taken seriously, were simply looked down on with a kind of irritated amusement. Rance thought them rather foolish people, yet he envied them, too; they claimed a freedom for themselves which seemed truer than the service to which he had dedicated himself. In the end, unable to dismiss them, he feared them — for what they were and for what he was not.

He lit another cigarette, the first still burning in the ashtray.

Isabel held knife and fork as if they were made of air, her movements liquid.

"They won't give it up, Isabel, that's the problem."

"Of course you are right, Rance. But they were many years fighting in the mountains —"

"— and they like the comforts of the presidential palace —"

"You think this is news to us? We have eyes, we have ears."

"Then you understand our —"

"But what gives you people the right to impose —"

"— encourage —"

"— and that is why *Cuaderno* opposes them all —"

"You supported the rebels —"

"And now that they're the government —"

"You oppose them —"

126

"Yes! Yes! Why not? We oppose all tyranny, the right, the
left, the *norteameri* —"

"Sometimes the centre is the most dangerous place —"

"But the only sensible —"

"Not if you don't survive."

"We get no support from you people —"

"What d'you —"

"You gave the generals guns, you trained their —"

"Security considerations —"

"— and you co-operated when the rebels won, at first.
Economic aid —"

"But then we saw the tyranny growing —"

"Yes, but because they wouldn't play your game —"

"You don't like them any more than we do —"

"No, they jailed my father, too, just like the generals —"

"Even though you supported them —"

"You're repeating yourself —"

"— and they confiscated your newsprint —"

"— and they shut us down for weeks at a time. Yes, yes,
I know!"

"So —"

"But that's our problem, Rance, *no entiendes?* Maybe we
had a chance with them, but then you — Cómo se dice?
Apretar los tornillos —"

"Put the screws on."

"*Sí*, you put the screws on them —"

"They decided on their own to turn to Fidel —"

"— but they didn't turn on you —"

"I don't believe you're defending them —"

"Not defending! Never!"

"This stuff you write, who cares —"

"The people read us —"

"The people?"

"They keep us going."

"Pawns —"

"That's the trouble, no? The people — everybody's pawns."

"Well —"

"Well what?"

"— that's reality. Political reality."

"No, Rance. That is not reality. That is games, that is greed —"

"So what's reality, then?"

"Reality? Reality is simple. Food, drink. Love and laughter. And politics is just about getting there."

"Or not."

"Or not."

Rance filled their wine glasses. He knew he was falling in love with her.

He left the movie halfway through. The off-duty Marine guards, passing a bottle of tequila from hand to hand, kept up a steady commentary on the film, conversed with the actors, answered their questions, improvised dialogue. Normally he enjoyed the spontaneity of their humour, but this evening their young voices grated on him, their laughter was intrusive.

He took the elevator up to his office from the basement, sat at his desk to try to compose his weekly report. There was little new and he found himself repeating phrases, entire sentences, from his last several cables. The bared shelves, the collapsing agriculture, the growing fiction of restaurant menus. Discontent, and a creeping weariness with the war. All reasons for joy, but he knew that, for the men in the windowless offices, it would be like getting into bed with their wives. All was as it should be, but there was no edge of excitement.

He knew he should tell them about Isabel. A new contact, a new source to be courted. Possibilities of future usefulness. Part of his job this, what he had been trained to do: traders in secrets kept no secrets. But he didn't want to. He told himself he didn't yet know whether Isabel could be turned into an asset, and to mention her would be premature. True enough, but not good enough. What would he tell them, anyway?

He poured the last of the gin into a glass, tossed in a couple of ice cubes, added a dash of flat tonic water, shrugged off the lack of lemon. He had developed a taste for gin and tonic during his stint at the Madrid embassy — his tennis partner from the British embassy ended every game with a couple of tall ones — and he had come to think of it as the perfect warm weather drink, refreshing, with a bit of a buzz. Curious, though, the way many of his compatriots reacted to the drink. They preferred bourbon, scotch, vodka, tequila, spirits they understood. The gin and tonics lent him, in their eyes, a certain eccentricity. Rance wondered at the pauses, the puzzlement, the brief frowns. The first time he ordered one here, the Marine guard tending bar remarked in surprise that the gin was reserved for foreign visitors. The ambassador, chewing at the olive from his martini, chuckled and said it was all right, they'd get some more in. Rance was amused by his own unease — dare he tell anyone that he also enjoyed the occasional Ricard? — but learned soon enough to enjoy the game. To fix an exotic drink, or to order one, was to indulge in a scintilla of defiance.

He took the drink to the window, let his gaze roam over the spotlit back lawn. He was on an island looking out beyond the edges to the darkness that swallowed horizons. He felt his isolation, felt Isabel's isolation, knew it was this that attracted him to her.

Isabel had a quality rare in this country. She refused to deny complexity. She rejected the simplification of vision that formed hard and irrevocable around power, around the having of it and the wanting of it. Ideology, of the right or of the left, was here veneer, a thing to cloak yourself in depending on your aims and on who was prepared to support your struggle. You hung it around your shoulders, and soon it trapped you in its clasp. But the truth was that, in the harsh world of black and white politics, beliefs were like bullets: they were, in flight, indistinguishable, and they respected no flesh. It was, to Rance, an almost paralysing realization. Money was funnelled, arms procured, troops trained — but it all had very little to do with the country involved. It all had to do, instead, with his father, his fears and his obsessions. It had to do with anxieties dressed up as policies and plated in ideology: a pretending at higher purpose. It was where religion and politics met, the fear of Hell leading to the contemplation of Heaven. Protect your money the way you protect your soul: camouflage the essential in a scaffolding of philosophical intricacies. It was why Rance didn't like his informers. They were not men who believed in liberties; they were men who believed in power. And cash spoke to them in wondrous tongues.

All this, Isabel understood.

He went back to the desk, wrote her name. Looked at it there on the yellow notepad and felt, after a moment, like a teenager surreptitiously scribbling the name of a secret crush just to see what it looked like, to see if in the letters he could divine marvels and promises for the future. The pen moved as of its own accord, his hand its appendage, decorating the letters, shadowing them, adding curls and flourishes. Then, feeling foolish, he scratched the name out, rendered it illegible. Isabel was a contact he wanted to keep from them; she was a contact he wanted to keep all for himself.

"What is this place, Rance?"

"A safe house."

She walked carefully around the darkened room, drew a finger along a table, examined it closely. "A dirty house, too."

Rance regretted he hadn't had a chance to come by before to clean up a bit. The place hadn't been used in a long time. Many people had been through here, but it had never felt peopled before.

"So how many other women have you brought here?" Her tone was teasing, but underlaid with tension.

"You're the first."

"I must believe that?"

"It's the truth." It was, and he cared deeply that she know it. "You do believe me, don't you?"

But she didn't reply, just continued her wandering through the dark, almost sensing her way, her hands touching, feeling, making an elemental contact. It was as if she were seeking the spirits of the place.

Rance went over to the window, gingerly raised the blinds

part-way so that the movement would be imperceptible from the street. The dull light of the streetlamp showed deserted sidewalks, and he thought almost with a touch of nostalgia of Tweedledum and Tweedledee sitting contentedly outside the embassy gates, secure in its illuminated inanimation.

"Do you believe in reincarnation?" she called from the bedroom.

He gently closed the blinds. "The great assembly-line of life?" He'd wanted to keep it light, but he'd spoken too quickly, failed to blunt the edge of his sarcasm.

She was silent for a moment. Then, with a light chuckle, said, "I knew you were going to say that."

He was flattered.

The bedroom light sluiced on. Rance hurried in, panic subsiding only when he saw that the blinds were down. Isabel was already stripping the bed. "Sheets?" she said, and it sounded like shits. Smiling, he pointed to the closet.

She stayed beside the bed, the dirty sheets bundled in her arms. "Well?"

"How domestic," he said, but didn't move.

Her face went serious, and she flung the sheets to the floor. "No soy tu criada, mierda!"

His hand reached up, flicked off the light. "No," he said. "Of course you're not my maid." He padded by instinct over to her, slipped his arms around her waist, pulled her close. Her body was firm and warm against him, her breath hot on his neck. Her hair smelled of the heavily perfumed local soap. He kissed her eyes, her nose, tasted inexplicable tears on her cheeks. One of her hands grasped his shoulder, the other rose to the back of his neck, pressing, urging his lips to hers. Grasping him, holding him there, claiming its rights with a tender insistence.

An eternity of telescoping time. The mind converging on sensation, wet and urgent.

Forever later, the ticking of the mattress rough on their bare skin.

The phone was heavy in his hand, hot against his ear. The sunlight through his office window burned white.

"What do you expect me to tell you, Señor Grimaldi?"

"Confirm the rumour for me, Señor Rance: yes or no?"

"I don't know anything about this."

"A list, Señor Rance. You have seen no list?"

"I've seen lots of lists, but none of the kind —"

"Come on, Señor Rance —"

"I shouldn't even be talking to you."

"Are your phones tapped? You have the technology —"

"That's not the problem. I have nothing to tell you."

"According to my information, a list has been drawn up —"

"Who by?"

"— of prominent people marked for assassination."

"I said, who by?"

"You tell me, Señor Rance."

"I resent the implication, Señor Grimaldi."

"What implication, Señor Rance?"

"We have nothing to do with assassinations."

"I didn't say you did. I'm just looking for confirmation —"

"How can I confirm the existence of something we —"

"It's your business to know things, Señor Rance."

"Yours too, if I'm not mistaken."

"A little co-operation —"

"We know nothing about assassination —"

"Let's be frank, Señor Rance. That's only because you're not very good at it —"

"I'm not about to dis—"

"— but your various proxies —"

"We have no proxies."

"— there are no controls —"

"Señor Grimaldi, you said you had a question. You asked it, I —"

"The mayor of Altamira was shot last night, and the mayor of —"

"Ask the government."

"My information is that it's the other side, your people."

"We have no people."

"It is your money that pays for —"

"Señor Grimaldi, *por favor* —"

"Señor Rance —"

"This conversation is over, Señor Grimaldi."

Rance hung up, briefly, never removing his hand from the receiver. Dialed, waited impatiently through the clicks and buzzes of the ancient phone system, and when a male voice answered said simply, "Luna."

Isabel had once been married. Still was, as far as she knew. She hadn't heard from her husband in years, and they'd never discussed divorce. "So I am," she said with a glimmer of mischievousness, "semi-detached."

He was a Canadian, someone she met while studying

134

English in Toronto. She was young at the time — "Another life," she sighed, but not with regret, "another Isabel" — but her parents had not been displeased. It was a particularly dangerous time in her country, the war intensifying, the killings becoming more blatant, less discriminating. Her father, at her mother's behest, took to moving around with armed bodyguards, his car never left untended.

The husband's name was Philip, but she called him Felipe, after the character in the *Mafalda* comic strip. He was, she said, what the comic-book Felipe would grow up to be — thin, earnest, with a naive social idealism and a greater intellectual urge than his capacities could accommodate. He was not particularly good-looking, she said, his face too long, teeth too prominent; but his animated spirit coupled with his physical frailty to create a certain allure.

"Many times I have thought that if I write the story of my marriage — and I will one day, when we can contemplate such things in peace, when it will not be immoral to spend our days obsessed by the personal — but if I write this story, I will call it 'No Effort Required'. It tells all. We were not rich, Felipe and me, but we lacked nothing. A movie a week, a restaurant a week, dancing from time to time.

"He taught two courses of poetry at the university and he wrote science fiction in his spare time. I worked part-time for a temporary agency, office work, filing, typing. I left my brain at home every morning. This, or go crazy.

"I volunteered at an immigrant women's centre, spent a few hours a week counselling Spanish-speaking women, helping them through the bureaucracy, listening to their stories. Sad stories, frightening stories. It was good work, important work, but it was like working with glue, Rance. It stuck to you, it went home with you. You slept with it, ate with it, made love with it. After a month Felipe asked me to give it up. Not for me, but for him. He couldn't support it any more, the stories I brought home, the 'long face' I showed. So I quit, for him, for us. He got me a dog to occupy my time. I named him Ananás, because his face reminded me of Noriega. It was around then that my mother had her stroke. She lost the use of a leg, an arm. She could only mumble. My father told me not to come.

"One afternoon not long after, I was out walking Ananás when he suddenly pulled the cord from my hand and ran into the street. A car was coming, too fast. I dashed after him without thinking. The car missed me, but by very little. I fell at the edge of the sidewalk, not hurt, just frightened. The driver stopped long enough to swear at me. Ananás was on the sidewalk looking at me with his tongue hanging out. People came out from a house, tied Ananás to the fence, took me inside, gave me some water. I heard someone calling the police. But I didn't want that, there was no point. And just the word 'police' makes me shiver. Yes, I know it's stupid, it makes no sense, the Toronto police are not the police of my counry. But still, some fears you don't lose. So I got up — just like that — got up and walked out of the house.

And I walked past Ananás to a little park just a bit down the road. I sat there on a bench, partly hidden by a tree trunk. Waiting for the police to come. Watched the policeman examine Ananás, while the people from the house looked around. Looking for me, I knew, so I hid behind the tree. Watched the policeman go into the house with the people, come back out again a few minutes later, speak into his car radio, put Ananás in the back seat of his car, and drive off.

"I went home, packed a suitcase, and was on a plane home that night. I didn't forget Felipe. I left a note. He knew I was safe.

"Irresponsible? Yes, it was. But, I've told you, that was another Isabel.

"Cruel? How dare you talk to me about cruel. Happy *norteamericanos!* You people will never understand. Maybe what I did to Felipe was cruel in your context, Rance, but not in mine. But you will never understand that, you will always be too much of a *yanqui.*

"Yes, of course, that was Felipe's context too, and yes, it was cruel for him in his context. But he solved all that. He's found someone else, I hear, has a child, is even an assistant professor. But the cruelties of my context — the one that makes me everything I am — those are still with us, worse than ever.

"Abandoning Ananás, leaving Felipe: I know when I talk about it, it all sounds easy. But you're a fool if you think it was. Sure, I wish now I had done the right thing, the logical thing, the kind thing. But sometimes our need is stronger than our logic. Don't you see, Rance, I just don't have the luxury of being able to wallow in it. Felipe's context allowed him a happy ending. In my context, people are still dying."

They never exchanged pleasantries, rarely watched each other.

Rance handed over the money, rolled tight in a rubber band. Luna — it was how Rance had trained himself to think of him, only by the name assigned to the file — swiftly pocketed the roll, as if wishing to thrust from sight the tangible acknowledgement of his betrayals. The surreptitiousness of the movement always reminded Rance of his predecessor's wry comment that Luna first came to him through patriotism, continued coming to him through greed.

Luna, as usual, remained close to the door. A nervous silhouette, slender in clothes baggy and shapeless.

Rance said, "Tell me about the list."

"What list?"

"Starts with the mayors of Altamira and —"

"What about it?"

"Who drew it up?"

"Don't know."

"Don't bullshit me, Luna."

"I don't know, I tell you."

"You've seen it?"

"No."

"So how do you know it exists?"

"Talk."

"Talk means nothing."

"Talk from the right person means everything."

"Who?"

"You don't know him."

"What's his name?"

"His name will mean nothing to you."

"His name, Luna."

"Lope de Vega."

"You're bullshitting me again."

"It's the name he goes by."

"What's he do?"

"Courier. Always back and forth. Stinks of the jungle."

"Why'd he tell you —"

"News, *hombre*. Just news."

"They're not exactly keeping it quiet —"

"Part of the game, no?"

"Part of the game. Right." The game, Rance thought, the endless fucking merry-go-round of lies and deception and intimidation.

"So who is on it?"

"Many names. Many, many names."

"You sound sad."

"I should dance about this?"

"So who?"

"Fernandez, Lacruz, Tarradellas —"

"The poet?"

"The same."

"Why a poet?"

"Why not? His pen is his weapon."

"We don't take poets that seriously where I come from —"

"That's because your poets can afford to sit around playing with themselves —"

"Who else?"

"Catedrales —"

"Which one?"

"Agosto —"

"But he's just —"

"I know, a singer —"

"— and not particularly good, either —"

"— but he appears in public with the wrong people, sometimes. Waving and smiling —"

"He has a following, you'll alienate —"

"Young girls, middle-aged women. We don't need their sexless romance."

"Who else?"

"You don't need the names, you'll find —"

"The names, damn you!"

"I'm go—"

"Wait, Luna, I'm sorry. I didn't mean —"

"*Bueno, bueno.* But the time. It is getting late —"

"Who else?"

"Who else? I don't know. Ruiz-Mateos, Carrillo, Grimaldi —"

"Grimaldi? Which Grimaldi?"

"The newspaper Grimaldi —"

"There are two —"

"I don't know which —"

"Man or woman?"

"Man."

"*Cierto?*"

"*Cierto*. Lope said no women this time —"

"Absolutely certain —"

"No doubt, I tell you —"

"When?"

"Don't know."

"Find out. I need to know."

"Who knows? When the chance comes —"

"Find out, Luna."

"You must not interfere —"

"I never interfere, you know that. Just let me know when."

"If I hear —"

"Just let me know, Luna."

"Okay, okay. If I know, you'll know."

"Good. Enough, Luna, enough. Go now."

Luna didn't have to be pushed. He turned the doorknob

and was gone, like a shadow slipping between two pages of a book.

Rance took out a cigarette, lit it. We are, he thought, like firemen. We put out fires when we can, create firebreaks and conduct controlled burns when we can't. But sometimes the flames get away from us, they burn where they want to, and there isn't a damned thing we can do about it.

He was truly beginning to hate his job.

"You have a funny accent when you speak Spanish."

"What's funny about it?"

"It's the Spanish equivalent of an English lord —"

"You mean —"

"— *onthay, dothay, trethay* —"

"I learned Spanish in Madrid —"

"And did you visit *Barthaylona* many times?"

"You've got to admit it's got one advantage —"

"And whath's thath?"

"You're impossible."

"Grathiath —"

"That's 'grathias' —"

"— but you're not the first to dithcover thath."

"Spelling. You people can't differentiate between z, c, s —"

"And how do you differenthiathe between z and c?"

"It's —"

"Admit it, Ranth, I goth you."

"Come here. Here, like this. Now — you've got to admit, I goth you, too."

"Mmmm?"

"Like thith."

"Mmmm."

"And thith."

"Mmmm."

"And thith —"

"Ahh, Ranth!"

Rance liked Grimaldi despite their mutual suspicion. He was a short, tub-like man, his ready jolliness a camouflage for the gravity of a deeper intelligence. He seemed to be always perspiring, his forehead slicked and beaded in any light. His body, internally battered by intermittent bouts of prison, contained a combative spirit. As a young reporter, Grimaldi had indulged in a lively, engaged journalism, with no pretence at objectivity. It was a virtue, he once said to Rance, that he could not afford, evenhandedness found not in balanced articles — "The left-wing death squads said, the right-wing death squads said" — but in equal reporting of their atrocities. He showed Rance death threats he had received, neatly typed letters remarkably similar in language and spirit, differing only in ideological perspective. "This is our tragedy," Grimaldi said. "It has not changed through the decades."

And nothing else had, either. Insurgencies had come and gone and come again; governments had risen and fallen and risen again, all with casual regularity. But this remained a land of implication. Nothing could be confirmed because everything was deception; no sooner was it there than it was gone, there but not there. Even the rumours of minefields: nobody knew for sure, not State, not Langley, whether mines had been planted. It was the best kind of rumour, indistin-

guishable from truth and therefore, for all intents and pur-
poses, truth itself.

All was truth, all was falsehood, all reality, all fantasy.
This was the key, Rance felt, to the country, and perhaps to
the entire continent; the key to the failures of policy developed in more settled northern air. And it was in the midst of
these shifting spectres that Grimaldi fought, a man thrashing
around at fact and fiction.

Rance wrote a report, dispatched it. God alone knew what
they would make of it up there.

So far away.

He lights another cigarette, blows the smoke towards the
ceiling.

Her face lies hot against his chest, her skin moist and
clinging as if melting into his. He smells her hair, tastes her
still in his mouth, hears still the gasps and babble of her
yearning.

"Don't you ever worry about your father?"

"What do *you* think, Rance?"

"These days — "

"You mean the mayors?"

"Yes."

"Is he in any more danger now than he's ever been in?
For people like my father danger is a given — "

"He's learned to live with it?"

"Don't be stupid. He's learned to live despite it."

"I don't want to go back," Rance suddenly blurts out.

"So don't."

"What do I do? Just disappear?"

"Cómo no?" She snapped her fingers. "Presto!"

143

"I'm serious."

"It's easier than you think, Rance."

"Come with me."

"You know this is not possible."

"How do I know that?"

"My mother—"

"And your work?"

"That too."

"You could be a journalist elsewhere. Maybe even TV —"

"Yes, and file stories for dinnertime viewing."

"Upset a few people."

"Spoil their dinners, so click, click, look, baseball!"

He knows she is right, knows he has to be blunt. "I'm asking you to be selfish. For me."

Her body stiffens, creates a psychic distance between their pressing skin. "But you don't understand, Rance. I am already selfish. For me."

"You're right, I don't understand."

"I do what I do because I have to satisfy myself."

"Don't you ever dream of a normal life? House, kids, cats and dogs?"

"That is what you dream of?"

"I never did before."

"I think about it sometimes. But there are other dreams too, *entiendes?*"

"Sí," he says after a moment. "Entiendo." And he tongues a curl of her hair into his mouth.

He has been sitting at his desk since Luna's call. The time. The place. Adiós, Grimaldi.

144

Twice he has dialed Isabel's number, and twice he has hung up. He has not been tempted to call Grimaldi himself; he is too well trained for that.

He has sat here as the darkness encrusted itself around the compound, patched itself around his office. Sits now in light of a different quality, less diffuse than daylight, its reach ending just beyond the sill, giving the office window a glow as from a television.

He waits, sitting at his desk, calmer, he thinks, than he has any right to be. Two cigarettes burn in the ashtray. His throat is dry, and he wishes he had a full bottle of gin. The beer he has settled for is forgotten hot and half-empty on his desk. Its aftertaste, a sour coating on the flesh of his mouth, will not go away.

Eventually it comes, the dull and distant thump of an exploding bomb. Hardly a lethal sound. Like a wall of wood hitting the ground.

The sound of goodbye: how can he face Isabel now?

He waits the few minutes until the sirens reach him, their thin wail more alarming than the explosion itself. Then he stands, slings his travel bag onto his shoulder, and takes the stairs down to the basement. Pads softly past the rec room where the Marines are improvising dialogue, to the steel door that leads to the tunnel, long and dim, walls spectacularly cracked by seeping water. The ceiling is high enough for him to walk erect but instinct causes him to hunch over.

Emerges from the tunnel to the nighttime effacement of blackened forest. Senses arrested: where is up? Where is down?

He is blind, he is spinning. The ground?

The building anchors him. Through the fences, past the

security strip, it sits there glowing, boasting of its invincibility. He has never before looked at it from here, never paused to examine it through the rip in the foliage, his vision intent, determinedly narrow. There is his office window, an opaque rectangle. He imagines for a moment that he sees himself peering through it: an uneasy ghost fading into the glass.

It is a life he is leaving behind, abandoning choices and possibilities by making the only one he can. His functions — this self that has been fashioned by training — are too deeply ingrained. He cannot turn his back on them, and is appalled that his betrayal of Isabel comes more easily.

He cannot imagine a future, doesn't want to remember the past. Thinks with a tremor of the revolution groupies.

Isabel. He will carry her face with him, always, her face as he imagines it now: tear-stained, crumpled in grief, warped by the horror of the inevitable he has watched evolve. There are some things, he thinks, that even love cannot conquer.

He switches on his flashlight, searches the ground for the pieces of tile imbedded in the earth that lead the long way out. There are, on this continent, villages, towns, countries where a man can easily disappear.

He firmly grasps the strap of his bag and, flashlight in hand, walks into the forest.

In the darkness, he feels the arctic landscape high above pressing down on him. Startling. Imposing.

He feels himself beginning to shatter.

Cracks and Keyholes

AS USUAL, BARNABAS sittin' on the narrow bench in the bus shelter outside the Riviera, his plastic left leg, lookin' like somebody chop it off at the knee from a store-window dummy, prop up beside him. Before, he use to be able to see me comin' a long way off, from the moment I turn the corner from Yonge Street, and he did have time to strap on the leg and limp to the entrance to wait for the cigarette I does give him.

Every day, the same thing: he take the cigarette in his open hand as if is something holy, wipe his long moustache with his other hand, wet his lips with his tongue and put the cigarette between them, half-close his eyes and wait for me to flick the fire on the end o' the cigarette. A deep-deep puff. Then he take the cigarette from his mouth with the thumb and first finger of his left hand, open his mouth and pull every last curl o' smoke into his lungs; he hold it for a good ten-fifteen seconds before he blow it out slow-slow, watchin' it stream out in front. Then he did always say, "You not having one, Lenny?" He's the only person who does call me Lenny; for everybody else is Leonard. And I always say, "No, man, later." But I never tell him I doesn't smoke. And every single time he did come back with, "Well then, you can give me the one you're not going to smoke." And it a'ready in my hand. He take it: "Thanks, Lenny." Limp back to the seat and, without strapping the leg, lose heself in the cigarette and the smoke.

But that was before. A little while ago they put up a big ad — a big, bright, colourful can o' soup that always look like it laughin' at people like Barnabas — on the side o' the shelter and Barnabas don't see me comin' no more. He does always look surprise and confuse when he see me in the door o' the bus shelter. He does reach for his leg — old beat-up pink plastic, leather straps, a green sock, a black shoe — tryin' to hide it, as if he embarrass for me to see it. I does feel bad for the fella — the leg does pain him a lot when he wearin' it — so I give him the cigarettes fast-fast, light one for him and take off for the Riviera as if I runnin' late.

At first I did hate that ad because it was takin' away the little bit o' dignity Barnabas use to bring to the whole transaction and it was blockin' his view o' Yonge Street in the distance: the lights, the cars, the gold decorations they hang across the street for Christmas. But then last night, walkin' to the subway after work, I take a good look at the decorations, the lights shinin' on the gold — wet snow was comin' down and the air was flowin' like water on me — and I realize it have few things more depressin' in this world than decorations that doesn't decorate; and them decorations across Yonge Street, old and wet and limp and mash-up, ain't have it in them to decorate. They does just hang there above the traffic like wear-out garlands somebody forget to take down after a party twenty years ago. Seein' them last night, I think maybe is a good thing Barnabas can't see Yonge Street and the decorations no more.

Barnabas is a piece o' the street in front the Riviera. I did find him here when I start my job just under a year ago; he still here; he probably goin' to be here till they take him away in a sheet. That bus shelter is like Barnabas' home. It have other people 'round here too but they does always be comin' or goin', old men and old women in older clothes, all walkin' as if the next step takin' them directly into the grave.

Is only in the last week or so that another man take up residence outside the Riviera, just a few feet away from the bus shelter. A fat old man with grey skin, wearin' a brown coat and a red wool cap pull down over his ears, he does spend the day in his wheelchair playin' tunes I never hear before on his mouth-organ. Over his legs he have a blanket the colour o' ashes and on the blanket he put a rusty biscuit tin with some change in it.

Before I light the cigarette, I ask Barnabas who he is.

"It's Noah," he say. "He used to be on Yonge Street, but they made him move." He laugh, lickin' his lips for the cigarette. "Not good for the conscience of the shoppers, don't you know."

"No, I ain't know, Barnabas. How they could do that to the poor fella? Christmas comin' tomorrow."

"So?" He screw up his face at me.

149

"Well, at least he playin' mouth-organ, not very good is true, but at least he not just beggin', he doin' something. Whatever happen to the Christmas spirit?"

"Why do you think they say 'spirit', Lenny? It's because the damn thing's dead — "

"He going to be lucky if he get fifty cents a day around here."

Barnabas look sour and wave his cigarette around in front of his face. "But it's just Noah. He's used to that, don't you know."

"But still — "

"It's just Noah, for God's sake!"

I decide to leave it there and light his cigarette. As I walk past Noah to the front door o' the Riviera, I nod at him and put a quarter in his tin. But he ignore me, just keep on playin' his mouth-organ. Except for my quarter and a few pennies he use to prime it, the biscuit tin empty. I open the door and go inside just as little bits o' snow begin driftin' down.

Is a good fifteen years I in Canada now, and I's livin' proof that not every immigrant is a multicultural success story. Maybe is a question of too much dreamin' and not enough doin'; maybe is a question of dreamin' the wrong dreams or doin' the wrong things. But before I arrive here, nobody — and especially nobody in the Canadian High Commission back home — really tell me much 'bout this country I was goin' to. It was all dream and gossip, what people say. They say, in Canada is: You want a job? Here's a job. You want money? Here's money. But I find out quick-quick that to get a job, you have to have the trainin'; to get money, you have to have money. And even then, it damn hard to hold on to the little you does manage to save. I recently close my chequin' account at the bank because they charge me for every cheque unless I have five hundred dollars in it. Must be nice to have five hundred dollars to just leave sittin' there. I close the account 'cause I ain't like their attitude: the more you have, the more you have; the less you have, the less you have. It ain't really a dog-eat-dog world, as my granma use to say. Is more a cat-eat-mouse world, and I ain't foolin' meself 'bout who is the cat and who is the mouse. The hard part is seein' the traps and avoidin' them or, the best, usin' them for your own good.

The only thing people was right about was the cold, although nobody ever mention the summer that could get hotter and stickier than back home. And nobody ever tell me neither that I might like the cold; nobody ever tell me that it don't drain away your energy like the heat.

So I arrive here a good fifteen years ago, knowin' little and not realizin' that that little was wrong. Maybe is a good thing, though, because maybe I never woulda come.

I never been back. I use to want to go back but I ain't never been able to collect the money for a ticket. I still ain't have the money, probably never will, but now I ain't have the desire neither. Fifteen years is a long time. Everything change: babies grow up, old people dead, friends become strangers. A dream does come to me sometimes: I back home and I standin' alone. I say, "Hello, everybody. I come back." Nobody answer. I say it again. And is only then I realize I standin' in a cemetery, all 'round me the graves of the people I use to know. I been away too long.

And in all this time, all these long fifteen years, I been driftin' from one cainin' minimum-wage job to another cainin' minimum-wage job, never movin' up, sometimes movin' down, usually just goin' along sweepin' floors or clearin' tables or washin' dishes. And this is how I end up livin' in a room above a milk store, workin' every day excep' Sunday here in the Riviera Nightclub and Tavern in a part o' downtown full o' people that Vince the disc jockey does call Yuffies and Vuffies, young urban failures and veteran urban failures. Vince think he funny but, if you ask me, Vince heself is a yuffie, he just ain't accept it yet. Because everybody here, includin' me, is a yuffie or a vuffie, more or less just survivin' in the middle o' the rich and shinin' city.

Inside, it warm and dark and I know, just by smellin' the air, that we ain't have too many customers: no cigarette smoke, and it not even a little bit stale. I walk from the lobby, past the sign that read *If total nudity offends you, please do not enter*, into the room full o' tables and chairs and loud music and flashin' lights. It have only five or six fellas sittin' around the stage watchin' Joan dance. Is her last song; I know this because she wearin' only shoes. She have her back to me, her long brown curly hair shinin' and her skin white-white in the light excep' for the butterfly tattoo she have on the right side just below the waist. I turn away fast-fast from the stage, walk behind the bar and through the door into the kitchen.

Frankie the manager, short and unfriendly and always tired-lookin', is standin' in front the packed sink tyin' on my dirty apron. In the fluorescent lightin' — only one bulb workin', Frankie say I doesn't need more light just to wash dishes — his skin take on a shade of very light olive green. He turn to me, more unfriendly than usual. "And where in hell have you been? Look at the time." He point to the clock on the wall above the sink. It sayin' five-fifteen.

"But Frankie, man," I say. "You know that thing always fast."

He untie the apron and throw it at me. "Don't forget we're closin' at six. You have forty-five minutes to wash up and mop out the place." He shake a finger at me. "And I don't wanna be late. My wife and kids are expectin' me for dinner." He walk off, out the kitchen, mutterin' to heself, but the music comin' in through the open door — mostly bass goin' boomboomboom — drown out the words.

I tie on the apron, turn on the hot water, pick up the soapy sponge and start washin' the only dishes it ever have around here: beer mug after beer mug after cainin' beer mug.

I suppose it have people who think I crazy, and I understand why. I know I does talk to meself sometimes, usually only in my head. But when I tired — five p.m. to one a.m. is my usual shift, washin' the mugs from the lunchtime rush before the evenin' rush arrive, washin' through the evenin' and helpin' Frankie at the bar, moppin' out the place after we close — or when it hot in the streetcar and the coat feelin' heavy on my back, my mouth does open up all by itself and out does tumble some o' the words runnin' through my head. I doesn't hear them till I see people givin' me funny looks and shiftin' away from me; then, as if somebody turn on a switch, I does hear meself sayin' things like: " — eggs, milk, bread — " Or: " — that cainin' son of a — " I does shock meself and half-wonder if I goin' crazy; and I does be glad for my granma who teach me how to cuss without cussin'.

Granma never put up with no bad word, four, five or six

letter. Instead, she did always use Cain name but, as she use to say, never in vain. When Granma say, "Get the cain out o' here!" everybody in hearin' distance did scatter. Or when she shout, "Where my cainin' belt?" it was time to stick a school book — the t'icker the better — down the back o' your pants.

Granma, short and thin and wrinkly, with sharp little eyes that always movin' in her head like they on springs, missin' nothing, seein' everything, had the cleanest dirty mouth I ever hear. Sometimes I does think that when I talkin' to meself is Granma I does really be talkin' to. She always there even if she long dead, like a monkey sittin' on my back, not a good monkey, not a bad monkey, but a strick monkey. She send me here in the first place and now is as if she here too, little eyes always on me, keepin' me honest.

It ain't been a busy day and workin' fast-fast — the soap and dip method — I finish the mugs in ten minutes. Frankie take them out in four big, drippin' plastic racks, to dry and put them away. Just as I start fillin' the bucket in the sink, Kim stick her head through the door. "Hey, Leonard. Coffee?" She short, blonde, with a tiny face, small body, and big moves. Fellas does pass up dollar bills to her when she dancin'.

"Sure, man, Kim. Double-double." I put my hand into my pants pocket for some change.

"It's on me," she say, givin' me a big grin. "Christmas present."

Kim is another one whose third dance I doesn't watch. She start workin' here just after me and she does come back regularly, just like Joan. I know Joan better — we does talk

154

more — but Kim, comin' from that time, link with her in my mind. For me, they different from the other girls.

When I go out, bucket in one hand, mop in the other, the last customer just puttin' on his coat to leave and the last dancer, a new girl, standin' at the side o' the stage puttin' back on her costume. Friendly Frankie behind the bar busy dryin' the mugs and puttin' them under the counter. The lights still flashin' — red, yellow, green, blue, white, flash-flash-flash of silver light, then around again on the empty stage. The last of the girls gather over in the left corner, some a'ready wearin' their coats, some still in their costume or half-out, just sittin' around talkin' and restin' their feet. Joan wave at me and I smile back. Vince, still in his control room behind the window of dark glass puttin' away his records, turn the music low-low. His little room is the only part o' the Riviera I not allowed to enter; Vince very particular 'bout his records and he does take the door key home with him every night.

I start turnin' the chairs over on the tables, takin' my time. The floor, red linoleum wear away to black circles in spots, not so dirty today and I count meself lucky. It snow only once so far this winter and that was on a busy night two weeks ago; afterwards the floor was like a sea, with sand, salt and water. It take me almost a whole hour to mop clean. So this evenin', as usual, I takin' my time. It ain't goin' to take me more than five or ten minutes in all. The Riviera not so big; is just the mirrors on the walls that does fool people. I workin' in a place that designed for that in every way.

Kim, tight in her black coat, come in holdin' a big bag from the all-night doughnut shop across the street. Her shoulders white and she shakin' water off her head. She say, "Looks like a white Christmas after all, you guys. It's really comin' down out there." Her high, piercin' voice cut right through the room and the girls in the corner cheer and clap. They start sharin' out the coffees.

I pull out a chair and sit down.

Frankie call, "Leonarrrd!" He sound just like Granma when she lookin' for the belt.

"Cool it, man, Frankie," I say without lookin' back at him. "I just goin' to have a quick coffee."

He say, "Six o'clock, Leonard. My wife and kids — "

" — expectin' you for dinner. I know, man, don't worry."

"I'm not waiting for you, Leonard. I'm lockin' up at six —"

"Jesus Ch— " Joan say from the corner. "I mean — " And she give me a big grin. "Oh cain, Frank! Give the guy a break. Let'im have his coffee in peace. Five minutes either way won't make no difference."

And Frankie don't say nothing back. I never hear him arguin' with Joan, or raisin' his voice at her. Sometimes, when a girl not movin' enough on stage, he does shout things like, "C'mon, move that fanny!" and worse. But never with Joan. The only thing I ain't understand is, if he 'fraid her, why he does continue hirin' her. Maybe is because he know she good, that it have guys who does come only when they know she here and not somewhere else on the circuit.

She come over to me, still wearin' her black baby-pyjama costume, two cups o' coffee in her hands, push aside my bucket with her foot, pull out a chair and sit down. She slide one o' the coffees across the table to me. "So how're you doin', Leonard?" She lift the strap o' her purse over her head — is a small black purse with a long string, the kind

156

all the girls does carry around their money in to prevent thiefin' — and put it on the table.

I take the plastic cover off the cup and I hear meself sayin': " — crick, crack, the monkey back — "

"What's that, Leonard?" She cross her left leg on her right, take off the shoe — black and shiny and with a heel that could punch holes in cement — and start rubbin' her red, hurtin' foot with both hands.

"Crick, crack, the monkey . . . bre'k."

"What in hell does that mean?" She pullin' and squeezin' her toes, long red fingernails bunchin' with the red toenails, rubbin' them slow-slow.

"My brain tryin' to remember something from when I was small." Is a rhyme Granma use to say, but it ain't comin'. Her voice soundin' far-far away in my head.

"You're workin' too hard, Leonard." She take a quick sip of her coffee and go back to her foot, squeezin' the heel, twistin' the ankle around. "You're — what? — thirty-six? Thirty-seven?"

"Seven."

She grin. "And your memory's goin' already." She switch legs, now rubbin' her right foot. She have corns on every toe, and every corn red and raw. "Or maybe it's just that all you guys from the islands are stupid."

I laugh. I know Joan just teasin' me. One time she do the nicest thing I ever see, and in this place you doesn't see too much nice things. One evenin', a first-timer was havin' trouble takin' things off. Two whole songs to get the top off, hardly movin' at all, only lookin' at sheself in the mirrors and ignorin' the fellas in the audience. By the time she had to take off the bottom, her eyes was full o' tears and her mouth was twitchin' like a little child. Suddenly, Joan jump up on the stage and start dancin' with her, as if they in a disco. The girl smile and manage to make it through to the end. And now that girl is a regular on the circuit, takin' it off with the best o' them.

The telephone ring over at the bar — a loud, long ring that does cut through even the poundin' music but that soundin' like a fire alarm with it turn down. Frankie answer it and call Joan: "Some guy named Sam."

She slip on her shoes, shake out her hair and walk over to the bar.

I turn around to watch her go and she give me a little wiggle and a laugh. Whenever I hear Vince announcin' her — "Okay, guys, put your hands together and welcome the sexy Candy!" — I does come out of the kitchen, stand behind the bar and watch her. Like most o' the girls, especially the hard-dancin' ones, Joan have a nice body and she know it. Everything in proportion, no fat, belly flat, legs long and muscular. But for me, is the face that's the standout. It round and, without the makeup that does add a good five or six years, soft. She have bright, brown eyes and thin lips that she does try to make thicker with lipstick.

Up there on that stage, swirlin' around and shakin' in her black pyjamas in front o' the wall that like a big lookin' glass, Joan is a woman of class, in control like none o' the other girls I ever see. Every fella in the room does feel she dancin' just for him, but if you watch her close and often, it not hard to see that she dancin' just for herself. Is why she so good; she does offer the best kind o' magic, the kind that does

158

make you forget is just a trick you watchin', the kind that does make you want the magician to fool you.

I does watch the fellas close too: businessmen in suits; Chinese grandfathers in sweaters; Yonge Street hustlers in leather jackets; Ryerson students trying to look like the Yonge Street hustlers. I does see all o' them starin' at her, some smilin' back when she lick her lips at them or when she lean over real close to shake her hair in their eyes; some stiff and stone-face — the dangerous ones, I think — as if their wife sittin' on their shoulder makin' sure they not enjoyin' too much seein' Joan becomin' Candy. When she take off her top, their eyes only on one place, as if they tryin' to make a picture of her chest in their head, followin' her fingers — the long, thin fingers; the red, red nails — as they rubbin' and squeezin' and feelin' and pretendin' to offer.

Is when she start takin' off the bottom, always with a slow, sexy song, that I does feel Granma heavy on my back and does slip into the kitchen, to the sink and the beer mugs. It have part of her I doesn't want to see, the part that is too much Candy and not enough Joan. So I never watch, because I does begin thinkin' that she's somebody daughter, somebody girlfriend, somebody sister, and none o' these guys here with their squintin' eyes and shinin' faces want to see their daughter or girlfriend or sister up there in the flashin' coloured lights feedin' other fellas' dreams. But all o' them sittin' there in front their beer, smoke driftin' 'round them, watchin' Joan become Candy, soakin' up the sexiness like dirt drinkin' fresh rain.

One time I break six mugs by accident just thinkin' about it. Friendly Frankie make me pay for every single one, and he promise to make me pay double in the future because he does have to go out and buy new ones.

Joan come back from the phone and throw herself in the chair. She less graceful off stage than on, more direct, more real. Some o' the other girls always the same, always like they on stage, walkin' around with half their assets hangin' out, goin' from guy to guy solicitin' table-dancin'. But not Joan. I see her slap a fella once when his hands get too free.

From the control room, Vince say, "Okay, girls, here's a little Christmas present for you." And he put on Bing Crosby singin' "White Christmas."

"White Christmas." Is a song that does take me back, to a little wood house light up by white candles and strings o' coloured lights, over in one corner a dry tree branch cover in strips o' cotton wool, the radio blarin' from the other corner and Granma singin' away. "That cainin' song jus' sound so cainin' clean!" she say one December before sittin' down to write ten different letters to the radio station requestin' they play the song over and over. Granma bein' Granma, of course she sign a different name to every letter.

The girls over in the corner start singin' along, but low and mournful, their hearts not really in it. Or maybe their hearts just too much in it, it hard to tell.

Joan lean over to me. "You guys have Christmas where you come from?"

"But all-you people could ask ignorant questions sometimes, yes!" I feel like teasin' her now: tit for tat, a eye for a eye, a toot' for a toot'. "I never meet people full o' stupid questions like Canadians. You know, people done ask me if we does wear grass skirts, if we have cars, what language we does speak." Now I grinnin' wide-wide. "Canadians always

160

complainin' Americans don't know nothing 'bout Canada but — I tell you — Canadians ain't know too much 'bout the rest o' the world either!"

Joan, rubbin' away again at her left foot, shake her head and roll her eyes northward to heaven — which in the Riviera is a ceilin' painted black. Then she give me a sour look and say in a half-vex voice, "So you guys have Christmas or not?"

"Of course we have Christmas! What you take we for?"

She lean over closer, brown eyes shinin' at me. "So you have Santa Claus, right?"

"Yeah."

"In a red suit and a white beard and Rudolph and all the rest, right?"

"Uh-huh."

"And it's a hot place, right? No fireplaces or chimneys?"

"But you bright, girl! Brighter than the sun that does shine on us!"

"So, Leonard," she say soft-soft as if she goin' to tell me a secret, "if you haven't got fireplaces and you haven't got chimneys, how in hell does Santa Claus get inside the houses?"

How Santa Claus does get inside the houses? What next from this woman? I take a sip o' my coffee, not sweet enough and just warm now. "But you so bright, Joan. You ain't able to figure it out yourself?"

"Well, Leonard, unless your Santa Claus is a B and E artist, I'll be damned if I know."

"Cracks," I say. "Cracks and keyholes."

"What?"

"He does make heself small-small and come through the cracks in the windows and the keyholes in the doors."

"Must've been a damn tight fit."

"No. He know how to do it, how to change heself so he could fit through any crack and any keyhole, go anywhere he want."

She look away, down at her foot. "I guess Santa Claus is a pretty smart guy. Here he can make his way down any chimney carrying a big bag of toys on his back, and he never gets dirty." She start rubbin' the bottom of her foot with her right thumb. "Must be nice." Then she go quiet, as if she thinkin'.

One day Joan ask me what race I was. Is the kind o' question people doesn't ordinarily ask; they too embarrass; they does prefer to ask you where you come from. But not Joan. When a question come in her head, it does pop out her mouth just like that. She examine me even as I explainin' that my mother was Indian and my father black. She feel my hair, twist a curl 'round her finger and say, "Think of all the dough you're saving on perms."

But that is what she like, this Joan: always askin' questions, always enjoyin' the answers in ways you never expect. This evenin' is the first time my answer seem to bother her. Is as if she seein' the cracks and keyholes, and she wonderin' if she could ever get through them herself.

"White Christmas" finish and Vince put on Elvis and "Blue Christmas", but after the first line o' the song, he suddenly take it off, say, "Just a joke, people," and put on "Jingle Bells".

The girls in the corner ignore him.

Suddenly Joan look up at me. "I'm thinking about not coming back, Leonard."

"To the Riviera?"

"To the business. I'm thinking of getting out."

"When?"

"This was my last shift, I think. I'll decide for sure over the holiday."

My finger run along the rim o' the coffee cup, hook over the edge and break off a piece. "How come?"

She look away, over my shoulder. "My son's almost three. Lives with my parents in Windsor. He doesn't hardly know me at all. I think it's time he got his mother back."

"So what you plannin' to do?" The piece o' styrofoam crumblin' between my fingers now.

"I'll probably stay in Windsor, find a job, bring up my kid."

"You think it goin' to be easy?" The bits o' styrofoam fall on the table like snow from my fingertips.

"It's gotta be better than this!" She wave her right hand around the Riviera, at the tables, the chairs, the mirrors on the walls. "I got into this game to make some big money quick. Thought I'd open a little boutique or something one day. But in two and a half years, I've managed to keep all of five hundred dollars. Most of the rest went to my parents to pay for the kid. And for hash and grass and liquor and presents for my friends. I'll tell you something, Leonard." She turn back to face me. "In this business, the more you have, the less you have. Two and a half years ago, there was almost a thousand dollars in my bank account." She laugh, but short-short. "And I'm planning to give my parents a colour TV for Christmas!"

I ain't say nothing. I not sure if I happy or sad, and I not sure what she expectin' from me, if anything.

She change feet again but now she not really rubbin', just

kind o' strokin' the skin with her fingertips. "Something happened when I was coming back from my stint in Quebec City two weeks ago. You ever been up there? Quebec?"

I shake my head — in all these years, I never been out o' Toronto — but she ain't lookin' at me; she not really lookin' for an answer.

"It's different up there. You gotta waitress. It's harder work, especially on the feet. But the guys are different, friendlier, more relaxed, even if you don't speak the language. It's just the way they look at you, you know? They don't take it serious like a lot o' the guys here. S'more like a party, somehow. That's why I like working in Quebec, even if there's less bread in it. Helps keep my perspective straight."

"On what?" The part o' the cup from where I break off the piece feel rough but soft under my finger, like the blade of a dull bread knife.

"On guys."

From the bar, voice cuttin' above the music, Frankie call out, "Fifteen minutes, Leonard!"

Joan, without lookin' up at him, say sharp-sharp: "I'm talking to Leonard, Frank!" And, amazin' to me, he ain't say another word.

Vince change the music again. Now, he deckin' the halls.

It seem to me, but I ain't know how or why, that it have something cruel in what Vince doin'. A couple o' the girls button up their coats and, without a word, without lookin' at nobody, leave together. A puff o' cold wind from the open door touch my skin.

"Anyways, I was on the train coming back. The day was grey and cloudy, heavy snow coming down, and I wasn't feeling too great. I spent my time looking out the window. Dreary, man, really ugly. Pissy little towns. Cemeteries. The world looking like the screen of a broken TV. After a while I couldn't stand it no more. And then I noticed this guy staring at me from across the aisle. But he wasn't just curious, y'know? Not like a guy showing interest. He had a kind of smirk on his face, a dirty, nasty little smirk, like a cat eyeing a mouse on the Saturday morning cartoons."

"You does watch cartoons on TV?" Is a strange picture my mind gettin': Joan, wearin' the black pyjama costume and high heel shoes, sittin' in front the TV watchin' Tom and Jerry.

"Sure, why not? My folks tell me that's what the kid always does. Maybe it's dumb, but it makes me feel closer to him." She say it in a way, with a strick voice, that show she don't want no argument.

And I doesn't give her none.

"So this guy keeps on staring at me, right?" she continue. "I stare hard right back at him — nothing like a good, hard glare to discourage a guy — but it didn't work. Then I realized that he recognized me, probably saw me at the club back in Quebec City, and he was one of those who have no respect, y'know? One of those guys who think that, because they saw you naked once, they own you and can do anything they want to you with their eyes.

"He had an ordinary face, forgettable. There was no way I could remember him, no matter how hard I tried. You know, you don't really see the guys when you're dancing up there. You look at them, you make eye contact, and they think you're seeing them but you're not. Know what I mean?"

"I think so. Is like washin' beer mugs. You does look at them but you doesn't really see them, just enough to do your job."

"Yeah. Maybe." She pick up her coffee cup, look down into it, wrinkle up her nose and put the cup back down on the table. "Well, it went on and on, till I just couldn't take the shit from his eyes no more. I grabbed my bag from the rack overhead and walked through the whole damned train until I found another free seat. I was half-bombed on beer when I changed trains in Montreal, and all bombed by the time I hit Toronto. I barely made it home.

"I haven't been able to forget that train ride, Leonard. I can't get the guy's smirk out of my head. It's like it's tattooed on my brain. And it's since that trip that I've been thinking of getting out, going back to Windsor. I don't want anybody to recognize me any more." She open her little purse, take out a cigarette and light it; her hand holdin' the gold lighter was shakin'.

I say, "You think you can go back?"

"Why not?" She throw her head back as if she feel I challengin' her and blow cigarette smoke up at the ceilin'.

"It not easy to pretend two years o' your life never happen."

"You don't think I can?"

"I ain't sayin' you can and I ain't sayin' you can't. I just wonderin', is all."

She flick ashes into the coffee cup. "Don't you ever want to go back to your island, Leonard? You haven't exactly made it big here."

"No reason to," I say. "My granma was my only real family, and she long dead. I's a stranger there now."

166

"But I still have my family in Windsor."

"Joan have her family in Windsor. What about Candy?"

"I'm leaving Candy behind. She won't exist after tonight."

"You think so? But she is you. Candy is Joan and Joan is Candy."

"It's not true." Her eyes shinin' with tears. She turn her face away. "I am going back."

I want to say: No, Candy goin' with Joan to Windsor and maybe they goin' to come back together too. Or maybe — and this is what I 'fraid most — maybe Candy goin' to come back alone. But why push it?

The sweet voice o' Nat King Cole roastin' chestnuts fill the room. A couple more girls get up and leave.

Suddenly Joan throw the cigarette into the coffee cup, open the little purse and take out a penknife. She open it, a bright tiny blade; say, "I *am* going back;" turn her left hands upside down on the table and quick-quick, before I even understand what she doin', slice off the long fingernails one after the other. Then, concentratin' hard, she do the same thing with the right hand.

I look at the pieces o' fingernail lyin' on the table. They remind me o' chip-chip shells cover in blood.

She say, "They're only plastic."

"Well," I say. "Maybe is possible for you to go back." And then, without thinkin': "You want to have dinner later?"

She give me a little smile. "Thanks, Leonard, but I have to go." She look at her watch. "In fact, I better get ready." She close the penknife and put it back in the purse.

Just as she about to stand up, I say, "Tell me something, Joan. I just curious, but how come you does boss Frankie around like that? Nobody else does talk to him like you."

She wrap the long string of the purse 'round her left hand. "I've known Frank for a long time. I started dancing here."

"Yeah, but sometimes I does think he not only don't like you too much but he 'fraid you, too."

She stand up, straightenin' the pyjama top. "I suppose." She look away to the bar, where Frankie finishin' the mugs. "You see, he's my brother."

My body suddenly go cold. I ain't have nothing more to say and, after a moment, she walk off barefeet to the change room, shoes swingin' from her right hand. I keep thinkin': I wish I didn't ask, I wish I didn't ask. . . .

Finally, I find it in meself to stand up, turn the rest o' the chairs over on the tables and start moppin'.

Vince turn off the music, lock the door of his control room, wish Frankie a merry Christmas and leave. The rest o' the girls follow a few minutes after him, all ignorin' me except for Kim, who wave and wish me a good holiday.

The moppin' go fast. I suppose I miss some spots but not too much boots and shoes pass through the Riviera today. After the room, I start doin' behind the bar, Frankie standin' on the other side frettin' and hurryin' me up.

The front door open and a man come in, snow on his head and coat.

Frankie say, "Sorry, man, we're closed."

The fella brush the snow from his head. "I'm meeting Candy," he say.

I look up from the floor. I recognize the fella, a regular customer, one o' the stone-face ones I doesn't trust, the kind that does carry their fantasies in their pockets.

Frankie just stare at him for a couple o' seconds, turn away, walk 'round the bar on the wet floor and disappear into the kitchen.

168

"She's still here, ain't she?" the fella say to me.

In his big sheepskin coat, it take me a minute to remember that he does usually be wearin' a three-piece suit. "She comin'. She just changin'."

Joan come out, all dress up in her grey coat. Usually she does clean off the make-up and tie her hair in a ponytail before leavin' but not this evenin'. She come straight over to me and just stand watchin' me.

I lean on the mop. "Joan."

"Leonard."

"Friend o' yours?"

"You could say so."

And then a question come into my head and it pop out my mouth just like that: "How much?"

"Three hundred." She ain't bat an eyelid.

I just look at her: once more, nothing to say. But in my head I hear Granma sayin': You happy now? You happy now, you cainin' fool?

She say, "I have to pay for that colour TV, Leonard."

I get the feelin' she dyin' for me to say, yes, Joan, is awright, Joan, I understand, Joan. But, instead, I say, "See you, Candy."

Her face go blank. Then she turn away from me, walk up to the fella and take his arm. "How're you doing, Sam?"

I go back to my work, my eyes wet and burnin'.

I hear the fella say, "Who's Joan?"

And I hear Joan say, "Nobody."

They open the front door and slip out together, while Granma whisper in my ear 'bout cracks and keyholes.

Frankie lock the door behind us and, without a word, head off for the parkin' lot behind the building. It dark out and the snow still comin' down in big, slow, heavy flakes. Everything cover in white and it impossible to see where the sidewalk end and the street begin. I pull my wool cap low down over my ears and start walkin' towards Yonge Street. The snow on the ground cover my boots and the bottom of my pants start getting wet. I step into the dark bus shelter, knock my boots against the frame to get the snow off and bend over to stick the pants legs into the top o' the boots.

"You gotta put them in *before* you go out, don't you know."

"Barnabas?" He catch me by surprise. He still sittin' there on the narrow bench, his leg next to him. "But what you still doin' here, man?"

"What's it look like I'm doin'? Getting a bloody suntan?"

I straighten up, the cold water a'ready soakin' through the socks and bitin' my skin. "You better get movin' soon, Barnabas. If you fall asleep here, you ain't goin' to get up in the mornin'."

"But it's not cold, Lenny. It's never cold when it's snowing, don't you know."

"Yeah, man, but afterwards — "

"By afterwards I'll be tucked away warm as toast in some little cot at the Mission. Yep, warm as toast." He cough, a deep rattlin' that sound like it comin' all the way up from his toes. "But in the meantime, a little smoke'll help keep the cold at bay, I'm sure."

I take the cigarette pack out o' my coat pocket and toss it to him. He catch it with both hands. "See you in a few days, Barnabas." I stick my hands in my pockets and turn to leave.

"One more thing, Lenny," he say just as I put my foot out into the snow. "Noah wheeled off a few minutes ago. Keep an eye out for him, will ya? Make sure he doesn't get stuck. His legs ain't as good as they used to be."

170

"No problem, man. You just take care o' yourself."

I step out into the snow and look ahead. Everything deserted, no cars, no people, only the white, white snow on the ground and fallin' from the sky, hidin' even the ugly decorations hangin' across Yonge Street. I walk fast, lookin' ahead for Noah, thinkin' about buyin' meself a nice dinner in some restaurant. It early still and I ain't feel like goin' home yet to the little room.

And then I spot Noah, a big black bundle in the white distance movin' slow-slow, elbows pumpin' out to the sides. I shout out his name but he ain't hear me. I still too far and maybe the snow too t'ick.

I start walkin' faster. When I get a little closer I see that he no longer pushin', takin' a rest, I think. But then . . . eh, eh, what this is I seein'? *The man standin' up.* He standin' up, he turnin' around, he foldin' up the wheelchair, he pickin' it up with one hand and he walkin' away easy-easy.

I start runnin' towards him, his big body walkin' slow-slow away from me, wheelchair under the right arm, blanket over the left shoulder. I have to see his face. I slippin' and slidin' on the snow but I keep on runnin'.

His back comin' closer and closer. His brown coat look like it made o' skin, from some dead animal, but is old skin, dirty skin, skin that a'ready take a lickin' on several backs.

I pass him, turn 'round, stop. And I look him straight in the face: this old man with red eyes, veiny nose, no lips, and cheeks that ain't seen a razor in two or three days. Now he seem less grey than this mornin', less old. He just look tired and, seein' me, frighten.

We stare at each other for a long, long time.

Then, feelin' Granma on my back, the strick monkey who always get through cracks and keyholes, I take a ten-dollar bill from my wallet and hold it out to him. He reach out and take it, but as if he just holdin' it for me, as if he expect me to take it back. When I put my hand back in my pocket, he look down at the money he holdin'. Then, slow-slow, he look up at me, but as if I crazy, his face screw up, only one eye open, as if he peepin' at me through a keyhole.

I give him a grin. "Merry cainin' Christmas, man." I turn around, walk away headin' for Yonge Street not too far now — I beginnin' to make out the ugly decorations — and suddenly I hear Granma talkin' in my head:

Crick, crack,
the monkey break he back.
Five, six,
pick up sticks.
Seven, eight,
lay them straight.
Nine, ten,
the monkey play again.

I find meself laughin' out loud, like a madman, but I ain't care. The snow comin' down heavier than ever, big balls o' wet cotton wool, fallin' on the buildings, fallin' on the street, fallin' on me. Barnabas right: it never cold when it snowin'. I pull off my wool cap and look up into a streetlight. The snow divin' down like a million shootin' stars comin' directly at me. And I think: is the most beautiful thing I ever see.

A Life of Goodbyes

"DANNY THE DEAL-MAKER. *Walk in, Drive out!* Can I help you?"

"Hello. Dan?"

"Yep, who's this?"

"Alicia."

"Alicia. . . ."

"Your wife. Remember?"

"Alicia! Hi —"

"Hi. . . ."

"So. I guess you got my letter."

"Took a couple of months, but it caught up with me. Thanks."

"Hey, what are estranged husbands for."

"How is she?"

"Getting weaker. Nothing dramatic but, you know, I just thought you should know."

"Has she asked for me?"

"Your mother doesn't ask for anything, Alicia."

"Or anyone?"

"You got a place to stay?"

"My mom's —"

"Alicia, she's been at Shady Pines for the last two years. She couldn't take care of herself any more —"

"Why didn't you let me know?"

"How long you planning on staying?"

"There's a train back to Toronto tomorrow morning —"

"You can stay at the house, if you like."

"Thanks, Dan, but —"

"I really don't mind."

"Well, you see, I've got someone with me."

"A guy?"

"We're sort of travelling together."

"Sort of?"

"Okay, so we're travelling together."

"I see. Well, you're still welcome, both of you. There are things we should talk about, anyway."

"Like what?"

"Just things."

"Things, eh? Things to clear up?"

"Eight years is a long time, Alicia."

"Ages, Dan. Ages and ages."

She had forgotten how small the town really was. From the car, it was easy to see that it had changed little and grown not at all in the eight years she had been away. This was no surprise; it had changed little and grown not at all in the thirty-seven years she had spent here, from birth to departure. Tree-lined streets, sculpted lawns, neat houses. The movie-house, the tavern, the shopping centre. The glutinous companionship of community in a small town that was all suburb.

Dan said, "Business is good. I bought out the dealership in Belleville a couple of years ago — "

"A real little empire, eh?" She spotted a Chinese restaurant that hadn't been there before.

" — and we're looking into a doughnut franchise —"

She had come here, had *returned* — although she resisted the word, for it seemed to imply that she somehow belonged here, that the place retained a claim on her even after all this time — to see her mother. They had never been particularly close, no more and rather less than other mothers and daughters she had known. But when Dan's letter, crushed and soiled, caught up with her on the fishing boat off Suva, offering in his crabbed handwriting brief details of her mother's illness, she knew it was time to retrace steps to the ruins of an abandoned life she had thought long effaced: to acknowledge, to bid farewell. There had been no urgency to the summons. Her mother's illness was neither dramatic nor immediately perilous. But it marked, she feared, the beginning of a final decline.

" — got a few investments here and there, nothing grand, but you never know when downturns will hit —"

So she had taken her time, the young man in tow, landing on the west coast and slowly making her way east through a late-summer heat, living off acquaintanceship the way others still lived off the land: lunching here, dining there, sleeping some other place, reaping and occasionally exhausting goodwill.

" — usually head down to the condo in Florida for a couple of weeks every February —"

By the time she and the young man drew closer to her

little town — she could not refer to it as "home", called it instead "the place I was born" — the heat of the day had given way to the early blasts of winter. She had forgotten the peculiar pain of iced breath, and it gave rise to a terror she knew to be irrational: she could picture the blood freezing in her veins. Yet, by the standards of the place, it wasn't cold. People still wore light summer clothing; the trees, still fully garbed, only hinted here and there at the change of colour that would inevitably come. She thought: I am more of a stranger here than elsewhere.

" — a few games of tennis, a couple rounds of golf, baking on the beach — "

The young man's muscles had begun aching. His movements slowed down: he might have been walking through water. "Only one night," she had promised as they prepared to board the train in Toronto. "It's all I need." And the young man, sulking, had agreed; he had had no choice.

Dan, she noticed, kept looking into the rearview mirror, not split-second glances of reassurance at the road behind but lengthier examinations of the face in the back seat, broad and fleshy and brown, stiff with an enigmatic unhappiness.

"You haven't changed much."

"Haven't I?"

"Travelling must be good for you."

"It has its ups and downs."

"And me?"

"You look — " She considered his profile. He had put on some weight, greyed somewhat. He dressed more stylishly, the plaid sports jacket and open-necked shirts replaced by a three-piece suit and maroon tie. A large gold watch hung from his left wrist, a large gold i.d. bracelet from his right. "You look content."

"Not too bad for a man of fifty, eh?"

They turned a corner and there it was, the house she had never managed to grow fond of, white, wooden, two-storeyed. Alicia felt unease cramp her stomach.

Dan pulled into the driveway, turned off the car. They sat quiet for several seconds, the rumble of the engine replaced by a deep silence. Dan's hands gripped the steering wheel. "Alicia," he said. "Before we go in, there's something you should know."

She looked straight ahead, at the garage door, waiting for him to go on.

"I have some more news." He cleared his throat. "You see, there's someone in my life."

She wasn't surprised.

He took a deep breath, wet his lips with his tongue. "His name's Mac."

"A son?"

"No. Not a son."

Alicia looked sharply over at him. In the confusion of her emotions, she chuckled.

Alicia settled the young man on the sofa for a nap and sat quietly in an armchair across from him. Her stomach was in knots, but what from — the impact of Dan's news, the prospect of seeing her mother — she wasn't sure. She felt, strongly, that it had been a mistake to come here, not just to the house but to the town itself. It always seemed to do this to her: to cut her breath in half, hem her in, tie her in knots that she couldn't unravel.

Dan, moving briskly, had let them into the house, given her keys, towels. He nodded sharply when she apologized for chuckling. She wasn't laughing at him, she said. But he'd cut off her explanation by saying he understood, it was how she'd always reacted to the unexpected. She said he had nothing to feel guilty or ashamed about, and he replied he didn't feel guilty or ashamed; it was just that small towns demanded prudence in certain matters. Then he'd hurried out, back to the dealership. Not once had he looked at her. She hadn't even had a chance to introduce the young man properly.

The living room was not as she would have expected. The low, indirect lighting; the walls of a deep absorbent blue; the furniture of grey felt; the gleam of chrome in straight, clean lines: it was all too modern, too sleek. It was not Dan, at least not the Dan she had left behind. Other tastes, it was clear, had dictated here.

When the young man's breathing had settled into a regular rhythm, she eased herself from the chair and padded to the front door.

Outside, she walked along familiar streets, past familiar shops. She recognized houses, trees, cracks in the sidewalk. There were few people about, but she kept her gaze averted. She didn't want to see anyone, or to be seen.

And then she was there. Shady Pines. With its semicircular driveway, picture windows, and name in stainless steel, one of the grander buildings in town. She asked directions from the receptionist, turning away just in time from a nurse, plump in near middle age, who had been a friend in grade seven or eight. Several flower arrangements, plastic-wrapped and tagged, were lined up on the desk.

The room was two floors up and at the end of a long hall. A blend of hospital sterility and homey gentility.

"Mother?" Alicia stood beside the shrunken woman in whose features she recognized her own. Here, the physical change, age marking itself with a slackening of form, flesh melting against the bone like wax down the sides of a candle. Her hair had thinned, whitened. Alicia leaned over, pressed her lips briefly to the dry cheeks. Saw recognition form in the melting eyes. Saw too the quick hardening into resentment.

Through the window, the town glimmered in the pale afternoon sunlight: the giant chicken bucket, the golden arches, Danny the Dealmaker.

Alicia forced a smile. "Mother."

Her mother, blinking, watched as Alicia pulled a chair up to the bed. Watched as she sat and laid her sunburned arm on the white bedsheets.

"How are you, mother?"

Her mother, alert, tight-lipped, focused on the small television suspended from a metal arm just above her head. But she held the earpiece in her fingers.

"Mother?"

Her right hand wound the grey cord around her left hand.

"I've come a long way to see you, mother."

She inserted the earpiece into her ear.

"Look, mother, I know I haven't been the perfect daughter. I haven't been a daughter in any sense of the word —"

She pulled the television closer.

" — that you understand."

Turned up the volume.

"I went away to Italy, and I never came back. I don't

179

expect you to understand, and I don't expect you to forgive me. But, you know, mother, I've seen some wonderful places, and I've met some wonderful people — "

And even though she knew it to be pointless, Alicia told her mother about her travels. Most of what she told was true, and most of what was true she told. Her invention was judicious, revelation weighed against discretion. If she added a little here, trimmed a little there, if she heightened, softened, shaded, it was to try to penetrate to a part of her mother never before touched. It was to try, through a tale well told, to offer a part of herself so essential that, eight years before, she had had to run without explanation and without excuse in order to preserve it.

Her mother had no questions, no reactions. She stared unmoving at the television screen. Yet, Alicia felt, she was listening. Or at least hearing. She continued to talk.

She spoke for over an hour, her throat growing sore. Her mother remained impassive. Alicia realized that her words were performing no magic. She could no longer fill the silence. Let it come.

Let it stretch out, grow thin. She could hear the sounds from her mother's earpiece, like the crackling of a distant fire.

Mother and daughter. Yet, with time and space, there had been a kind of dissipation. They were even beyond accusation.

Outside, the light was fading.

Alicia stood to take her leave. "I've got to go now, mother." She leaned forward to offer a kiss, but then pulled back: a kiss would have been too untrue. She gave instead a light pat to the veined and spotted hand, turned and walked quietly to the door.

"Alicia — " The voice was strong.

"Mother?"

"How *old* are you?"

"Forty-five."

Her mother seemed saddened by the answer. She adjusted the earpiece and looked away. Her hand wiped stiffly at her eyes.

Alicia said, "I'll be back, mother." But as she walked from the room she knew it was a lie. As, she suspected, did her mother. There were some goodbyes that simply couldn't be said.

The excuse, initially, had been Italy and art.

It had come as no surprise to Dan, her sudden decision to go, alone, to Italy for a month. He knew of the fantasy that had begun at the age of sixteen when, impressionable yet, life experienced only in the rigid confines of home and school in the small town, she had been seduced by a young Italian, the eldest son of one of the first foreign families to settle in the area.

He was confident with the ease of wealth. His father, neatly greyed and gentle with reserve, had flourished with a single machine in a single room making a single computer part. The son drove a red sportscar that purred with power; wore his sweaters, soft and furry affairs of brilliant colours, thrown casually over his shoulders, the sleeves loosely knotted on his chest.

He had spoken to her, in his soft voice, of Italy: of the sky and the light, of the feel of the air on the skin, of water and mountain. He had conjured up paintings and statues in sumptuous detail, his mouth, finely shaped, seeming to water as he sought to transmit just the right shade of red, just the right fold of garment. The word gold was deliciously molten when it came from him.

And so, with his words, he had eased her into actions that the other boys, with rougher hands and cruder, more familiar words, had failed to inspire.

But the thrill of conquest quickly drained the energy that had electrified him. He became ordinary. And it wasn't long before she realized that he had experienced none of it: he had been too young. Every word, every pretty picture, had come to him through his mother and father, through books and family albums fat with yellowing photographs, through the nostalgia of weekend visitors, aunts and uncles who, less moneyed, had settled into the Italian section of Toronto, living in sombre apartments above the little vegetable shops and import outlets they had established.

Yet, even as her passion for him evaporated, the web of his words retained a hold on her. His images, so intricately wrought, remained alive in her mind, brilliant, vibrant. And they came in time to form a new fantasy: a dream of that air, that light, that sky, the water, the mountains, and, above all, the promise of colours only imagined.

Italy, then, had provided the excuse when she needed one. It was an escape to promise, to sights and sensations only hinted at.

It failed, as — she understood only later — it had to. The red turned out to be not so lustrous, the fold of the cloth not so delicate, the air not so silken. Rome was garbage-strewn,

Venice sat in a heavy cloud of poisoned vapour. And as for the art, there seemed an excess of it, statue and painting and ruin dispersed in profusion throughout the dingy halls of a decaying museum. She stopped seeing, and left the country after three weeks.

But not for her little town. With the fading of her fantasy, she realized, other links had gone too. She boarded a freighter and when asked where she was headed replied, "Away." She had learned to keep words to a minimum. She had come to distrust the power of their artifice.

"Just what exactly were you doing over there, Alicia?"

Sometimes, even when Dan asked a simple question, he made it sound like an accusation. It was a quality Alicia had enjoyed when they first met. There had been, at the time, no edge to it, no challenge beyond the teasingly sexual. But now — maybe it had always been there — she detected a touch of the acerbic.

"Working on a boat," she replied with studied dispassion. "Collecting tropical fish."

Mac said, "Is that where you picked *him* up?" He was young, short, with bleached, unhealthy skin and roughly cut, dirty-blond hair. Alicia didn't know what she had expected — she hadn't really been able to think about it — but Mac, in any case, was a disappointment.

"It was his boat."

Dan said, "And his island, too, I suppose."

"Why not? He's a king."

"Aren't they all?"

Mac looked over to the young man. "Are you really a king, Fred?"

The young man nodded, his big dark head moving slowly in the dim light, as if rousing himself from slumber. On the boat he was quick, agile, his strengths well matched to the tasks at hand. But seated in the small living room, he merely gave an impression of great bulk, of muscle and fat ladled with generosity onto an ample human frame.

Dan chuckled. "King Fred," he said, almost to himself.

They were having drinks, martinis for Alicia and Dan, scotch for Mac, orange juice for the young man. The window, a large rectangle of double-paned glass, looked out onto shrubbery and patches of dark pavement lit by the glow of an unseen streetlamp. An autumn wind howled through the deserted streets. As she watched the helpless, frenzied shivering of the shrubbery, Alicia thought of hurricanes.

"Fred isn't really his name, you know," she said. "I just call him that."

"So what's his name?" Dan leaned forward in the armchair, hands placed delicately, expectantly, on his thighs. He had changed to slacks and a t-shirt, and Alicia could see just how much weight he had put on by the roll of fat that bulged above the waistband. He had been proud, way back when, of his trim figure.

"You'll never be able to pronounce it."

"Try me."

"Even I can't pronounce it."

Dan turned to the young man. "So what's your name there, ahh, Fred?"

With his loose pose — forearms perched on thighs, fingers curled around the glass held between his widely spaced legs — the young man diminished the low sofa. "Call me Fred," he said in a deep, quiet voice.

184

Mac chuckled.

"I told you," Alicia said. But she knew Dan better than that.

"No, no, no," Dan said, stiffening his back into the chair. "You must tell me your real name. Fred is —" He shook his head. "Fred is a *silly* name."

"*Also sprach* Danny the Dealmaker," Alicia said, sipping her drink.

Mac slapped his thigh. "Uhh! At last! Someone else! I don't know why you don't just change that silly title of yours, Dan." He looked over at Alicia, winked and nodded.

Dan took a deep breath, looked through the window in mild annoyance.

Alicia followed his gaze. A dead leaf, one of the first of the season, slapped against the glass, danced for a moment like a trapped butterfly, then skipped back off into the night. Refuge sought; refuge denied.

Mac said, "You heard Alicia, Dan — "

"Lay off, Mac. If I've told you once, I've told you a thousand times —" He faced Alicia. "That silly title is worth a million bucks."

Alicia wondered whether she was supposed to be impressed.

"Your name," Dan continued, turning back to the young man, "your *real* name, is a valuable possession. It is yours, it says who you are. You must let no one take it away from you —" His eyes flickered towards Alicia. "— no matter who —" Then back to the young man. "Now, tell me."

"Go on, tell him," Alicia said. "Both barrels."

The young man nodded at her. Then, evidently amused, emitted a sound that gave shape to a string of full, rounded gutturals.

Dan listened intently. It sounded to him like the mixture of a growl, water chugging down a drainpipe, and an extended belch. "Could you," he said evenly, "repeat that please?"

Alicia couldn't restrain a smile as the young man repeated the name.

Dan once more leaned forward in his chair, lips moving silently, with hesitation, trying to reproduce the sounds he'd heard.

Mac said, "Don't strangle yourself, Danny."

But Alicia would have expected no less of him. Names, especially difficult, foreign ones, had long challenged him, but not for the reasons of self and identity he had offered. That, she was well aware, he had fudged together in the same way that he had once put together an outfit of tennis whites for summer without either acquiring a racket or intending to step onto a court. It had come, rather, from the car dealership. An aggressive and wily salesman, he prided himself on charming his way into a sale by his attention to detail, significant, insignificant, and invented. He would, on the spot, fabricate nieces and nephews to sell clients with children on the family uses of a particular model. Would conjure up aged grandparents to convince hesitant clients of the roominess and comfort of another. With newcomers of unusual name, he would pay close attention to the correct pronunciation. It provided humour, he felt, and relaxed the client, even nudged the ego a bit that he was careful and interested where others were often careless and uncaring. And it worked. His client list could easily have been mistaken for roll-call at the United Nations. The salesman's ploy had, over the years, become habit, and a point of pride. It was not, Alicia thought, an entirely unattactive quality.

The young man grinned. "My name too hard for you people to say." He spoke slowly, almost with difficulty, as if his tongue were heavy and thickened, lacking in flexibility; but he spoke, too, with a pride that Alicia knew would be a challenge to Dan.

"Maybe you could write it out?" Mac, coming to Dan's rescue, said anxiously.

"Give it up," Alicia said. "You see —"

The young man frowned at her.

"— he can't read or write."

"We not need it in my country," the young man said too quickly.

Alicia grinned.

Mac snorted skeptically. "Oh yeah?"

Dan nodded thoughtfully, his eyes moving in puzzlement from the young man to Alicia. "I see," he said, finally. He turned back to the young man. "You hungry Fred?"

The young man looked at him, nodded.

There was something in the slight, almost imperceptible dip of his head that Alicia didn't like. It was, it seemed to her, a curiously helpless gesture.

"Things organic, hold the plastic. Stir my glands, unwashed hands." Dan stood at the kitchen sink peeling carrots. "Do you still buy vegetables caked in dirt, Alicia?" He didn't wait for an answer. "Alicia used to have this thing about plastic, did you know that, Mac?"

"Sounds kin-ky," Mac responded as he carved carefully at a chicken. "Doesn't it, Fred?"

Dan reached for a fresh carrot. "Do you know what plastic is, Fred?"

Alicia clicked her tongue sharply in disgust. "Don't be stupid —"

The young man, seated across the kitchen table from her, was frowning.

"— it's a poor country, not a primitive one."

"But Alicia —" Mac, the knife dangling in his hand, turned to face her. "— he doesn't even know how to read, it's a fair question."

"They've got a seventy-five percent literacy rate, after all," Dan added.

"How'd you know that?"

"I did some checking. I keep this reference book at the office —"

"Well, bully for you."

"It comes in handy. This guy from Bhutan came in the other day. I popped into the office for a second, checked it out. You should've seen his face light up when I asked him if he was from Thimbu. That's the capital, you know. One of the quickest sales I've ever made. Doesn't take much sometimes."

Always the salesman, Alicia thought. She wondered what Dan would do to try to impress the young man if he walked into the showroom one day. Or her.

"And did you know," Dan continued, "that they're cannibals?"

"*Were.*"

A chuckle suddenly rumbled from the young man.

"What's the joke?" Mac asked, neatly severing a leg from the chicken.

"My grandfather." The young man chuckled again, the

188

sound — a leisured thunder rolling from his chest — calling
to Dan's mind a picture of lava boiling and bubbling its way
along a seam deep beneath the surface of the Earth. "My
grandfather, once, when he is a boy, he try to eat a missionary's sandal."

Dan laughed. "Didn't the missionary object?"

"Not possible. They already eat him."

"Oh God." Mac slapped the knife down onto the counter.
"Is that a true story?"

Alicia nodded. "They have the sandals in the museum.
You can still see the teeth-marks."

"Oh God."

"Oh, quit complaining, Mac," Dan said. "After all, you
like chewing on certain parts of the human anatomy."

"Now, now, be nice, Danny —"

Alicia's jaw tightened.

Laughing, Dan turned away from the plate of fresh vegetables he was preparing. "Fred, how'd you like to slice the
bread?"

"Subtle-subtle." Mac picked up the knife, probed at the
chicken. "As someone once said, there are some questions
best left unasked and some stories best left untold."

"Who said that?" Dan took a long French stick and a
breadknife from the cupboard, placed them on the table
before the young man. "Inch-wide pieces would be fine,
Fred."

"Probably my mother," Mac laughed.

The young man looked hesitantly at the bread and the
knife, as if they were objects unfamiliar to him.

"Mine too," Alicia said.

"I just don't want you to feel left out," Dan explained to the young man. "This way, Alicia'll be the only one doing nothing. But then, she's used to that."

"Fuck off," Alicia said easily, with only a hint of irritation.

The young man reached for the knife.

"Don't pay any attention to her, Fred," Dan said. "You just go ahead." He held his thumb and forefinger an inch apart. "About so big."

The young man glanced uneasily at Alicia. She raised her eyebrows once, then turned away.

"In my country —" the young man said. Then he stopped. His eyes, small only against the field of his wide, fleshy face, hardened onto Dan.

"Yes? In your country?"

"In my country, it not polite to ask the guest to work." He spoke slowly, pronouncing each syllable fully and with care.

Dan, perplexed, stared wordlessly back at him.

Mac, knife poised above the carved carcass of the chicken, gazed back over his shoulder.

After a moment, Alicia reached across the table and roughly took the knife from the young man's hand. She began hacking away at the bread. Shards of crust flew into the air.

The debris of the meal littered the plates and tablecloth. The young man peeled a last strand of meat from a bone with his teeth. "In my country," he said, "we not have traffic jams."

"There aren't enough cars to have a decent one," Alicia shot back.

"Our life natural, our rules simple. I know what I must do, my father and my mother know what they must do, my

190

sister know what she must do. In the mor-ning I go on my boat and I collect fish. In the after-noon when the sun hot, I rest." He bit off the soft head of the bone, chewed at it with relish. The interior of the bone, grasped delicately between the tips of his fingers, showed red. "In my country, woman respect man. If I sitting in a chair and my sister sweeping the floor, she know not to ask me to move my foot, she must wait. I am a man, and a king. I have my own island. She only a woman. She only have a broom." He licked his fingers free of chicken grease, sat back in the chair, and sighed in satisfaction. "Life in my country more simple than life here. We wake with the sun, we sleep with the sun. Life happier."

"But there's no electricity," Alicia said. "Just these itsy-bitsy candles that couldn't light the path of an ant."

The young man grunted. "Better that way."

"The stars must be wonderful at night," Mac said.

"Sure, for the first two or three nights, but then —" Alicia opened her palms before her, as if in supplication. "— there's nothing else to do. You can't even read unless you're a cat. As a result —" Her palms faced each other, then came slowly together. "— their minds go like this."

Mac, picking absently at a piece of bread, nodded.

The young man paid no attention to her.

Dan smiled.

"With electric-city," the young man said, "people stay awake late. For what reason? They go to the rum shop, they get drunk, they go to the bad woman, they get sick, they cannot work. No, electric-city not good."

"And you like to sleep," Alicia said sweetly to him.

He shrugged. "I work hard."

"But you sleep harder." She smiled.

"Still," Dan said, "it must be fun catching tropical fish for a living."

"It's hard work," Alicia said.

"Is it lucrative?" Mac asked.

The young man looked at him, puzzled.

"Do you make a lot of money?"

"They pay me ten cents a fish,' he said, disgruntled. "Then they sell them here for thirty dollars each." He leaned forward, elbows on the table. His hands, large, with fingers like sinewy sausages, stirred agitated at the air in front of his face. "But here they not know how to take care of fish. The tanks so dirty sometimes you see dead fish floating on the water." His eyes reddened, moistened.

"I made the mistake of taking him to some pet stores," Alicia said. "Disgusting."

Mac nodded sorrowfully. "The kittens kill me," he said.

Dan drained the last of the wine from the bottle into his glass.

"But what they care?" the young man continued. "They sell the fish for thirty dollars each. And they pay *me* —" His large right hand, fingers splayed, slapped his chest. "— a king in my country, ten cents a fish."

"It's called marketing," Alicia said, a slight impatience bracketing her voice. "Free enterprise, or something like that. They can get people to pay thirty dollars each. And they can get you to accept ten cents each. Because they know — and you know — there are hundreds of other boys just like you who'd grab at ten cents a fish."

"That not make it right," he responded quietly, in an aggrieved voice.

"I know you, Fred." Alicia glared at him through eyes

192

narrowed and suddenly malicious. "If you could force them to pay fifty dollars a fish, you'd do it. You'd exploit them as much as they're exploiting you. But you can't, you don't have the power. You have no choice. And until I brought you here and I took you to the pet shops and I showed you the prices, you were very happy with your ten cents." She clamped her teeth tight, lips downturned into thin, angry strips, and took a deep breath.

The young man leaned back in his chair, hands settling quietly on his lap. In his sudden deflation, the impression he gave of physical bulk was strangely heightened, untensed muscles jellying under the overlying fat. His chest, tight against his green t-shirt, sagged to the sides like small, sad, unsupported breasts. "It not fair," he pouted, eyes falling to the floor.

"It doesn't matter," she said, suddenly gentle. "It's just a different world, that's all."

Her words seemed to mollify him. "But why the fish die?" he said. "I not going to fish no more. I not want to send them here to die."

"Don't be stupid." Her voice hardened again. "What would you do without those ten cents a fish in that penny-sized island of yours?"

"I would —"

"You would what?"

"I would live."

"You would *live*?" She laughed a sound brutal and incisive.

The muscles of his hands tensed on his lap.

Dan rose, began clearing the table. Mac and Alicia joined in. The young man, at ease, watched them.

Afterwards, when they'd all settled back into the living

room, when Mac had rolled a joint, lit it, and passed it around, the young man fetched his guitar with its one broken string and sang softly for them, sad and lonely songs of languid love and lost sailors.

As he sang — his deep, raw voice resounding in the room — Alicia studied the faces of Mac and her husband. She could see on them, clearly written, bemusement and a smug contempt. She was embarrassed — for the young man. And she was angered — but with whom, she wasn't quite sure.

The walls of the bathroom had been redone in tiles of lustrous pink. Neatly folded towel sets hung from shiny chrome rails. The shower curtain exploded with an imitation sunset of pink, red and orange. It was extravagance of a kind Alicia neither needed nor understood, but had stopped questioning the day she walked out of Dan's life.

She stripped off her clothes and began hanging them on the elaborate chrome hooks screwed into the back of the door; but then, with a satisfaction she knew to be childish, she changed her mind and threw them onto the floor.

Alicia had no illusions about herself. She knew that her face, small and round, elfin-like in her youth, had weathered through travel and the deprivations of climate. At the age of forty-five, her face suggested fifty-five, and if, as Dan fairly claimed, her mother wore her life on her face like a badge of bitterness, then it could be justly said that Alicia had assumed a road-map.

She hadn't noticed the process. In all the places she had been — communes, collective farms, vineyards, sugar plantations, fishing boats — mirrors, and the time to contemplate oneself, had been a rarity. But now, standing naked before the full-length bathroom mirror in the probing glare of two fluorescent tubes — in the silence, she could hear them hissing — she thought herself somehow desiccated, an ageing gnome almost sexless with a strange mixture of the feminine and the masculine: veined arms, muscled shoulders, small firm breasts, trim stomach sloping down to sparse, almost childlike pubic hair couched between pared hips.

As she turned and twisted, viewing herself from the left, from the right, from over the shoulders, she saw that from certain angles she might have easily been a boy.

She stepped to within an inch of the mirror, grasped her hair, already short, with the fingers of her right hand, and pulled it severely back. With her left, she brushed the rest of her hair behind her ears. She gazed at herself for a moment and began to understand why Dan had always insisted on her having it cut shorter than was stylish at the time. Something — she couldn't name it — flared within her.

With trembling hands, she reached into the shower and turned on the water. She wanted it to be hot and powerful enough to be painful: it had to strike very, very deep within her.

Mac had gone to bed. The young man had gently fallen asleep on the sofa, his chest rising and falling rhythmically, a soft snore riffling from between his lips. The guitar, broken string curled serpentine around the neck, lay at his feet.

The wind outside had subsided. The shrubbery sat inert in the heavy yellow light of the streetlamp. Alicia thought she could see the lateness of the hour in the air: there seemed a greyness to the night, as if it were suffused with the finest smoke.

Dan helped her unroll their sleeping bags onto the floor.

"I have to admit, it feels strange," he said when they were done.

Alicia shook her head. "You think it's strange for you?"

He smiled sadly. "Who would've thought? Eight years —"

"I can't think about it, you know."

"What?"

"Your going to bed with another man."

He walked over to the window, tapped at the glass with a finger. "Maybe if you'd wanted to have children, Alicia —"

"You've never understood, the dangers at my age —"

"I was willing to chance it."

"You were." She clicked her fingers at him in a derisive, incredulous gesture. "You see, that's why I had to leave. Besides, kids wouldn't have made any difference."

"Wouldn't they? I don't know, Alicia —"

"Come on, Dan, what would you have done if I hadn't left? You are the way you are. You should thank me for leaving."

"Was it all bad, Alicia?"

"You know it wasn't. A lot of it was good." She wondered suddenly whether that was true for him too. "But I needed more." And then the question that had been picking at her since her shower asked itself. "Dan, did you know Mac before I left?"

"No." He shook his head. "I never lied to you, Alicia. I never did anything that I'm ashamed of. Mac and I met at the auto show in Toronto the year after."

"And?"

His eyes glittered sharply at her. "And I guess we all choose our freedoms in the end, don't we."

"Yes. Don't we."

After a moment, Dan glanced at the young man. "Why'd you bring him?"

"No ulterior motive, if that's what you're wondering."

"Really, Alicia? You sure he's not just your little travelling road-show? Come see the cannibal —"

"That's not fair." But, in truth, it was how it had worked out. Curiosity opened doors.

"So what's he doing here? He's a child, Alicia. How old is he? Twenty-five? Twenty-six? Isn't he just another piece of exotica you've picked up in your endless search for God knows what?"

"You sound jealous, Dan."

"Give me a break."

"I'm just repaying a debt. You see, I lived with his family —"

"His family or him?"

"There's that jealousy again." It was the only word that occurred to her, for what she heard in his voice was the old tone of accusation edged with sexual challenge. And she felt the thrill of it enough that she had to turn away. "He lives with his family, you see. I stayed six months with them. I helped him on his boat, but I felt it wasn't enough. So I invited him to come with me, I thought I'd show him a bit of Canada. He's never left his island before." She looked over to the sleeping young man. "It's been a bit of a shock, I'm afraid. For both of us."

"Is he your boyfriend?"

"You mean," she said flatly, "do I sleep with him."

He nodded.

"No and yes. He's not my boyfriend, but I sleep with him." She shrugged. "It's the least I could do."

The young man stirred, grunted, shifted position on the sofa, and slipped back into a deep sleep.

"His parents expected it, you see. Not of me, but of him. We all slept in the same room, different beds. But I remember the first night we made love, his parents were in their bed next to ours pretending to sleep. I knew they were awake, I sensed it. And I knew they were watching. But they weren't seeing me. They were observing their son, assessing him, reassuring themselves that when the day comes he'll be able to perpetuate the family. I was incidental."

"So how'd it feel to be a piece of meat?" Dan's mouth twisted in disgust.

"Great. I enjoyed it. I like being watched without being seen."

"Alicia." Her name was like an expression of exasperation. "So what's next? You planning to settle down or anything like that?"

She frowned, shook her head. "I can't stay anywhere longer than a few months. Don't know why, but I need to keep moving on. New things, new places, new faces. I get bored."

"What are you looking for, Alicia?"

She considered the question. "I don't think I'm looking for anything. I think —" She gestured, as if stirring a cauldron of possibilities with her hand. "I think it's just that I've built a life of goodbyes, and I don't know how to stop."

"It's a sad way to live a life."

"I've seen worse."

"You going back to his island with him?"

"No." She had come to the decision without ever asking herself the question. "It's time for a change. He's tired of me and I'm tired of him. Do you know the joker swears he recognizes the fish individually? And all that crap about how superior his damned island is —" She shook her head, bit at her lower lip. "No, I'll be sending him back soon with a pile of disposable diapers, a box of baby food, and instructions to get on with his family. He faces obligations and expectations. He's got to fulfil them."

"Do you think you'll ever come back? For a visit, maybe?"

"I doubt it."

Dan stuck his hands into his pockets.

"I've been wanting to ask you," she said. "How does my mother pay for it? Shady Pines isn't a cheap place."

"She manages."

"Not that well."

"I help her out a bit."

"How much?"

He shrugged.

"Thanks, Dan —"

"It's no big deal, I can afford it."

"You know, I'll never be able to pay you back."

"I'm not looking to be paid back."

"How come you're doing all this, Dan?"

"Somebody had to."

"You son-of-a-bitch."

"I didn't mean that as criticism, Alicia."

"Didn't you?" She stepped closer to him. "You know, I really came here for one reason."

"I know. Your mother."

"No. She was the excuse, not the reason. I understand that now."

He waited for her to continue.

"I —" Did she dare? How could she tell him that part of her still loved him or, at least, still loved the man he had once been? And how could she explain, without making an utter fool of herself, that it was this love that made what he had become so hard to take?

"Yes?"

"You're going to laugh —"

"No, Alicia —"

She stepped right up to him and, in a swift movement, tugged his lips to hers in a firm, hard kiss. He struggled to pull away but she held him tight, the tip of her tongue playing furiously on his clamped lips. When she felt them part, when she felt her tongue brush against his teeth, she pushed violently at him, breaking their embrace. Her hand rose swiftly from her side, arm uncontrolled in a sudden burst of energy, and cracked sharply onto the left side of his face. She felt her index finger slap into the fleshy softness of his eye.

Dan raised his hand to his temple. His left eye went red. "What was that for?"

"You'd haul me into bed in a minute if I let you, wouldn't you?"

"I won't deny it."

"And Mac?"

"What about him?"

"Where does he fit in?"

"He's not the jealous type."

She couldn't help snickering. "We can get a divorce if you like."

"What's the point?"

"Someday you might meet a woman. . . ."

"No, Alicia. I've said goodbye to that part of my life."

"But I'm a woman —"

"I've just said goodbye to that part, that's all. The part you fit into."

"So there's no point, is there?"

"As I said." He gently rubbed at his eye. "People are complex, Alicia. Even in piss-ass towns like this."

"That's usually when I leave, you know. When things get too complex."

"Or too simple?"

"Then, too." Her hand reached up, caressed the redness around his eye. "Are you happy, Dan?"

A look of sadness came to his face as he considered the question. "Yes," he said finally. "It's not the way I used to picture it but, yes, I am." And he took her hand from his face, kissed it. Then, without looking back, he walked from the living room and went upstairs.

Alicia wiped her eyes on her sleeve, let herself fall slowly into the armchair, listening to the alien silence of the house, watching the gentle rise and fall of the young man's chest. It was so easy, when you lived an itinerant life, to forget that the rest of the world changed too. It didn't just sit there, inert, waiting for you to reinsert yourself. Your own place grew fluid, eventually — as she now understood — erased itself. She'd never before realized that her wanderings had come so easily largely because of that vague notion of a centre, a place to go back to. And she knew, sitting there in the muted light, that she would one day settle down, but it wouldn't be in any place, or at any time, that she could imagine now.

She sat there for hours, the night transformed into a lingering moment pulsing with images of movement and transience.

When she sensed a lightening of the sky, when she saw the dimming of the streetlight, she roused the young man and had him help her roll the sleeping bags back up. Then she hung their backpacks on him and led him, bewildered, into the dawn.

The Power of Reason

PLATES OF CHIPPED porcelain peppered with toasted bread-crumbs, smeared at the edges with jam and peanut butter; coffee cups, of various shapes and colours, with rings of hardened 'scum clinging to the insides; cutlery scattered around in casual disorder: Monica knows that the breakfast dishes will probably not be done by the time she returns home this evening. They'll still be there, piled in the sink and on the counter next to it. But Monica likes to think of herself as a woman of infinite patience, a woman persistent with a deep belief in the ultimate power of reason.

So she does as she does every morning before leaving for the day's labour. Places herself squarely in the doorway to the living room — small, crowded with mismatched furniture — and calls out in a voice loud and hectoring to her three sons, a voice calculated to cut through the hubbub of the television before which they are gathered: "Charlie. Andy. Eddie. The dishes. You not goin' to forget, eh?"

There is neither reply nor acknowledgement. But that is expected.

"Charlie. Andy. Eddie. All-you goin' to —"

"Nora will do them when she get up, Mammy."

"Is not Nora job, you know that, Charlie."

"Is woman work." Andy: he speaks with his father's voice, at least his voice as Monica remembers it. But that was so long ago.

"Work is work, Andy. It ain't have no man or woman in it."

"So why Nora can't do it?" Eddie: her youngest, the one in whom she had, briefly, the most hope, and the one for whom she feels, deeply, the greatest despair.

"Because Nora shift finish at twelve o'clock last night and it was double shift that she work and she startin' again at four o'clock this afternoon." Monica hears her breath shorten — she is protective of her daughters — but she manages, in the briefest of pauses, to snatch it back. "You think Nora goin' to want to wash your breakfast dishes when she get up, young man?"

"And Sandra?" Charlie's eyes do not leave the television screen. "She ain't have too much to do when she come home from school."

Monica sucks softly at her teeth. "Your sister have studyin' to do." They cover the same ground every morning, in one variation or another.

Eddie snorts in the dismissive derision with which he distances himself. "Some psychologist she goin' to make, eh, fellas?"

Charlie ignores him.

Andy, irritated, says, "All-you can't shut up? I tryin' to hear the TV."

His brothers fall silent. Andy has somehow evolved into a kind of leader. Monica cannot understand the deference Charlie and Eddie and their friends show him. He is a sullen boy given to keeping his counsel, but when he speaks the others listen.

Monica casts a sad look around the living room: at the sofa, tattered and colourless, diminished by her sons. At the uncertain television, brash and noisy, hectic with exercising women. At the dining table off to the side, a construction several hands old of faded formica and corroded chrome. At the calendars and glow-in-the-dark paintings — lakes, trees, mountains — that clutter the walls.

Then her eyes move beyond them, leave them behind in the knowledge that she is doing the best she can; focus with what feels like finality on the drapes still drawn to the day. They are floor-length, of a white lace that admits the light but provides privacy from the prying binoculars of a man in the building across the way.

"Charlie," she says. But her voice is half-hearted. "Andy. Eddie."

They ignore her. They may not even have heard her.

Before slipping on her shoes and picking up her bag, she looks again at her sons, at their blank, absorbed, strangers' faces. Knows that, as usual, she has failed to penetrate the shell they have encrusted around themselves.

Not a minute later, as Monica waits for the elevator down the dusky corridor, a cockroach scurries across her shoe and cowers against the wall. It is not a cockroach as she knew them, is only half an inch long and lacks the aggressiveness of its tropical cousins. But the thought of its ugliness, the knowledge of its invincibility, infuriate Monica. Even as the elevator door opens, she pursues the snippet of spurting shadow, snapping at it with her shoe; lets the elevator continue without her until she has ground the creature into the dingy carpet. She wants to bang her head against the swirling graffiti, rip down the peeling wallpaper. But she settles for hitting the wall. Once. With her open palm. A dry, unsatisfying slap.

Another defeat for the power of reason.

Today is Tuesday. It is Ms. Galahad's day. The subway ride, to Monica's regret, is not long. There is barely enough time to close her eyes, to seek the composure that seems more and more to elude her. Like the sightless, she counts the subway stops as they go by, wringing from the sounds of each — the trundling of the doors, the shrills of the conductor's whistle — the precious seconds of delay.

But before she is ready, she knows she must get off — either that or spend the day riding the train back and forth from one end of the tunnel to the other, cushioned in the rhythm of its sounds. Pure temptation, this, but frightening in the power of its fantasy. She forces her eyes open, forces herself up, and dashes without thinking through the closing doors of the train, up the escalator, up the stairs to the street.

Ms. Galahad's house is in an older section of the city, although it is, in spots, being renewed. There are no trees, but few of the buildings reach higher than two or three storeys. The preponderance of red brick — some blackened, some blasted back to freshness — is interspersed with walls of mildewed stucco and, more rarely, painted wood. Convenience stores, the older displaying newspapers and buckets of cellophaned flowers out front, the more modern being miniature supermarkets of glass and plastic, sit at every corner and midway along the longer blocks. Monica has often wondered how they all survive, competing with each other to sell loaves of bread or cartons of milk or packets of cigarettes.

The neighbourhood is, Monica knows, full of the sort of young working couples, insistently professional and tenacious in their habits, who employ women like herself to clean their houses and look after their children.

It is part of her distress: to see, in mid-morning or mid-afternoon, the leisurely roamings and sidewalk congregations of young women, some black, mostly Filipino, to whose society she once reluctantly belonged. Two years of living in a strange room in a strange house, in a strange city in a strange country among strange people, ministering to their needs and the needs of their young. She, too, has walked sidewalks with her fair-haired charges, holding back as best she could the enervating thoughts of her own offspring left behind, seeking others of her station with whom to chat, before whom to flash the worn photographs, in whose ears to whisper the fears and the resentments, from whom to seek solace and the necessary reminders of the permanent visa and the reunions to come. Two years of long hours, low pay. The gentle bondage that was the price of a future.

But Monica has never been able to decide whether the price was too high, whether the final, still unfolding outcome is but a twist of a knife that was being driven in bit by bit during those two years; that was inserted even as she accepted the offer to be a nanny — a word unknown then, but glamorous in the dictionary definition at the local library — to the fine young couple in distant Canada. So she avoids them now, these young women reticent with fears but eager with expectation, shies from the chatter of the children not theirs, from the constrictions of their indentured lives, the uncertainties of their distant tomorrows. She walks past them with eyes averted, is grateful when, as she makes her way to or from Ms. Galahad's house, they are not around.

This morning the street is deserted. She even hears the knock of her shoes, man's shoes, the only kind that will last, on the sidewalk, on the concrete path to Ms. Galahad's house, on the wooden stairs to Ms. Galahad's porch.

She takes the key from where it always is, under the frayed upper-right corner of the hemp doormat. Today it is wrapped in a note that tells her Ms. Galahad wants her to distribute discreet doses of powdered poison around the kitchen. "The cockroaches," the typed words read, "are getting out of hand. God knows where they come from. Professional exterminators cost an arm and a couple of legs. I want them eradicated. Have a nice day!" The note is signed, in violet ink, *Christine*, the name which Ms. Galahad keeps pushing at her and which she, in her horror of familiarity with employers, insists on resisting.

Monica crumples the note. She isn't happy with the order, although she prides herself on not being difficult. She'll do windows, floors, will even polish silverware for an extra fee. But this order to play exterminator does not please her. It brings to mind the building in which she lives, rekindles the sense of helplessness she struggles to leave behind every morning. But she needs Ms. Galahad, needs her house and the dust that it kicks up, needs, even, the cockroaches: how else would she earn her living?

Whenever Monica enters Ms. Galahad's house, once she has shut the door behind her — "Listen for the click!" Ms. Galahad insisted the first time with a touch of hysteria, opening and closing the door again and again. "The click! The click! The click! Understand?" — she feels the house close in around her, feels it pull her into its own alien world.

It is in no way an exceptional house. Two storeys. A roof of green shingles slipping at the edges. Living room, dining room, kitchen. Bedrooms upstairs. A yard out back the size of a grave. Ms. Galahad grew up here, one of two children. Her father, an electrician, died years ago. Her mother, senile and incontinent, lives in a "home". Her brother, younger, is "somewhere on the west coast dealing drugs"; she hasn't seen him in years, expects never to see him again. Ms. Galahad has been alone in the house for a long time. And yet she has changed little. The curtains in the living room are new, most of the furniture has been reupholstered, her bedroom contains a waterbed. But everything else gives the impression of having been there for decades: chairs and tables and cabinets of dark, heavy wood oiled and gleaming, much of it crawling with intricate carving, all of it making Monica's job more difficult.

Monica finds it strange that Ms. Galahad, so young (at least with her makeup on; without it, Monica suspects, less so) and so modern (she buys her clothes only at "boutiques"; Monica has seen the extravagant bills and the stacks of designer bags) and so much the single, successful entrepre-

neur (she owns a catering company, Whims and Fancies, that
services the rich and idle), strange that she never updated the
house, never remade it more in her own image.

She begins where she always does, in the bathroom on the
second floor just at the top of the narrow staircase. It is a
small room, amateurishly tiled in blue halfway up — Ms.
Galahad's father's handiwork — and painted white above,
that smells subtly of Nature's Perfume, the potpourri in a
lace sock hanging on the wall. A small window of patterned,
opaque glass opens to the muddy backyard, a third of which
is taken up by Ms. Galahad's herb garden. Ms. Galahad
enjoys showing off her little cultivation. She took Monica out
on her first visit, Monica protesting that she didn't do gardens,
Ms. Galahad laughing at the thought and assuring her that
she employed a weekly gardener for that. Monica was impressed by Ms. Galahad's knowledge; she knew the name
and origin of every plant, knew how each grew — this
one had to have its tips pinched, that one had to be left
untouched — and how each was to be used. But Monica saw,
too, that when Ms. Galahad reached in among the plants with
her slim fingers, her touch was tentative, as if she was more
at ease with the theory than with the practice. Monica envies
her that freedom. It is a luxury she herself can ill afford and
she yearns, in the recollection of that whiff of unknown
pleasure, to slam the window on it. But no, the window is
fragile, the putty cracked, the wood rotting, and to slam it
would be to shatter it. She leaves it as it is.

A little triumph for the power of reason.

She shakes open a green garbage bag and empties into it
the contents of the wicker basket that sits beside the toilet

bowl. Next she washes the toilet, scrubbing it with a brush and an abrasive cleanser, then rubbing it down with a liquid disinfectant, the scent of the potpourri momentarily overpowered. There is a rust stain on the lower neck of the bowl that won't come off. When she sponges the base and the tiled floor around, the sponge comes away black with dust and fallen hair.

The only disadvantage to this job, as far as Monica is concerned, is that it fails to occupy her mind. She considers this a dangerous drawback for, no matter what she does, the repetitiveness of the tasks cannot prevent her thoughts from roaming into areas she would rather avoid. Cannot keep buried images of the man so long absent.

Rudy. Rudolph. Rudolph Augustus Spears. A slight man, unimposing. And not a handsome man, or a particularly strong man, not a man exceptional in any way. But, on the whole, a good man. A dependable man, in the right circumstances. A hard-working man, but not a lucky one. Fathering six children, five of whom survived, made him less proud than he made out before his friends. With them, he played at a boastful modesty. With her, he made no pretension: dogs did it, he said, and cats and chickens and frogs and alligators. And somehow, when he said it, his words were not demeaning; they implied no judgement of her maternity. Monica liked this about him, this deeper modesty. She liked many things about him.

So she was not consciously resentful of his decision to return to the island. She understood that he needed more from his life. Needed his friends, his knowledge of island workings that was a kind of self-sufficiency. Most important of all, he'd needed a certain thrill, something indefinable that came from his familiarity with the island, from the feel of its air, from its very odours, which evaporated when he, with the children in tow, boarded the plane to fly to her, the wife and mother unseen for more than three years. She understood his inability to relax in this place so new and so different. To adjust after his customs officer duties to dishwashing and floor-sweeping and garbage-handling. To accustom himself, when it was all said and done, to Canada: after all, this place was really just a job to her, too. So when he announced his decision to go back, leaving the children with her, she knew it was the right one for him. Accepted it with equanimity, and with an effort of reason.

But even reason has its bite: Monica still feels the wound, knows it will never heal, knows the best she can hope for is a dimming of memory and a dulling of the pain.

After dusting the tank and neatening the stack of magazines, *Chatelaine, Vogue, Ms, National Geographic*, that sit ripped and dog-eared on it, she pushes aside the shower curtain of transparent plastic and gets down on her knees to scrub the tub. The porcelain, like that of the toilet bowl and the sink, is old, has lost its shine and is pitted where the water hits. Ms. Galahad never cleans the tub after her shower. By the time Monica reaches into it to do the weekly scrub, several layers of scum have formed around the sides, working themselves into the rashes of decay. She turns on the tap briefly to dampen the porcelain, sprinkles around a generous amount of abrasive cleanser — she likes the way the blue crystals explode against the white when touched by water — and lays into it with the stiff-bristled scrub brush gripped tightly in her hand.

The job has its drawbacks. But not as many as the others she has held. The couple in whose home she spent two years of sixteen-hour days — cooking, cleaning, ironing, looking after twins, with only the occasional Sunday off to spend a little of the money she had not sent to Rudy and the children — were not bad people. They were just people who lived by only their own, deeply held priorities, people in whom — and she knew, with delight, that this would wound them — the spirit of slavery was not quite extinguished. Leaving them with her newly won visa for a secretarial course and part-time labour in a restaurant was not difficult, was like liberation.

Only, six months later, in the placement found for her by the secretarial school, to run into Mr. Youseesee. This was how he was known to the typing pool at the insurance company because of his constant references to his son's private school, Upper Canada College. He had come from England about ten years before, a big balding man with a moustache and a curt manner. Monica took a dislike to him on his first day in the office when, on being told that she would be his secretary, he said with eyes assessing and critical, "She'll do, I suppose." He did not offer his hand, did not even smile.

Mr. Youseesee was a stiff, unreasonably demanding man. He never took off his jacket, never loosened his tie, sat upright in his chair as if pinned to it. If typed letters or reports showed even minute evidence of correction he returned them scrawled *Unsatisfactory Do Again.* He wanted them fast and he wanted them clean; he insisted that anything he signed look as if printed. Monica's tension rose; her typing rate slowed; she required extra hours at the office to complete her work.

One day Mr. Youseesee brought in a silver tea service still

in its Birks box, put it on her desk, and ordered that she prepare his tea every afternoon at three o'clock. She did as instructed, following the specifications he had printed in fountain pen on a sheet of typing paper. Yet her efforts merited neither words of gratitude nor acknowledgement of effort. Monica took a little revenge each day by spitting juicily into the pot before filling it with boiling water. But vengeance in small doses, unnoticed, soon proves unfulfilling. Monica knew it was time to depart the day she thought of urinating into the pot. She typed up her resignation letter, put it on Mr. Youseesee's desk, mistakes and all.

Bosses are not among Monica's favourite people, and she has come to see this cleaning of other people's houses, at first so demeaning, as a form of freedom. No bosses, but instead clients to whom she owes nothing: she even dropped two when their demands grew irksome. Freedom: that was what Rudy was looking for, even if the word itself never occurred to him; and that is what, in earning her living on her own, Monica wants to believe she's found.

The tub done, she turns her attention to the bathroom mirror, spraying the glass from the side, concealing it in a film of cleanser so that she cannot see herself reflected. When she wipes the film off, the dry rag scrubbing away the white dots of spattered toothpaste, sharpening the green-edged decay behind the glass, she keeps her eyes on the coating of liquid, looking instinctively beyond where she has already cleaned. Monica doesn't want to see herself in the same mirror in which Ms. Galahad gazes every morning. It seems somehow too personal, an intrusion, like digging through a drawer of someone else's underwear.

After the mirror, the shelf below. Long and narrow, the sliding doors enclosing the cabinet beneath unsteady in their runners, it is crowded with boxes and bottles and fancy glass containers: cold and allergy medicines, antacid tablets and constipation pills, perfumes and powders and skin creams, lipsticks and rouge and eyeliners in profusion, styling mousse and tanning lotions and contact lens solutions. Brushes thick with matted hair lie in disarray — in the cabinet, kept always out of sight, are the bottles of hair tint Ms. Galahad uses to camouflage the revelations of age — and propped precariously at one end is a curling iron, its cord wrapped loosely around the shaft.

So much equipment, Monica thinks, her eyes darting with distaste the length of the congested shelf. So much time, so much effort, for both Ms. Galahad and herself. The cleaning of this bathroom shelf, so small in itself, is in its tiresome way the most onerous part of the job. This simple but irritating task, this minute and concentrated labour of many minutes, seems to take longer than anything else, longer even than the monthly polishing of the wooden floors. But Monica knows it is not the work itself that annoys her. It is, rather, this contradictory accumulation of revealed confidences that is only a beginning. As she makes her way around the house she will come across, in this simple act of cleaning, more little revelations of intimacy, more of the little things that, together, create the Ms. Galahad no one else sees, and they are truths Monica would rather not know.

Once the bottles and containers have been replaced, the

sink remains to be scrubbed, the toothbrush holder to be wiped, the floor to be mopped. Monica bends reluctantly to the floor, her mind, restive, swimming along unsought channels.

Ms. Galahad's bedroom is next to the bathroom. It is not a large room, but has been given the illusion of spaciousness by the sparseness of its decoration. This is not the result of decision, the effect is one of omission rather than of deliberation: Ms. Galahad has simply never bothered to furnish it beyond the basic necessities.

A waterbed: Why this? Monica always wonders, dissatisfied with Ms. Galahad's explanation that it is good for her back, suspecting that, like the food processor in the kitchen and the herb garden in the backyard, a waterbed is a necessary fixture for people like Ms. Galahad. It is flanked by two white night-tables with lamps, only one of which has a bulb. A dressing table, grotesquely ornate, of wood painted a plasticized white and lined with gold trim, squats laboriously in the corner to the left, beside the lace-curtained window.

Monica moves cautiously across the wooden floor — the silence of the house seems most profound in this room, bare and inanimate — to the dressing table with its oval mirror dark and aqueous in the subdued light. Monica looks into the glass, at her image half-lit by the light from the window, fatigue and coarseness of skin smoothed away, hair once more totally black, years and pounds stripped off. The walls of the room contract, a familiar mustiness suffuses the air. Monica senses a comfort that she knows to be deceptive, but she revels in it. Sees herself as she once was. Sees herself, after a moment, as her daughter Sandra, with hopes and

216

dreams and years yet uncluttered by events and the unyielding impositions of acquired responsibility. Glimpses what she only half-acknowledges as a subdued jealousy of her daughter, of the possibilities open to her. It is a feeling Monica would never admit to. But she knows, too, that she is not yet old enough to take pride solely in what she has been able to provide for her children. As accomplishment it is too selfless; as autobiography, too despairing. It is a boast that reflects the twilight of life, and Monica feels her sun to be still bright. Sandra's she pictures as the soft iridescence of advanced dawn, her own as the harsher glare of early afternoon, but nowhere does she sense the thickening of twilight's shadows, only the inexorable advance of her day, the growing lateness of her hour. The initial pleasure at illusory youth gives way to a keen dissatisfaction. It creates envy, and envy makes her irritable.

Monica turns quickly from the mirror to the dull glow of the window, tugs the curtains aside. Where's the power of her reason in all this? she wonders, impatient with herself. Her reason has been her most virile pride, the source of the strength to leave behind those dearest to her, to abandon without even fleeting hesitation the comforts of the birthright, meagre but tangible, that was hers. Her reason: Monica feels the power of it as she pounds across the floor back to the door, reaches up for the switch on the wall and, with a snap of her finger, splatters a dull light around the bedroom. The walls expand as if shoved by a great force, the mustiness evaporates. The room reverts to neutrality, reclaims its flatness.

Monica moves briskly, cloth and dust spray in hand, to the night-table with the lamp that works. Both its drawers are hanging half open, evidence of haste. In them are Ms. Galahad's romance novels; her serious, hardcover books are displayed on a small bookcase in the living room. She firmly closes the drawers, sprays and wipes the tabletop, the base of the lamp. Moves now in a growing blur to the other night-table and lamp, to the dressing table littered with fake fingernails, boxes of eyelashes, sticks of lipstick, coded containers with coloured contact lenses. Her cloth brushes objects aside, crowds them pell-mell into the corners, against the sides.

And when Monica next glimpses herself in the oval mirror, she too has reverted to neutrality, she too has reclaimed her flatness.

Lunch time. Monica sits at the table in the dining room, before her a plate and crystal wine glass from the packaged sets Ms. Galahad keeps in the cabinet to the left, silver-ware — knife, fork, hefty and solid — from the velvet-lined box in the drawer beneath. She unwraps the small bundle she has brought with her from home, places on the plate two thick slices of homemade bread, buttered and lightly sprinkled with red-pepper sauce. She carefully folds the aluminum foil, flattens it with her palm, and puts it back into her bag on the floor beside her. Takes at the same time a warm can of cola, cracks it open and empties it into the glass, puts the empty can into her bag. Sits back in the chair — it rocks uneasily under her — admiring the setting she has created for the only quiet meal of her day.

This elevation of simple nourishment to ritual is how Monica treats herself. She relishes its precision and control. It would be so easy to gobble up the bread, a couple of minutes of quick chomping and swallowing while leaning against the kitchen counter. So easy, Monica knows, and so joyless.

She picks up the implements with care, the smooth, heavy silver radiating warmth into her hands. The fork sinks into the corner of one of the slices of bread, pinning it firmly to the plate. The knife blade hovers for a moment, selecting its angle as her eye instinctively divides the yellow, red-speckled expanse into nine equal squares.Then, slowly, it presses down, sinking firmly through the butter, through the bread until it makes contact with the hardness of the plate. Swiftly now, with greater assurance, the blade slashes at a right angle to the first cut, severing the pinned corner of bread.

Monica's mouth waters in anticipation as she raises the morsel to her lips, the scent of sweet butter and spicy pepper, contradictory and enticing, tickling her nostrils, arousing a gleeful tightening of her stomach. She hooks the bread off the fork with her tongue, lets it sit there growing moist in the bubbling saliva, the butter and the pepper prickling and teasing her palate. As the bread threatens to dissolve, her tongue presses it against the roof of her mouth, squelches the juices out of it, the butter melting, the pepper nipping into her flesh. She carefully slices off the next square, places it in her mouth, tosses it onto her teeth and slowly masticates its softness. The bread crumbles and squelches, the butter coats her tongue, the pepper explodes. And when she sips the warm cola, the liquid enveloping her tongue, its bubbles fizzing and bursting, it is a moment of abandon, a glimpse of ecstasy absurd and unreasonable, but for these few moments she does not let herself care.

Blue, alive and luminescent. Immense. Wet. A field of movement suggested rather than apparent. The soles of her feet cool on the gentle grit of dampened sand. Her cheeks brushed by a soft, hot wind. Vision recedes, pulls back further into herself: The water surges towards the shore, a submerged monster determined to beach itself; hesitates, back arching as if in fright; reaches back into itself, curls back into its belly, spitting and fraying in sudden dissipation. For many long minutes the water breathes in her mind, its body pulsing imperceptibly, its edges heaving themselves in languid, ragged frenzy at her. And she knows, sensing their pull, that she knew then that she would one day leave them.

Switches, even as the thought forms: to a yard of hardened brown earth, a grizzled grapefruit tree to the right and a barren mango tree to the left holding a house of grey and weathered wood in leafy parenthesis. It is a small house of a kind now found mostly in watercolours produced for sale to tourists, a roof of corrugated iron rusted red, windows, also of wood, hinged at the top and held open at the bottom by sticks jammed against the sill, hanging open like heavy eyelids.

Then inside: through the little living room with its Morris chairs and doilied coffee table and religious calendars, past the two tiny bedrooms with their unforgiving beds and inadequate wardrobes. At last, she can smell the comforting, slightly sour odour of dry earth, old wood, and new dust. Granny is in the kitchen, her dress faded and loose, tufts of stiff silvered hair peeking from the bandanna tied around her head. A pot bubbles on the stove, vapours sinuous and substantial in the thin light. Granny stands at the counter in front of the window that looks out into the backyard, beside her on the floor a bucket brimming with water fetched earlier from the standpipe fifteen minutes down the unbordered road. She is washing the dishes in her unhurried, methodical way, taking them one by one from the red plastic bowl on her right, dipping them into the enamel bowl of soapy water in front of her, rinsing them in the green plastic bowl on her left. She hums quietly to herself as she works, a dirge unidentifiable in the sounds rising from her throat.

The window beyond her allows a glimpse of the backyard: exposed earth, straggling grass, a stand of unhealthy sugar-cane farther on and, just off to the left where it adjoins the house at the side, the wash-shed with its deep basin of cast concrete that her mother had installed when the dirty laundry she took in exceeded the capacities of her wooden tub and scrub board. Reaching into the basin, two bare brown arms — Monica can't see the face, doesn't have to, knows the muscles well, knows their shape and movement, knows the way the light glistens off the wet skin — knead vigorously at a dripping garment. Monica is not tempted to peek beyond the hanging window shutter to the face; it is already so familiar in its fatigue, she has no wish to sweep further into its distant insufficiencies. For she recalls vividly her fears that the sterility of this yard, and the inestimable depth of that wash-basin, would for ever be hers.

After carefully wiping the glass and the utensils clean — she does not wash them, sees no need for putting soap and water to them — and replacing them in the cabinet, Monica fetches the vacuum cleaner from the broom-closet in the kitchen and sets about cleaning the living-room rug, a rectangle of unpatterned white large enough to create an impression of voluptuousness but small enough that it remains just an impression. No guest's shoe — if Ms. Galahad ever has guests — can touch the carpet, so small is it, so distant from the sofa and the armchairs forlorn in their updated upholstery. Careful not to set her own shoes upon its ageing virgin plushness, Monica vacuums from the edge with a delicacy that she believes unwarranted but unavoidable.

Her sons. Charlie, Andy, Eddie. They are what Monica has been struggling not to think about. But as the day wears on, as fatigue grows, her resolve diminishes. They come to her, her sons, as a group clustered on the sofa before the television, speaking in whispers to one another, more garrulously to others.

Monica doesn't understand her sons. She knows this is not unusual — neither her mother nor her grandmother understands her; neither has ever quite accepted her decision to emigrate from a warm country to a cold one. Life held an envious certainty for them. They demanded little of it, and usually got more than expected in return. She, on the other hand, grew up with dissatisfactions that would never have occurred to either her mother or her grandmother. Dissatisfactions that have led her to her present life in a city she still does not really know, in an apartment less spacious than the cramped wooden house left behind, with five other people leading different and independent lives, three of whom stretch her reason in ways never anticipated.

It began, simply, with their language. There were times when Monica couldn't follow their words, couldn't read their gestures. At home, there was no problem. They retained, in privacy, the island accent and what they remembered of the slang. It was as islanders that they argued with their mother, growled at their sisters. But outside, hanging out — her word would have been *liming* — with their friends on the sidewalk or at the shopping mall, they speak in a dialect not of the island, not even of Canada, which would not have surprised her, but of black America. Their speech slows to a drawl, takes on a pointed, railing inflection. *Fella* becomes *bro'*, *mahn* becomes *mehn*, depending on who they're with. Even their way of walking changes. At home, they move with a painful lethargy. In the street they swagger and strut, their bodies boastful, as if moving to an unheard music, the urgings of dance barely restrained. Monica does not enjoy encountering her sons in public. They are at their strangest to her at these moments; are like people who have climbed out of a television set, minor characters from some police series set in a New York ghetto.

They dropped out of high school, one after the other, despite her opposition. But not, it soon became clear, in order to work. They seemed, in fact, to do nothing. They hung out, they hung around. They ate, they slept, they watched television. Yet, as time went along, they remained always well dressed, new clothes appearing with a striking regularity. They freely bought jewellery — chains, wrist bands, lumpy rings — and snack foods — cookies, chips, cases of soft drinks after Monica banned beer.

She wondered more than once about the source of their money but found her questions rebuffed with irritation and noncommittal mumbles. One evening she pressed, deflecting their evasions, demanding details; pressed to the point of explosion, their shouts of anger evoking bangs of protest from the apartments above and beside. Her sons stalked out of the apartment as a group, and by the time they returned two days later — with no explanation of where they had been or what they had been up to — Monica had decided to let things be, accepting in this way the distance her sons had established.

It would never have occurred to her to ask them to leave had Sandra not suggested it. And even if it had, she would have dismissed the thought as quickly as she in fact did. To throw her own sons out! The idea was scandalous to her, as it would have been to her mother and grandmother and any other family members who heard about it. But the idea did occur to Sandra; and Sandra was able to suggest it to her mother, their mother, almost matter-of-factly, one morning as the two of them were leaving the apartment together. Monica remembers her horror at this simple jettisoning of flesh and blood, this willingness to abandon her brothers to the streets. For the first time, Monica understood her daughter to be cold-blooded. Her words to Sandra, their harsh tone, still rang fresh in her mind: "I bring those boys into the world, jus' as I bring you and your sister. So what to do 'bout them is up to me, and me alone. You hear?" Sandra said nothing, just picked up her pace until she had left her mother far behind.

Monica resigned herself to living with, and providing for, three strangers.

But she is no fool. She realizes that her sons are up to something she would rather not know about. She hasn't missed the late-night phone calls, the huddled whisperings, the strangers coming to the apartment at odd hours. There is a furtiveness to their lives that Monica fears but before which she feels helpless, the power of her reason disarmed, her maternal emotion remote. Inevitably, Monica must fight against a feeling of being trampled, against her sense of being used but not quite discarded.

She puts the vacuum cleaner back into its closet, back among the brooms and brushes that hang, bat-like, from plastic clips. From the shelf she takes a can of furniture polish and a chamois cloth and quickly swirls around the living and dining rooms spraying and wiping the dark, shining wood. She is tired now, has had enough of Ms. Galahad's house, its clutter and its pretensions. She just wants to get her work done, to pocket the envelope of money Ms. Galahad leaves for her on the kitchen table and return to. . .what? Her sons? The breakfast dishes? The scurrying of cockroaches? Yes, and yes, and yes. But to her daughters, too, girls — no, women — issued of her though different from her in inexplicable ways.

By the time the wiping and polishing are done, her hand is moving in a blur of fury and her fingers grip the cloth as if to strangle it.

Monica's hands are aching when she sits at the kitchen table. This ache: it must be similar, she thinks, to the arthritic pain both her mother and grandmother complain of in their infrequent letters. She examines her fingers, as if looking for the pain, and sees there — in the length and slimness of the fingers, in the broad flatness of the nails — replicas of her mother's, as she sees replicas of her own in Sandra's and Nora's. Continuity, even with change both subtle and glaring: she takes pleasure in that, even as the thought comes to her that her sons' hands owe nothing to her, owe their thickness and their short, hard nails to their father.

The ache in her hands eases, her fingers straighten out, stretch, regain flexibility. Ms. Galahad's envelope lies flat on top of a small white box. It is not the envelope that attracts Monica's attention — she knows well its silky feel, its contents hold no mystery for her — but the box beneath with its black death's head on a base of red letters reading DANGER.

Cockroaches. Ms. Galahad has cockroaches. Monica feels like laughing. She knows the corners and crannies of this house more intimately than Ms. Galahad ever will. She has come across the occasional silverfish in the bathroom, has slapped at the occasional housefly. *The cockroaches are getting out of hand*, Ms. Galahad wrote in her note. What cockroaches? Monica wonders. What hand?

She reaches for the envelope and the box, folds and pockets the first, tears back the top flap of the second. Inside is a sealed cellophane bag containing a white powder which, on closer inspection, brings to mind all-purpose flour. Monica weighs the bag in her palm, squeezes gingerly at it.

Monica pushes the chair back from the table, pauses momentarily, stands up. Her legs are shaky, she is drained in more ways than she knew. From a cupboard she takes a package of flour; from a drawer, scissors and a spoon; from a shelf, a sandwich bag. Cockroaches: they are her province, she knows what she has to do.

It is late afternoon when Monica returns home. The apartment is quiet. Sandra is at school, Nora on her way to work, her sons, well, somewhere out there being TV characters. As usual, the breakfast dishes are not done and the drapes remain undrawn, but the television is silent and, for a little while at least, the apartment feels unpeopled.

As Monica changes, she even allows herself to toy with a favorite daydream: changing the apartment, and so changing her life. Tossing out the dining table, replacing the old sofa, stripping the walls of their derelict decoration. Letting in the light and letting in the air, inviting in a sparkle that would, through sheer brilliance, be a deterrent to cockroaches.

But shuffling her feet into the ragged comfort of her slippers, she thinks of the drapes forlorn in the living room, thinks of the cost of replacing them, knows she can ill afford it, knows she can ill afford any change except in fantasy.

The light coming through the kitchen window is already that of dusk, brightness dulled high up by an invisible suspension of city emissions and further filtered lower down by the unbroken conglomeration of buildings to the west, buildings just like the one she lives in, multi-storeyed and grey, balconies cluttered with discards or strung with laundry lines. She switches on the light, and it relieves a little of the gloom. But it reveals, too, the work left to her; and the sight of the dishes piled helter-skelter in and around the sink drains her energy from her, leaves her limp with despair.

Is this what she has come here for, to this cold and wealthy land? she wonders. Is this truly the result of all she has put herself through? The alienation from those closest to her, two years of domestic labour, part-time waitressing and secretarial training, the travails of Mr. Youseesee, the inabilities of Rudy? Is this where it has all led? To a cramped apartment, dirty dishes, and domestic disarray?

She thinks of Sandra and Nora, and her strength surges. She thinks of her sons and the dishes, and her strength subsides.

A movement among the dishes catches her eye: the darting

227

of a shadow, a pause, and a renewed scurrying into the clutter of plates.

She picks up the frying pan studded with burnt egg and crashes it down hard on the plates, on the saucers, on the cups. Chips and shards explode into the air, cutlery clinks and clatters. Monica bangs and bangs and bangs away. Cups are reduced to powder. Forks and knives tumble to the floor. A piece of flying glass grazes her hand, draws blood. But she bangs and bangs and bangs away.

And when she is done, she takes a deep breath, relaxes her aching shoulders, feels the sweat drying on her skin. Her fingers release the frying pan, let it fall to the floor with a bang that is like an exclamation mark.

Contentment. Relief.

For, in the glow of long-sought accomplishment, she knows that the power of reason is back.

Sandra, slicing carrots beside her, is the only one who notices the strip of plaster on Monica's hand. When she asks what happened, Monica shrugs it off, says she scratched herself accidentally at Ms. Galahad's. But she is secretly pleased at the question, it reveals a usually unspoken interest.

And when, setting the table, Sandra asks about the missing dishes, Monica confesses only to an accident, embellishing the story — to her own surprise — with details that get them both laughing. They are, for as long as the levity lasts, not simply mother and daughter; share for these few minutes a greater intimacy. Monica realizes that, were they not related, she would want Sandra for a friend. Yet the laughter is tinged with sadness, for she is aware that at its heart lurks a lie.

From the living room, howls of irritated protest cut through their laughter, and Charlie or Andy or Eddie turns up the volume on the television set.

Monica sighs, looks up from the sink where she is peeling potatoes, through the window to the buildings hanging lit in the darkness. She sees others labouring in kitchens, drinking in living rooms. She sees one couple in vibrant argument, and another lighting each other's cigarettes. Is life different there? she wonders. Other people's lives always seem so much less complicated. But it is comforting to know they are not, reassuring to know that even Ms. Galahad secretes her discomforts below a layer of contrived simplicity, in bathroom cupboards and night-tables.

Sandra announces that the chicken stock is boiling. Monica instructs her to throw in the sliced carrots and then to get to work on the turnip.

"And the soup noodles?" Sandra asks.

"No. Later." Monica scrapes with renewed vigour at the potato in her hand. "And don't forget the salt and black pepper."

"Yes, m'am."

"I kill a cockroach today. Two."

"Yeah? Where?"

"The corridor. And here, on the counter."

"We should get some poison."

"Yeah. Poison would do it." Monica's hands begin to shake as she finishes the potatoes, washes them off. "How you doin' with the turnip?"

"Just about ready."

"Here." She piles the potatoes on the cutting board, passes it to Sandra. "Cut them up and throw them in. I going to put some flour in the soup."

"Flour?"

"Yeah. Flour." Monica looks around for her handbag, sees it. Hesitates. "Jus' to thicken it up a bit."

Her sons settle themselves in at the table, Charlie and Andy to one side, Eddie at the end. From their seats they have an unobstructed view of the television.

Monica takes her place at the head of the table, across from Eddie, while Sandra carefully sets the steaming soup-pot down in the middle. Leaning on the table, she ladles the soup into her brothers' bowls. They pay no attention to her, their eyes darting momentarily to each other's bowls, assessing the equality of helpings. To avoid protest, she is careful to fill the bowls to the brim, putting into each vegetables of the same kind and number, and equal amounts of meat.

Sandra serves her mother — Monica stops her when her bowl is half full — then herself. The remainder, enough for a small meal, she takes back to the kitchen to await Nora.

Monica picks up her spoon, lazily mashes the chunks of potato and turnip and carrot into the whitish liquid. This releases its aromas, a fragrance of peppers and spice. But she is uninterested in the food, her stomach tight and airless, as if it has collapsed into itself. Instead she watches her sons, observes their hungry slurping at the liquid, their vigorous chewing at the meat. They do not notice when the soup spills onto the table, palm it unconcernedly from their chins. Monica has never observed her sons this closely before, has never realized how much like their father they are, but without his natural finesse. There is a wolfish furtiveness to them; they seem to scurry at all that they do, living their lives secretly, always seeking the shadows. She feels the weight of her handbag, which is sitting closed in her lap.

Sandra returns from the kitchen, takes her seat. She stirs the soup with her spoon, looks quizzically at Monica, asks what's wrong.

"Wrong?" Monica says.

"Well, you have something on your mind, Mammy." Like Monica, she mashes her vegetables into the liquid. "What's with the handbag anyways?"

"Handbag?" Monica feels wrenched from her thoughts. Her left hand clutches the bag tightly. She stares at it, then slowly puts it on the table next to her soup. She suddenly remembers why it's there, what she had thought of doing. "Andy," she says evenly. "Turn off the TV."

Andy glares irritated at her from the corner of his eye, turns back to his food.

"Andy, you hear me?"

Andy drops his spoon onto the table, sucks his teeth.

"Turn off the TV, Andy."

His eyes narrow at her. "You jokin', right?"

"You see me laughin'?"

Charlie and Eddie, uneasy, glance over at her. Sandra puts down her spoon, sits back in her chair, expectant.

"Turn off the damned TV, Andy." Her voice remains controlled. "I not going to tell you again."

Andy sucks his teeth once more, strides noisily across the living room, slaps the television off. Then he stalks towards the front door, his brothers scraping their chairs back to follow him.

"Andy." Monica does not turn, stares past Eddie at a silver waterfall painted on black velvet hanging on the wall behind him. "Sit down, Andy. Charlie. Eddie. Don't move another inch."

Andy pauses, his hand on the doorknob, looking to his brothers. When they do not move, when their heads droop and they shrink into themselves, he comes cautiously back to his chair, stands behind it with his hands clutching the back.

"Charlie. Andy. Eddie." Monica speaks evenly, her voice soft. "I want to talk to you —" But the words are wrong, are a touch too gentle. "No. I ain't want to talk to you, I want to tell you something. I want to tell you —" She can't believe what she is about to say, can't believe she can have changed so much. "— that is high time you three — you, Charlie, you, Andy, and you, Eddie — is high time you move out and find your own place to live."

Silence greets her words. For many seconds, there is no reaction.

Then Charlie chuckles. "You jokin', Mammy."

Andy, incredulous, says, "You throwin' us out? Your own chil'ren?"

"No, Andy, I not throwin' anybody out. I just saying —"

Charlie says, "But —"

"No buts, Charlie —"

Eddie says, "Mammy —"

"And don't mammy me, Eddie." It is only at his look of boyish defiance that Monica wavers, but she is aware of her vulnerability to him, the youngest; will not let it deter her. "I just sayin', enough is enough. I sayin' that tomorrow morning, you, Charlie, or you, Andy, or maybe both o' you, I don't care, going to get the newspaper, you going to go through it and you going to find a place for the three o' you to live, you understanding me?"

Sandra, disbelieving, places her hand on Monica's shoulder. "Mammy?"

"Sandra?"

"What —"

"Oh yeah, the handbag." She knows it is not the handbag Sandra wishes to ask about, but she will not be questioned by anyone just now, not even a daughter she knows will approve. And before Sandra can interrupt, she opens up the bag and fumbles around in it. "Here," she says, putting the plastic sandwich bag fat with white powder into Sandra's hand. "Take this. Is for the cockroaches."

Sandra stares in incomprehension at the bag flattening in her hand.

Monica smiles at her, then turns with contentment to her three sons, to their looks of dismay and dissatisfaction. She knows that she loves them, as she knows she loves her mother and grandmother, but she knows too that she is beginning to understand, at least a little, what love means. And for that, she silently thanks God. For that, and for the power of reason.

Goodnight, Mr. Slade

I AM SIXTY-FIVE. I feel eighty-five. I have felt eighty-five since the age of twenty-five.

Mr. Slade, sitting behind his desk, says, "You understand our position, Gold."

Through the half-opened blinds behind him cars, vans, streetcars — flashes of red that cause a light tremble of the floor under my feet — slide by on St. Clair Avenue. It is a grey day, February in full tilt.

His breathing becomes audible in the quiet office. "We appreciate the service you have done for us, Gold. But, you know, it is impossible in this building, it is not a retirement home — " His voice breaks off as something within him — more than I would have expected of him, really — points up the emptiness of his words. His stupidity makes him aggressive. "You should appreciate the fact, Gold, that the company is not asking you to pay. You're lucky. The company is not heartless, you know, Gold. We own that building, there's room, so as a reward — "

And his voice hangs there in mid-air, giving me time to contemplate my ingratitude.

"Come, Gold, let us go." He makes no move to leave his chair, waits for me to signal my willingness. He says, in a voice tinged with impatience, "At least take a look, Gold. Try it for a month or two. An experiment. If it doesn't work out, we'll try something else. The company is not heartless, Gold."

His face, a mask of steadily fading youth, heightens in colour from his usual professional pallor. It is as emotional as I've ever seen him.

"Look, Gold, if it had been up to me — " There is controlled exasperation in his voice. "Let's go. Go get your coat." He leans over to his left and switches on the telephone-answering machine.

I stand and make my way from the office, floorboards squeaking rustily under me. As I open the door, he switches off the reading lamp on the desk, plunging the room into a greater greyness. The long corridor before me lies quietly dead in the fluorescent lighting, brightness absorbed by the cream walls, the green doors, the colourless carpet. And for a moment, closing the door behind me, I wonder why I want to stay in this building: there is no prettiness to it.

I fetch my coat from the nail of my "office", a little cluttered cubicle beside the glassed front doors. I struggle into the arms — it has grown tight for me — do up the buttons, except the second from the top, which is long missing, and stand waiting for Mr. Slade in the lobby.

Already he has changed the little sign that was displayed

236

at the entrance of the building for twenty years. The little
sign that read in black lettering:

SUPERINTENDENT

MR. GOLDMAN

APT. 101

The new sign looks the same but now the name is different.
I, Mr. Goldman, Gold to Mr. Slade, Goldie to some of our
older tenants, even Goldilocks — despite my almost total
baldness — to one young woman, have already ceased to
exist here.

Through the front doors, my eyes travel down the paved
walk that leads to the street; it is guarded at the sidewalk by
two concrete pillars surmounted by large, round globes that
glow warmly at night. Beyond them, the icy sidewalk, parking
meters sunk halfway into the dirty snow piled at the side of
the road. Cars, vans, trucks, streetcars, but few people. It is
midafternoon and everyone who doesn't have to be outside
is hunkered down at a desk in the monoliths of the oil and
insurance companies that line this part of the street.

Obeying a sudden need, I turn my back on the grey outside
and survey my silent lobby.

There are newer buildings. There are prettier buildings.
There are buildings with elevators that don't have to be
opened by hand, elevators with shiny stainless-steel doors
that slide silently sideways and not, like here, varnished
wooden doors that rattle and shake on their rollers. Buildings
with garbage chutes running like throats down through the
floors and not aluminum garbage cans set in the stairwell at
the end of every corridor.

But this building, this old, old building built in the thirties
when the shadows on the edges of life were only occasional

237

irritants; when futures seemed secure and assured in a Vienna of coat-tails and dining rooms; this old building is a repository of more life, of more *truth*, than any of its shiny new cousins will ever see.

For this building, its weathered brick, its dulled carpet, its unused milk boxes, is memory. And memory, in the end, is all that we are ever left with. And memory, ethereal and shifting, needs a hook.

I remember my ambitions. I had them back then, but I will not dwell on them. The memory of ambition unfulfilled carries with it a certain embarrassment. But I did have them, all the dreams and wishes and expectations of talented youth, and that is the important thing: it is enough.

Mr. Slade, dapper in his grey coat, pants stuck untidily into his rubber overshoes, stalks rapidly from the office. Pulling on his gloves, he says, "Ready, Gold?"

Spring, 1937. May, I believe. May, in Paris.

Pablo, surprisingly short, stocky with the build of a ditch-digger, standing before the canvas too large to stay upright in his studio, even stirred his paint with intensity. Intensity. That is what I remember best about him; that and the startling fact that anyone but him, about to set to work on an opus of destruction and death, would have stockpiled cans of red paint in a corner. But not Pablo, no. Blacks, whites, greys. We called it his newspaper vision; he had spent hours staring at newspaper photographs from his burning country, the static images of devastation transforming themselves in his mind into a frieze of allegory.

I was not an intimate. I was an acquaintance of an intimate, and this visit, when the canvas was yet blank, a wall to cry against, was the only one I made to his studio. I have seen the painting, itself exiled for so many years, only in photographs, and usually quite by accident. I find it nearly impossible to contemplate even in miniature and when, in an idle moment of dream, my mind projects it to the size I remember, my heart races and I feel the blood throbbing in my wrists and temples. It is as if, with an intuition that pierced beyond history into the eternal heart of man, he managed, years before the actual events, to capture the beginning of the end of my life.

But not then, not in spring, 1937. That was a spring of cafés and nightclubs, of bread and wine and cheese, of artists and writers, of would-be artists and would-be writers, of talk and argument without end. And, the biggest thrill of all to me, it was the spring of my wife, my new wife, of love at midmorning, midafternoon and midnight in the hard, lumpy bed of the little room we rented. The pretty, controlled, drawing-room lady that I married, surprising my friends, pleasing my mother, launched herself into this life with an enthusiasm that stunned. She laughed, she ate, she drank, she argued. It was as if, on shedding Vienna, she shed a shell of acquired habit and allowed all that bubbled within her to flow without restraint.

There had been hints before, in the eyes, in the nervous little movements that revealed a fervour constrained; and it was probably these hints, coming at me like sparks, that caused me to fall in love with her. Here, under this web of convention, they seemed to say, was gold. In Paris, free of the carefully cultivated social observances of Vienna, it revealed itself. Money was a problem, of course — my father, well off, held that generosity was to be tempered, luxury earned — but it didn't seem like a problem: poverty was part of the adventure, it was part of being young, it gave the illusion of the bohemian. And that spring we fed off each other's energy.

Because of her, because of the beauty she offered every waking moment, I did a less than commendable job of scouting new painters for my father's art gallery. I justified the failure with the thought that I had constantly with me that spring an art unequalled. It was an explanation only youth could view with equanimity.

Upon our return to Vienna, a city in which the violently multiplying shadows of politics were becoming difficult to ignore, my father stuck me in the office with the administrative work. It was a form of punishment, but one he imposed with an unconcealed bemusement. He understood, my father, and he insisted on the regimen of paperwork just because that was the kind of man he was. Enthusiasm, to him, was commendable, but only when restrained by responsibility; it wasn't, as to my mother, to be feared, but it was to be harnessed.

Mr. Slade leads the way in. He walks, here too, with an air of proprietorship. He knows the place, this tall, narrow box of new red brick, and he strides ahead of me with a haste that is probably nervousness. I take my time, exaggerating my slowness, looking at this Spadina Avenue that is like a world unknown to me. Wide, too wide, and wet with a slick oiliness. Unremarkable houses, some of garish colour like old women attempting to disguise decay with a burlesque of makeup, others standing with a kind of helplessness in their own collapse. The CN Tower, that eternally inescapable —

"Come on, Gold." Mr. Slade is standing at the door, holding it open. He stamps his feet as if in petulance, but it is probably just that they're cold.

I refuse to look at him as I enter the building.

The lobby, long and narrow, is lit by the same fluorescent coils the company installed in my building about three years ago, and it is to these, to their familiar shape and glow, that my eyes first go. Not with fondness, though, but with a vibrant animosity. Their shadowless clarity, exciting to Mr. Slade as a "building improvement", has done nothing to the corridors but bring out the dinginess of their age.

Not here, though. Here there is no age, no dinginess. The walls are of an electric white, the carpet a swept brown, and in the far wall, like the doors to a vault, are elevators of shiny stainless steel. To the left is a reception desk, on it a white telephone and a vase with a fake red rose. Seated behind the desk talking to two men in green work clothes is a woman; her face, flat, as if the features had failed to fully develop, is like a minimal charcoal drawing, cheeks, nose, mouth defined by streaks and smudges of the lightest grey. "Six-oh-one," she says to the men. I recognize them, movers, they have been to my building often enough. "It all goes to the Sally Ann. The family's already helped themselves but most of it's still there." She begins shuffling through a stack of papers on the desk before her.

Across from the desk, sitting pertly in a wicker chair, a woman physically diminished by age — hair thinned to the scalp, skin sitting like Saran wrap on veins and skull — is staring at the clock mounted on the wall behind the reception-ist. Her eyes, of a luminescent blue, are the brightest element in the room. She leans slightly forward, towards Mr. Slade. "Excuse me," she says, almost in a whisper. "Excuse me."

"Yes, ma'am?" Mr. Slade is solicitous.

"What time is it, please?" She speaks with a kind of vague desperation.

Glancing at his watch, he tells her.

"Thank you." And her hand, all bone and vein, clutches in anxiety at her cardigan. Her eyes return to the clock.

But she has caught Mr. Slade's attention. He tries to engage her in conversation. "What's your name, dear?" He has all the charm of a balding man with toupee askew. She doesn't hear him at first and the tone of concern in which he contrives to cast the question falters in its repetition. "I said, what's your name, dear?"

"Oh." She smiles. "Mrs. Daley. Yes. Mrs. Da— " She pauses, unsure. "Isn't it? Oh dear, I think it is. I don't really remember any more, you know. My name." She contemplates this mystery with puzzled serenity.

Mr. Slade smiles, looking a little paler, and glances towards the desk, for rescue, I think. But Mrs. Daley — the name, I reason, is as good as any other if she cannot recall her own — has lost interest. The clock behind the reception-ist has seized her.

The movers, hands stuck into their baggy trouser pockets, go off to the elevator and as they do so I hear my name whispered between them. I understand their surreptitious-ness; it must be unsettling for them to realize that, one day, they will be carting away my belongings to the Sally Ann. It is the kind of situation that makes a man contemplate his age, glimpse his mortality.

"So here you are at last," the receptionist says with a smile to Mr. Slade. And to me, "You must be Mr. Goldman."

I nod.

"Well," she continues with professional gaiety, "shall I give you the grand tour, or — " Her gaze shifts to Mr. Slade.

"I'll take care of it, June," he says.

"Have fun, then." And to me, "Welcome. I'm sure you'll like it here." Her smile follows us to the elevator.

Just over a year later, in the growing warmth of the summer of '38, we traded in the gallery in return for exit visas. My father had died two months before, while cleaning an SS toilet with his silk handkerchief. His heart stopped, it was as simple as that. They threw his body into the street, telephoned my mother, and told her to come fetch him. They neglected to mention his condition. My wife and I were at the time negotiating documents at Gestapo headquarters in the Hotel Metropole. My mother went alone. "A weak old man," they said when she got there, "a very weak old man." She lasted barely three weeks beyond that.

My wife and I, carrying a suitcase each, headed for Paris. We were too stunned to be wistful at leaving Austria. Paris, and thoughts of the previous year, shone like a jewel for us, the only glitter in that grey, uncertain time.

But Paris was tense. We were not tourists this time, poverty was no longer a game, and the sense of adventure we remembered from that now distant spring had warped and crinkled into one of tenacious anxiety.

Summer slipped into fall, fall into winter. We washed dishes, waited on tables, swept floors. Winter to spring, spring to summer. We relieved our exhaustion on a succession of ossified mattresses in cheerless hotels and we sought visas from any country that seemed far enough away to be a haven. But always the answers came: no, no, no, no.

As the months straggled by and the refusals grew into a litany, my wife began to wither. In little ways at first. Her thinness sharpened. Her laugh, nervous in its enthusiasm, almost manic even, lost the keenness of its edge. Her hair she let grow long; ever since our Paris spring she had worn it short, gentle curls rising from behind her ears and from the back of her neck, soft swirls of dark brown. She pretended she wanted to change the style. "It's my new look," she kept saying, making a transparent play at gaiety by holding up her arms, thin, so thin, and twirling around as if dancing. But it wasn't a question of style, it was one of money. One night I got out the scissors. I was no barber and as I clipped, fussing, the sharpness returned to her laughter.

But as France plunged into war and into winter, as the cold damp seeped into our room, settled into our bed like a clammy companion, her movements became slower, more pained. Her energy was quickly drained and I suspected that, even if anyone had wanted us, she would not have survived the inescapably rough journey to safety. Safety, at that point, was just too far off.

"This is the exercise room," says Mr. Slade. We have already seen the library, a small room with easy chairs, a few battered novels, and stacks of *Maclean's*, *Time*, and *Reader's Digest*.

"Of course, Gold," Mr. Slade said conspiratorially, "if you want *Playboy*...."

"Good afternoon, everyone," he says to the dozen or so people sitting on a row of chairs facing the front of the room.

"Good afternoon," comes the reply, the collective chorus, weak and unsure, conjuring up visions of a group of preschoolers.

"And how is everyone today?"

"Fine," one old man says flatly, "just fine."

A young woman in a blue jogging suit and running shoes hurries into the room. She smiles, professionally, and invites me to join the class. "You'll feel soooo much better for it," she says, squeezing my arm. I decline with a shake of the head and Mr. Slade, with a slight wave of the hand, discourages her enthusiasm.

She walks briskly to the front of the class. "Okay, everyone, shall we begin? Let us fly. We're going to fly and fly and fly." The exercisers, arms outstretched, draw circles with their taut fingers. "Come on, Mr. Henry, flap those wings. Don't be lazy now. Mrs. Grand, do be careful, we don't want to hit Mr. Sharpe again, now, do we? Come on everybody, we have visitors today. Flap, flap, flap."

Next, standing, they march in place, if not quite in time, then sit and are instructed to breathe deeply. No hearts will stop here, not if she can help it.

"Okay, everybody, it's time to row. Okay? Now. *Row, row, row your boat*...," she begins to sing. Picking up the tune, they move their arms back, then forward, then back again. "*... gently down the stream*...."

I look at Mr. Slade. Even he looks a little embarrassed. "Ready to have a look at the dining facilities, Gold?"

245

"*Merrily, merrily, merrily, merrily. . . .*"
I nod. We leave the room.
"*Life is but a — *"
Mr. Slade hurriedly clicks the door shut behind us.

June 15, 1940. Her twenty-fourth birthday. In the streets, German army units were settling themselves in. They had arrived the day before, marching, strutting, dispersing throughout the city like schoolboys on vacation. I remember my odd reaction when, serving a bottle of champagne to a group of army officers in the café where I worked, I had a moment of mindless joy on being surrounded by the German language. But only a moment. Joy changed quickly to fear and I found myself grasping at comfort. I thought: But we are in France, we are all guests here. The vision of the conqueror did not offer itself to me. How infantile the mind becomes when confronted by helplessness.

My wife — I cannot use her name, cannot think it — kept saying, "I'm just tired, only tired." I could no longer even say, yes, I know. I felt like a man trying to guard the flame of a match in a heavy downpour.

But it was her birthday. That night, after my shift at the restaurant, I got a square of flan, a small candle, and half a bottle of red wine. She sat up in bed; I sat beside her, legs crossed. She blew out the candle; we ate the flan, drank the wine. Maybe we spoke. I don't know. I don't remember.

Later that night, as we were sipping the last of the wine, a knock came at the door. Before I could get off the bed, the door swung open and two gendarmes stepped into the room. "Monsieur et Madame Goldman?"

"Oui." I was sitting on the edge of the bed.

246

"Vous devez nous suivre. Dépêchez-vous."

"Que me voulez-vous? Ma femme est malade."

A third gendarme came in. "Ferme ta gueule, Goldman. Allons-y!"

And without warning they were on me, seizing my arms, my hair, dragging me to a corner of the room. Two of them held me there, arms pinned behind me, head wrenched to the left by a hand that seemed to rip at my hair, setting my scalp on fire.

Through eyes clouded by tears, I watched as the third gendarme approached the bed and, without so much as a word, dragged my wife from it. She was too weak even to scream. That silence, like her laughter, resounds in my memory.

Mr. Slade decides we will stay for dinner and we sit, the two of us, alone at a table waiting for the others to arrive. Around us in the piercingly lit room — windowless, photographs of trees dying colourfully hung with a symmetrical severity on the walls — waitresses uniformed and hairnetted bustle about setting out cutlery, china, and little vases with fake red roses.

Mr. Slade clears his throat, undoes the button of his jacket. "Take off your coat, Gold. Get comfortable."

I remove my coat.

The residents begin dribbling in. First, in a group, come the exercisers. They seem hardly more animated now than before and settle, in a silence broken only by the slow scraping of chairs and the quiet sighs of effort, at two tables of their own. Others make their way in, singly or in pairs, helping each other, scattering with a kind of possessiveness to the various tables around the room. Two women leaning on walkers shuffle by, chattering quietly, neither listening as the other speaks. Following them is Mrs. Daley, hand still clutching tightly at her cardigan. She hesitates at the door, looks around uncertainly, then makes her slow way to our table. "Excuse me, please," she whispers, "may I sit here?" She is like a victim of famine, erect, but with a terrifying, tremulous frailty.

"But of course, of course!" Mr. Slade says heartily. He does not rise, though, and he does not help with her chair.

Two other women and a man join our table. Mr. Slade smiles brightly and nods at each of them.

Mrs. Daley, skull etched out under the white light, settles with her blue eyes on Mr. Slade. She has no lips left, they are lost in the welter of wrinkles bunching around her mouth, and when she moves them to speak, it is like a healed wound parting. "Please," she says, "please, what time is it?"

Mr. Slade tells her. He smiles.

She bites at her lower lip.

The man across from me, sitting straight-backed, his posture that of an alert pigeon, is trying to focus on a photograph he is holding at arm's length. The back of the photograph is light brown. He moves it around, now bringing it closer, now moving it away, searching for clarity. His hand, nails yellowed and in need of cutting, shakes badly.

One of the women leans over to him, steadies his hand, studies the picture. "Was she your wife?"

The man nods, holds the picture up into the light as if to animate the image.

And it occurs to me, reflecting briefly on her question, how easily, how naturally, the past tense presents itself here.

"Was she good in bed?" She laughs, a sharp, hacking sound.

The man, offended, palms the photograph and pockets it.

Then she turns to me. "What's your name, honey?" Her mouth, in a smile, is crooked.

When I do not respond, Mr. Slade jumps in. "Goldman. His name is Goldman."

"That's not his first name."

"No."

"Well then, what is it?"

"Joshua."

"Joshua. What's the matter, Josh? Cat got your tongue?" She laughs.

"He doesn't speak much," says Mr. Slade.

She ignores him. "So, Josh — " and the sound of my name is strange; for too long I have been Goldman, or Gold, or Goldie, or Goldilocks " — are you moving in or visiting?"

Mr. Slade says, "Visiting." This, I know, is for my benefit.

"Oh yah." She says it flatly, dragging out the sound, in a voice that implies, "you'll be moving in."

Mrs. Daley, clutching now at her napkin, stares at Mr. Slade. There is already on her face, despite the life in her, that stillness, the stillness that is without a buzz, the stillness that is like a definition of the absolute.

The waitresses bring dinner. We eat in silence.

Surrounded by others who, too, clutched at themselves or at each other, we stood waiting, shivering, in the pre-dawn darkness of a morning, of a year, distant enough now to return as yesterday. We had been among the first group off the train into the blue-tinged, dreamlike darkness of the searchlights, the rasping growl of dogs, the orders screamed from throats hoarse with impatience.

I saw none of it, none of the helmets, the uniforms, the guns, only heard them and felt them in the rattle of cowering fear that surged through us, making us move huddled together to the darkness beyond the wooden platform, like a shadow gliding through sun-suffused water.

I held my wife up. Held her against me. I could feel her trembling, not from fear but from the weakness that was eating its way, unrestrained, through her. She buried her head between the lapels of my jacket, grasping them tightly in her weakened hands, pressing them to her cheeks, cold, so cold, already brushed by an icicled breath.

And then she went slack. Went slack, just like that.

Fear. I grasped her to me: she was not dead, there was yet breath there. But then she began slipping from me, I couldn't hold on to her. Someone caught her, took her from me. And as I watched, choking, unable to move, hurried hands removed her jacket, pulling it roughly from under her so that her head and shoulders flew into the air, then rocketed back down into the total darkness at our feet.

And she was gone, lost in the swell of the burgeoning crowd. I pushed along, propelled forward by the growing numbers.

Mr. Slade drives me back. A storm has descended in a sudden furious blast of wind and snow. The streets we crawl along are deserted; parked cars have become shapeless mounds of white; sidewalk and road are merged. The wind drives the falling flakes at the headlights of Mr. Slade's car and it is as if the beams are absorbing them, sucking them in. The snow shoots dizzyingly through the brilliance of the streetlamps; the buildings that line the streets, lights glowing faintly like distant promises of warmth, look as if they are being erased.

Mr. Slade, eyes squinted in concentration, says, "They seem happy, don't they, Gold?" There is in his voice a straining animation, a forced liveliness: he is trying to sell me a life. "And think, Gold, you won't have to do a thing there. Everything is done for you, your bed made, your meals prepared. You'll have time to do all the things — "

He turns with caution, the car skidding, onto St. Clair Avenue. A streetcar glides by. We drive in silence past the oil and insurance companies, monoliths reduced to lit lobbies, and stop at the red light. Snow quickly builds up against the glass of the windows and it is possible, glancing sideways away from the labouring windshield wipers, to imagine that we are buried.

"Well, Gold?"

I shrug.

"Gold, your enthusiasm — " His voice drops off, sarcasm lost in weariness.

A bit beyond the traffic lights he stops to let me out. I undo the seatbelt, fumbling in the dark with the latch, and open the door. I brace myself, one hand on the dashboard, the other on the arm of the door, snow piling quickly onto my sleeve, ready to tug myself out. But then, unexpectedly, Mr. Slade puts out his hand for me to shake. I hesitate, he has never done this before. Silly man, I think, but then feel sorry for him and briefly put my hand in his. Snow tumbles off my arm onto the seat. "Goodnight, Gold," he says, and it is the first time in five years that he has meant the words.

I stand on the street and watch him fishtail his way from

the curb. I follow the tail-lights until they disappear in the falling snow. The corner of Yonge and St. Clair, not far away, is concealed; the flashing yellow light at the streetcar stop, the red, amber, or green of the traffic lights, the glare of the office buildings, they are all effaced.

Across the street, a stretch of white, is my building. The globes glow at the sidewalk, light fuzzy and animate; the lobby, indistinct, shows a dull yellow through the glass of the doors. I feel nothing now, looking at the building. It seems to have stepped into my past, but a past too recent to really matter much. It is a repository of memories, yes, but not of my memories, not of my vital memories. For these it has been but a framework, the parentheses between which I have managed through thirty-five years to preserve, to coddle, recollections of passion.

I turn away from it without regret and begin walking towards Yonge Street.

The next morning I was set to work at stones and boulders in one of the fields of the camp. Around me, wielding sledge-hammers, heaving rocks, other men in the same baggy prison outfits we had been given in place of our street clothes. Around us, unapproachable in a passivity that masked an abrupt ferocity, armed guards in greatcoats and steel helmets, German shepherds on long leashes squatting beside them. In the distance, low brick buildings with chimneys, purpose unproclaimed. Until, in whispers, a fellow prisoner explained the horror to which we had been brought.

And later that day, I watched as she was belched up through the chimneys in writhings of thick, black, oily smoke, spreading and thinning into the low, grey Polish sky.

That smoke, at that moment, made nonsense of my life.

The park, a layer of earth stretched like skin over the mid-city reservoir, is a massive gulf of darkness, and until my eyes accustom themselves I sense rather than see its snowbound expanse. Downtown, with its cluster of bank and department store towers, no longer exists. The snow, unseen, continues falling, flakes plunging onto my face growing numb, tickling past my nostrils, settling on my lips. The wind, given free passage, gusts and whips with a vengeful fury.

I head off into the vast emptiness before me, legs sinking to the knees into the snow. Each step is like falling, boot moving easily through the soft new snow to the hard layer crusting the old, hesitating, then breaking through and sinking in uncontrollable swiftness. After only a few steps, my body warms up under the coat and the cool dampness of perspiration breaks out on my chest and arms.

I make for the centre of the park, where I know there is a concrete wading pool overhung by a stainless steel structure that may be either a piece of public art or a fancy lamppost, possibly both. On summer evenings I like to sit on one of the park benches and watch the children splashing in the water, but it is not the pool that attracts me now, or the steel structure, or the memories of summer. It is, rather, a need, unexamined, instinctive, to move to the centre of things.

Puffing, feeling the exertion of walking through the snow, I at least reach the arm of stainless steel. The pool is gone, buried in snow and ice. I stand for a moment, eyes accustomed now to the darkness, the wind pushing at me, snowflakes jostling wetly against my face, skin chilled and prickling. There is nothing to see: intimations of movement, hints of shadows.

I remove my gloves, let them fall from my hands. I unbutton my coat.

I think: But you see, Mr. Slade, I am not old. I have seen the old. The old is Mrs. Daley. The old is June the receptionist. The old, Mr. Slade, is even you.

I remove my coat, let it fall from my hands.

Yes, Mr. Slade, my body is going. It has grown heavy and slow and awkward like a bear's. And at times, when I examine myself in the mirror, my mind does not register this face, this face with its features grown into a clotted roundness. Old? The physical cannot be denied, Mr. Slade. But I, at least, have lived. I have experienced passion. I am not one of those who must manufacture enthusiasm.

Slowly, my hand burning on the cold of the steel, I lower myself to the snow, turn so that my back rests comfortably against the base of the structure. The wind bites into my face, the flying snow stings my eyes.

I have carried on for long enough, Mr. Slade. There is strength left, but sufficient will only to refuse to allow my life to be turned once more to nonsense. I accept no more disruptions to my soul.

The snow and wind swirl around me in thick, white writhings; they are, through my squinting eyes, through the filters of my imagination and memory, like a dance of agonized smoke.

It is a long way that I have travelled. But now I am warm.

Things Best Forgotten

THE WALL, WASHED in white, reflects the sun. The door of heavy wood dark with age, iron fittings — hinges, ring — of roughly finished iron, reaches back to a time of lesser refinement.

"This is where I was born," he says, fingers reaching out to the door. In the brilliant sun that does not burn — it is dry here, air so devoid of moisture that the heat does not drain, rather vivifies even as it parches the throat — his face tightens under his head of carefully combed silver hair and, for a moment, lines appear, on his forehead, between cheeks and mouth, that reveal the age usually hidden beneath a trim exterior of energy and enthusiasm. With a nervous movement, he shrugs the strap of his camera case farther up onto his left shoulder. "It's open," he says unnecessarily, with just a touch of surprise, as the door gives a little under the light pressure of his fingertips. He glances at me. "Let's take a quick look."

He steps through the doorway with the certainty of possession, but quietly, shoes falling firmly and soundlessly on the red-bricked floor. I follow a few steps behind him, cautioned by my sense of trespass, into a large, unlit room, walls of stone, a gloomy antechamber to the courtyard that glows painfully through the unbarred doorway in the far wall. He pauses for a minute, looking around, peering into the empty darkened corners. And slowly, in the twilight, he engages memory. "I remember," he says. "It was different then. There were boxes piled on both sides with just a narrow passage between them. I ran through here —" and his finger traces a swift path from the courtyard door to the street door, "— after I learned my father was dead." He looks for a moment longer, clicks with the right side of his mouth — that click I know so well, a sound that comes at the end of conversations, at the conclusion of funeral orations, a click almost of regret that is at times a period, at times a miniature exclamation mark — turns with his characteristic abruptness and marches into the courtyard. It seems to me, watching his retreating back, that his shoulders droop more now than a minute ago.

The courtyard, expansive and open to the sky, floor recently red-bricked, rises four floors on all four sides, the walls washed in the same white as the street wall, a white so bright it seems to blend with the sunlight that is pouring in. The wood — framing the windows, hung in shutters, coursing the walls in partially imbedded beams — is of a rich, natural red. It all looks bright and new and clean.

He stands in the sunlight looking up, hands on his hips,

eyes squinting, examining with manifest wonder a place no longer totally familiar. His small paunch, usually held tightly in to give him a stiff-backed, military look, tightens his shirt and protrudes a bit beyond the top of his belt.

After a few minutes — minutes during which I observe him observing this place I cannot connect with him, it looks too new, seems too far from the darkness of the age in which I can picture him young — he points to a window on the third floor. "That's where we lived," he says. Then, unexpectedly, he falls silent staring at the window and, with that click of regretful dismissal, turns away ready to go.

I sense, without knowing why, that he is leaving with disappointment, not in the changes he has seen but in the words he has failed to pronounce. It is not by accident that he picked this town to stop at, not by accident that we find ourselves at the house of his birth. But as usual, he holds back, stops short. I know him: in a few minutes he will be once more jolly and energetic, as he has always been. If I were still young, he would pull me out into the street, buy me an ice cream cone or a piece of marzipan, and manufacture excitement over his latest photographic gadget. Our albums at home spill shots of me, aggrieved, holding a cone or chewing on a chunk of candy.

Now we will return to the car and continue our trip along the winding, dusty backroads of the interior, stopping at unlikely places in the wake of subdued exclamations from one of us to photograph folds and angles of arid mountains, or ruins of castles and forts standing in useless dejection against the cloudless, blue August sky. We will listen to music from the cassette deck and when we talk, if we talk, it will be about lenses and filters and film speeds. He will film and I will snap and in this way we will continue meeting, as we always have, only in this passion for mechanical, manipulated vision that we share.

He walks slowly back towards the entrance, checking himself so visibly that I want to shout, to throw my camera at him. But that is not my way, never has been. I have always glowered — witness the photographs — but I have never, so far as I recall, engaged the dramatic: in the end I always ate the ice cream, always coveted the candy to its last. I think that, in growing up with him, I have come to distrust the dramatic; I see it as a kind of public display, emotions forced into animation for the scrutiny of others who, in the final analysis, neither matter nor care. My father, it must be said, is well loved by family and friends.

Unwillingly, as if moving through air sudddenly viscous, I begin following him towards the door.

"What do you want here, gentlemen?" an aged female voice suddenly demands. It is a suspicious, unfriendly voice, the *gentlemen* at the end adding bite to its tone of unwelcome.

My father hesitates, caught unawares, the observer finding himself unknowingly observed. Then — I see it, appearing like a twinkle and growing instantaneously — his summoned animation: the smile, the stiffening of the back into dignity. There is someone here to charm.

The door closest to the entrance, on the left, is ajar enough to reveal about halfway down, at the height of a child, half of a shadowed face: head loosely scarfed; tufts of grey falling untidily onto the forehead; one eyebrow; one eye darkened by wariness; half a nose; half a mouth; half a chin; and, below this, four fingers clutching tightly at the door.

"Buenos días, señora," says my father turning, towards her. "Do you live here?"

She looks for a moment with that one dark eye, gaze flickering from my father to me and back again. "Of course. How can I help you?" Her hostility has already diminished. My father's charm is working its magic.

"Martín Domínguez Segura," my father says with the practised theatrical flourish that lends weight to his name. He indicates me with a wave of his open palm, adds, "And this is my son," words he always manages to pronounce with an overstated pride, although he seldom remembers to give my name. "I used to live here," he continues, "when I was small."

She opens the door a little wider, so that all of her face and half her body are exposed. The suspicion that has been cramping her features gradually gives way to curiosity and an effort at recollection.

The door opens all the way to reveal a man, tall, gaunt, in a white shirt that emphasizes his thinness and his hollowness of chest, standing behind her. He gazes at my father. Runs his right hand — long fingers, crooked, broadening at the nails —through his stiff, uncombed grey hair, while his left hand fumbles in his shirt pocket at a pack of Marlboros. He slowly repeats my father's name to himself, then he smiles and whispers to his wife, jabbing the red and white pack in the direction of my father.

As she listens to him, she too breaks into a smile and her eyes widen with a kind of wonder. Together they step out into the sun and approach my father. "Yes, yes, I remember," she says. "On the fourth floor —"

"Third," my father mumbles.

" — there!" Her finger points to a window across from the one my father had pointed out.

"Not exactly —"

"*Bueno, no importa.*" She shrugs off her mistake. "I remember —"

"There, that apartment," my father insists.

" — your father was an electrician or a plumber, a tradesman of some kind. And your mother, your mother —"

Her husband, breaking in, introduces himself, Eutimio Angeles Contreras, and his wife, Vicenta. He offers cigarettes, lights them with a match held with a studied steadiness.

"Your mother was a beautiful woman," Doña Vicenta continues. "A fine woman. How is she? Is she —"

"Yes," my father acknowledges, nodding gently. "She died many years ago."

"*Sí, sí, por cierto.* It's been a long time since —"

"Come in, come in, please," her husband urges, sweeping his arm towards their apartment. "Have a beer." He squints, smiling at me. "A nice cold beer. What do you say?"

"No, no, thank you," says my father. "We shouldn't. The time." But I can see, as I'm sure they can, that he is playing the social game. I sense his delight, restrained as it is, cautious, almost wary of itself.

But the couple will have none of it. Theirs, too, the social game, and they are less subtle than he tries to be. They are loudly insistent, reaching out now to my father, casting polite glances at me, including me peripherally.

Chuckling, my father drops all pretence at hesitation and allows them to lead him to the door of the apartment. Just before entering, he turns around to make sure I am following — I am, hesitantly — and he gives me a quick smile that mingles apologetic tension with relieved anticipation.

We are shown into a tiny room, windowless and unlit, that is not their living room, as I expect, but their kitchen. On the right are a fridge and a stove, ancient and spottily rusted. The floor, of green tiles, feels gritty under my shoes. On the left is a sink full of unwashed dishes.

Sitting at a tiny painted table are a young girl — fourteen or fifteen, breasts rising voluptuously from her pink halter top — and a man older than old, ancient, sunburnt skin laboriously wrought with wrinkles. They are finishing their lunch, the girl holding the plate up to her neck and shovelling quickly with her fork, the ancient man bending low over his, eating with a mechanical, uninterested motion.

Doña Vicenta introduces them as her father, who looks wordlessly at us and continues his meal, and her granddaughter, who smiles, flirting with lips and eyes that are those of her grandmother. Doña Vicenta explains to them who my father is. "Don Martín was born here a long time ago," she says. The ancient man reveals no interest. The girl smiles — it is, I decide, her standard response — and nods at my father. She hurriedly finishes off her food, clatters the plate into the sink, and runs off.

"Sit down, sit down," Don Eutimio urges my father, indicating the chair abandoned by the girl. But my father, ever the gentleman, insists that the wife take the free chair. Don Eutimio disappears behind a faded blue curtain that hangs in the doorway to the next room and returns a moment later with two chairs, twins of those at the dining table; the kitchen is too small to accommodate them all.

Having seated my father before the blue curtain and me in front of the door, he opens the fridge, removes four small beers that he uncaps with deft twists of thumb and index finger, and distributes them around, to the ancient grandfather, to my father, and to me. Shyly he says, "Salud," and takes a long swallow that empties more than half the bottle.

During all this, Doña Vicenta has been fidgeting, eager to get to the topic of the past. Her father, on the other hand, has continued his steady eating, absorbed in the mechanical. He pays no attention to us, does not even acknowledge the beer his son-in-law has placed on the table before him.

Don Eutimio once more passes around cigarettes. Doña Vicenta, holding hers inexpertly between the tips of the first three fingers of her right hand, begins seeking the major lines of my father's autobiography.

Yes, he's married, well, he was but his wife is dead, you see. Several years ago, in a car accident. Yes, it's too bad, but what can one do? Life is full of the unfortunate. He's found other things to occupy himself — photography, travel. Retired? No, no, not yet, but soon enough. He's an accountant for a fairly large company. Yes, it's a good job, not too exciting but the money's not too bad either, it allows him to indulge his interests. Ah, yes, he was young when they left here, nine or ten at the most. Yes, it was just after the end of the civil war. They went to live with his grandparents on the coast and he's made his life there.

As they talk, I drink my beer and smoke my cigarette. The husband, listening to the conversation more intently than I but still the attentive host, reaches for a clean ashtray from on top of the fridge and passes it around with an almost ceremonious solicitude. The nail of his left thumb, I notice, is deeply cracked down the middle, but it is an old wound, bulbously healed. The grandfather, plate empty, sits quietly with a cigarette clamped betweeen pinched lips. He has not touched his beer. I cannot tell whether or not he is paying attention to the conversation but he seems to be looking — not fixedly but mistily, seeing without observing in the way of the near-blind — at my father's face.

"My father?" my father continues in response to another question. "Well, no. He didn't go with us, no. It was after the war, you see. . . ." His voice trails off, leaving it to the simple statement of historical period to explain the circumstances. Knowing him, I expect to hear that regretful, dismissive click, but it doesn't come. He is, I realize, deliberately not putting an end to the subject.

"Ahh, yes, I remember now," says Doña Vicenta contemplatively. The ash on her cigarette, long and curved, cracks and falls to her lap, rolls off onto the floor. "It was when the Reds came during their last retreat. They took him, poor man. I remember, I was sitting over there —" and she points to where I'm sitting "— drinking my first coffee of the morning, that terrible coffee we had during the war, when they came for him. Your mother, she remained calm. But you were in bed still, it was very early."

"Yes," my father says softly, looking at me through pained eyes. He knows this is a story I have never heard. He has always told me simply that my grandfather died during the war, leaving it to my imagination to pencil in any details it wished to conjure up; and I have always fancied that that nameless, faceless soldier captured in his explosive, ecstatic moment of death, throwing his arms open to the heavens and photographically transformed into a central image of our war, was my grandfather. "Yes," my father repeats, returning his attention to Doña Vicenta. "It was as if he'd simply disappeared." And he snaps his fingers.

"We did what we could," she continues. "We tried to make your mother comfortable. That evening we gave you wine to help you sleep. You were a good boy, though, you gave us no trouble." The butt of her cigarette begins to burn and the noxious smell brings her husband with the ashtray. The grandfather, too, takes the opportunity to extinguish his cigarette, pounding with unexpected vigour into the ashtray. Then he leans back in his chair, working his mouth with a self-absorbed satisfaction.

"But your poor father," continues his daughter. "There was nothing we could do, really. The Reds put him in prison with so many others. And by the time the Movement took the town, it was too late, they had already —" She shakes her head in regret and my father, with that slow twist of his head, at last clicks.

Period.

The Movement, the Reds: words familiar to me only as history, my generation already more detached, using words — the Fascists, the Communists, or the Nationalists, the Republicans — more neutral, merely descriptive of ideology and less laden with judgement. So that the language, almost archaic to my ears, alienates. Yet this is my grandfather they are talking about. Questions present themselves, questions which, unformed, will remain unasked and so unanswered. It is difficult to imagine it can be otherwise between my father and me.

The grandfather shuffles, pushing back his chair. He

stands with difficulty, reaches for the cane leaning against the wall in the corner behind him. He limps sluggishly from the table towards the door — I shift my legs to let him pass — and leaves without a word. He has small, glittery eyes, with a touch of panic to them.

Don Eutimio once more offers cigarettes, but no one accepts. My father takes a business card from his wallet and scribbles our home address on the back. He hands it to the husband. "If you're ever there . . . ," he says, knowing they never will be — they probably haven't left this town since before the war — but fulfilling nevertheless the dictates of social intercourse with a straighter face and a greater sincerity than I will ever be able to manage. Then, forgetting nothing, he asks for a photograph, to which they pretend to agree reluctantly, and we troop out into the courtyard where the light is better.

My father selects the spot. "Here," he says, striding across the red bricks to the far wall and placing himself squarely before the large wooden door that leads to the stairway to the upper floors. He directs the couple, Don Eutimio to his right, Doña Vicenta to his left, and he wants me to take a picture of them from about ten feet away, directly in front of them.

Only as I frame the photograph in the rectangle of my lens, bringing them into focus, do I begin to understand why my father wants me so close that I cut them off at the knees. I have seen this photograph before, in faded black and yellowing white, my father in early youth between two older people before this door, less lustrous then but with the same heavy curls embossed on its surface. It is a little joke he is playing, I think; he will slip this one into the album next to the

265

original. But I also suspect it is a joke with complexities I cannot begin to appreciate, not now, not yet. I snap the photograph.

We walk them back to the door of their apartment, conclude the formalities of thanks and goodbye. My father promises to send them a copy of the photograph, which he will do, eventually, in his methodical way, with the date and place inscribed on the back. In silence we make our way back through the empty antechamber into the street.

Once on the sidewalk, the door securely pulled in behind us, I turn to my father, facing him as never before, the question shaping itself with only the greatest of effort: "Why didn't you ever tell me about this? About my grandfather?"

He is silent for a moment, his eyes skimming the wall. He shrugs the strap of the camera case farther up onto his shoulder. "Because I think there are things best left behind, things —" He swallows air, shrugging, "— best forgotten." His eyes are beyond me, searching the air, the sidewalk. "You know, it wasn't so much that I didn't want to tell you. It was more that I didn't want to hear myself telling you." Slowly his eyes travel up to mine and, for a second, it is as if we have switched roles, I the father, he the son, and there is between us the pain of a secret revealed. Then my father's eyes settle on me, hard, brilliant, speaking to *me*, his *son*, as never before: "Listen," he says. "She got one detail wrong. She —"

"You look like your father." The voice cuts him off. I turn around and find myself facing the ancient grandfather. He hobbles up to us leaning heavily on his walking stick, looking even smaller here in the narrow street than he did in the tiny kitchen. I begin to react to his words — the polite smile I always use when people throw this compliment at me — when I realize he isn't talking to me but to my father. "His hair wasn't silver like yours but then he was younger, he never had the chance to get old enough for his hair to turn." He walks past me as if I'm not there, right up to my father as if to confront him. "My daughter," he says, "has a very bad memory for some things."

My father, squinting at him, nods slowly.

"I don't." The old man is almost aggressive. "I remember things the way they were. She remembers things in a —" He shakes his head from side to side, working his mouth as if to get rid of a bitter taste. " — in a, let's say, convenient way."

My father smiles thinly. "Or maybe in a diplomatic way," he says. "You were in the Movement, weren't you." The way he says it, it is less a question than an accusation. I have never heard my father use this tone. It is cold and unfriendly; even his voice is different.

"Yes."

"So you know it was the other way around?"

"Yes."

"You were there?"

"Yes." The old man begins to cough, a rumble that begins in his stomach and works its way, bubbling, up to his throat. "A cigarette," he says. "Do you have a cigarette?"

I give him one, light it.

He takes a deep puff, allowing the smoke to flow uninhibited from his nostrils and mouth. "It's the only thing that stops this goddamn cough." He takes a second puff, exhales strongly, and, pointing up the street with his stick, says, "Come, let's walk."

Obeying, my father falls in at his side. I follow closely behind them up the cobbled street.

After a minute the old man says, "Yes, I was there. I was one of the guards. And when it was necessary, I was also a member of the firing squads." He pauses, taking a last puff from the spent cigarette. "It was often necessary." He flicks the butt away, following its arc with his eyes.

I find myself becoming impatient. Just what are you getting at? I want to say. Did you shoot my grandfather? Is that what you want to get off your chest? But I hold myself in check.

"What do you know of your father's execution?" he demands suddenly, eyes surveying the street ahead.

My father, also looking into the distance, replies, "Almost nothing. We didn't find out until after the war that he'd been shot, and by whom. When, where, why — those were extraneous details to those who could tell us."

"When and where are easy," the old man says. "Two weeks after he was arrested, in the prison courtyard. Why? There was a war on, and he was on the wrong side. War simplifies things, even death. You're either in the wrong place at the wrong time, or you're on the wrong side. That's usually all there is to it."

"Is that all there is to my father's death?" There is disappointment in my father's voice.

"No, it's a little more complicated. But that requires —"

"What?" interjects my father. "Surely not money."

"No," says the old man, a laugh making his words tremble. "No. The price is another cigarette." He lets his laugh run free. "My sense of humour," he says, choking.

Unamused, I give him my pack. My father, unsmiling, adds his disposable lighter.

The old man, fumbling, lights a cigarette, pockets the pack and the lighter. "I was one of the guards, as I've said. We had little to do. We gave the prisoners a sip of water now and then, some bread. I even passed around cigarettes once in a while — I was a great smoker back then, not like today. But that was about it, really, there was nothing else to be done for them. They had chosen their side at the beginning, they knew what they had coming at the end." He pauses, tongue probing around the cavity of his mouth, and swallows. "Your father was in a cell with about twenty others. Reds, every single one of them. It was a small cell, four would have been comfortable —"

"My father wasn't a Red," my father interrupts. "He belonged to a union, that's all."

But the old man seems not to have heard him. "The thing is, nobody really knew why we were holding them. Waiting for the orders, I suppose. To shoot them, I mean." A nervousness enters his voice and he begins coughing, less to clear his throat than to dissipate the tickle of trepidation. "And one day, the orders came. I don't know why just then, I don't know why we didn't just shoot them at the beginning as we usually did. Confusion of the war, I suppose."

"Yes," my father says bitterly. "I suppose."

"Anyway, we began taking them out by fives. Your father was in the second group and we, his firing squad, waited with them while the first squad completed its task. It took a little while because they were having trouble with a couple of the prisoners. Reds are afraid to die. They don't believe in heaven so they don't know where they're going when they stop breathing. Things grew pretty tense, I don't have to tell you. So, for something to do — there was nothing to say —

269

I started handing out cigarettes. To the guards —" His right hand flits before him, as if he is scattering grain. " — and to the prisoners. Everybody took one except your father. And this is why I remember him: nobody but your father, not the other guards, not the prisoners, allowed his eyes to meet mine. And in your father's gaze, I saw that he was the first man — there have been others since — to truly hate me. It is a look that I have never forgotten. It gave me nightmares for weeks afterwards."

We stop walking while the old man gropes for a cigarette. My father looks silently at him and, in this instant, I frame them in my lens and snap a shot.

"Did you shoot him yourself?" my father finally asks.

The old man squints through the smoke. "No. I couldn't, you see. Not after that."

We have walked a couple of short blocks. Before us is a small, grassless park dusty in the thickening afternoon sunlight. In the shadows of the few trees, old men in dark clothes — blues, greys — lounge on the park benches. Over in one corner, other old men stripped to their undershirts are rolling their steel balls along the ground to little cries of delight and derision. Our red car, its shine dulled by days of deposited dust, sits in the street behind them.

We stop and idly watch the old men at play. My father puts out his hand to the grandfather, who takes it and says, "She is ashamed of me, my daughter. She belongs to the Movement, but she is ashamed of the role I played in the war. I never saw combat, you see. Whenever I fired my rifle, it was always a one-way arrangement. And now she remembers things the way she wishes they had been."

My father listens to him, nodding. Then, with a twist of

his head, he clicks, and the traces of a smile creep across his lips.

We leave the old man on the sidewalk and make our way across the park towards the car. The old men call out to us as we walk past them and my father, with a touch of theatre, acknowledges their greeting. I stop long enough to take two photographs, then join my father in the car. He is sitting behind the wheel, looking through the cassettes.

As I settle myself in, he says, "You know, I was always a little ashamed of him. I thought he must have been a coward." He smiles, his eyes glittering with moisture. He starts the car, slips in a cassette, and pulls out into the street. We drive slowly around the park. Up ahead, on the sidewalk, we see the grandfather leaning on his walking stick.

"Take a picture of him for me, will you?" my father asks quietly.

As we drive past him, I raise my camera and freeze the coughing old man in the frame of my lens.

Neil Bissoondath

A CASUAL BRUTALITY

'In Neil Bissoondath's fine new novel, the atmosphere of paranoia and tension created by the death-throes of a short-lived financial boom on the small Caribbean island of Casaquemada is sustained throughout by a tone which is both passionate and ironic . . .

   'As the story of a Casaquemadan doctor, Ramsingh, returning from Canada, progresses, his gradual induction into the reality of living in an increasingly anarchic and unstable society is conveyed in sharp jolts of incident.

   '*A Casual Brutality* is very much a description of colonialism gone wrong . . . The false economic boom on Casaquemada has become like a cancer: the island is dying but a "cure" would almost certainly kill. It is this dilemma that Bissoondath writes about with great sensitivity and realism.'   *Guardian*

'A marvellously assured performance'   *Financial Times*

'The book builds to a shattering climax. Like Naipaul, Bissoondath is excellent at atmosphere, at place, at detail' Hanif Kureishi, *New Statesman*

'An absorbing and very readable novel written with intelligence, conviction and wit . . . "Promise", the usual word for first novels, would be an insult here; this important book is a complete, mature achievement' Hilary Mantel, *Weekend Telegraph*

'A disturbing, original voice'   *Independent*

Nino Ricci

LIVES OF THE SAINTS

'Simple, moving and compelling' *Spectator*

'Ricci belongs on the shelf reserved for writers such as Chatwin, Ondaatje and Flannery O'Connor' Timothy Findley

'A début of shining promise' Francis King

'A first novel with hardly a false note' *Observer*

'A more than promising first novel, with a velvety tone to the writing that is eloquent but not precious'
Isabel Quigly, *The Times*

'There is an inner strength in Nino Ricci's prose which is apparent on every page . . . an outstanding first novel, acutely and sensitively observed' *The Tablet*

'An impressive début' *Guardian*

Set in Valle del Sole, a village nestled in the folds of the Italian Apennines like a world forgotten, *Lives of the Saints* tells the story of young Vittorio Innocente and his mother Cristina, whose affair with a blue-eyed stranger abruptly shatters the innocence of Vittorio's childhood.

This powerful first novel won Canada's most prestigious literary prize, the Governor General's Award, as well as the W. H. Smith/*Books in Canada* First Novel Award.

Susan Minot

LUST & OTHER STORIES

'For all the New York chic which surrounds them, the situations and dilemmas of Susan Minot's women could hardly be more classical. The women know they are going to lose and several of them try to guard themselves against attachment, to stay free, but their hearts are not in it. They know there is not much they can do about it, once a look, a touch, a night out changes everything. It's a bleak situation, but talking about it doesn't appear to help, and writing about it doesn't either, beyond a certain point, soon reached. The terseness of these laconic tales has its own telling decorum' *London Review of Books*

'A sort of tenderness in the writing reminds me not a little of Raymond Carver at his best' *Guardian*

'Susan Minot's prose is a rarity in this windy age. It is clean, shapely, with the directness and precision of a child's letter' Penelope Gilliatt

'This collection of acrid little love-hate tales passes on the bad news about relationships in the barest, most unselfpitying of prose styles' *The Times*

Helen Simpson

FOUR BARE LEGS IN A BED

'Absolutely brilliant . . . the only book this year that's made me sick with envy' Julie Burchill

'These stories of sex pack a truly original pungency . . . kicking off belly-laughs or melting you with an apt phrase, Simpson makes a delectable debut' *Mail on Sunday*

'She can be sparingly tragic and unsparingly funny . . . a unique writer' Ruth Rendell

'Outstanding . . . You should read her' *The Times*

'Dazzlingly original . . . Simpson's black-hearted humour is something to relish' *Sunday Times*

'Stories told in such succulent prose that you wince at their brevity . . . a most exceptional debut' *Evening Standard*

'Deserves all the literary prizes she will get' *Daily Telegraph*

Eva Figes

THE TREE OF KNOWLEDGE

'This is a woman's version of literary history, a deeply felt response to the smug argument that "genius" is something to be pampered and cosseted . . . As a commentary on the domestic and intellectual deprivations suffered by women during (and not only during) this period, *The Tree of Knowledge* is totally compelling: but its ambitions go further than that. It is not simply about "knowledge" in the sense of learning because, as the final chapter makes movingly clear, Deborah Milton has been denied not only her education but the very right to give voice to her knowledge of herself' Jonathan Coe, *Guardian*

'In fact, Milton's daughter was discovered in poverty and then kept by the charity of the curious. Her grandfather was ruined in the Civil War. He never paid John Milton for his daughter's dowry, and she was persecuted for the want of it. A woman without property had no prospects, except marrying an old man with desires no lower than his stomach. With a humane comprehension of right speech, Eva Figes makes Milton's daughter breathe again, and deliver a homily against male oppression, which her father would never have admitted, for all his talk of freedom for men and the right of divorce. This is the apple of wisdom that the serpent of experience has given to this new Eve, who cannot regain the paradise that men like her father have lost for her' Andrew Sinclair, *The Times*

Christopher Hope

A SEPARATE DEVELOPMENT

Wole Soyinka

AKE: THE YEARS OF CHILDHOOD

'What if V. S. Naipaul were a happy man? . . . What if Vladimir Nabokov had grown up in a small town in Western Nigeria and decided that politics were not unworthy of him? . . . Aké locates the lost child in all of us, underneath language, inside sound and smell, wide-eyed, brave and flummoxed. What Waugh made fun of and Proust felt bad about, Mr Soyinka celebrates . . . Brilliant' John Leonard, *The New York Times*

'A superb act of remembrance . . . dazzling reading . . . Aké has an enchanting effect . . . Soyinka's memoir makes everything seem wondrous' *Village Voice*

'A beautifully drawn picture of childhood, by a man with a prodigious memory and by a writer whose sense of the comic and tragic have combined once more to make a major contribution to contemporary English literature that will surely number among the classics of childhood' *The Standard*

'An exhilaratingly *glad* contribution to the literature of childhood . . . a marvellously rich and amusing book, with not a dull paragraph, let alone a dull page' *New Society*

'Enchanting' *The Observer*

'Gentle and lighthearted . . . a joyous celebration of childhood that is neither sentimental nor clichéd . . . There are few books that succeed so admirably in capturing the joys, hopes, fears and frustrations that are part and parcel of growing up' *Newsday*

Wole Soyinka

ISARA: A VOYAGE AROUND ESSAY

In 1984, two years after writing his classic childhood auto-biography *Aké*, Wole Soyinka opened a tin box that had belonged to his father, a schoolteacher during Nigeria's Colonial period. The simple contents of this box – 'a handful of letters, old journals with marked pages and annotations, notebook jottings, tax and other levy receipts, minutes of meetings and school reports, programme notes of special events' – provide the fuel for this second instalment of Soyinka's memoirs: a son's fictionalised 'voyage' into the life and times of his father.

'The book yields the bounties of a superbly-orchestrated narrative. The gentle laughter of hard-won wisdom pervades its pages. It grows on you later with the loveliness of a life well lived, with a hint that fulfillment is in contentment and that life's pleasures are won slowly . . . Excellent' Ben Okri, *Daily Telegraph*

'It goes beyond a homage; it supplies the essential ingredient missing from history books – not only the Zeitgeist, but the heart that propels the spirit' *New York Times*

'Instead of offering a merely wistful or elegiac portrait of a lost father-figure, it pays him an even more handsome tribute: it celebrates the life of the mind, and nails down a moment in history, with a wit, accuracy and intelligence which our own writers would do well to emulate' Jonathan Coe, *Guardian*

'A beautiful, loving book' *Times Literary Supplement*

A Selected List of Titles Available from Minerva

Fiction

☐	7493 9026 3	**I Pass Like Night**	Jonathan Ames	£3.99	BX
☐	7493 9006 9	**The Tidewater Tales**	John Bath	£4.99	BX
☐	7493 9004 2	**A Casual Brutality**	Neil Blessondath	£4.50	BX
☐	7493 9028 2	**Interior**	Justin Cartwright	£3.99	BC
☐	7493 9002 6	**No Telephone to Heaven**	Michelle Cliff	£3.99	BX
☐	7493 9028 X	**Not Not While the Giro**	James Kelman	£4.50	BX
☐	7493 9011 5	**Parable of the Blind**	Gert Hofmann	£3.99	BC
☐	7493 9010 7	**The Inventor**	Jakov Lind	£3.99	BC
☐	7493 9003 4	**Fall of the Imam**	Nawal El Saadewi	£3.99	BC

Non-Fiction

☐	7493 9012 3	**Days in the Life**	Jonathon Green	£4.99	BC
☐	7493 9019 0	**In Search of J D Salinger**	Ian Hamilton	£4.99	BX
☐	7493 9023 9	**Stealing from a Deep Place**	Brian Hall	£3.99	BX
☐	7493 9005 0	**The Orton Diaries**	John Lahr	£5.99	BC
☐	7493 9014 X	**Nora**	Brenda Maddox	£6.99	BC